SEP 20 2001

BISON
BOOKS

W9-BGO-799

9/27-1015

Mark Twain

HOW Nancy Jackson Married Kate Wilson

AND Other Tales of Rebellious Girls & Daring Young Women

Edited by John Cooley

UNIVERSITY OF NEBRASKA PRESS

LINCOLN AND LONDON

Acknowledgments for the use
of previously published material
appear on page 255, which con-
stitutes an extension of the copyright page. Copyright © 2001 by
the University of Nebraska Press

Library of Congress Cataloging-in-Publication Data
Twain, Mark, 1835–1910.
How Nancy Jackson married Kate Wilson and
other tales of rebellious girls and daring young
women / Mark Twain ; edited by John Cooley.
p. cm.
Includes bibliographical references.
ISBN 0-8032-9442-5 (paperback : alk. paper)
1. Humorous stories, American. 2. Young
women – Fiction. 3. Girls – Fiction. I. Cooley,
John. II. Title.
PS1302 .C66 2001 813'.4–dc21 2001027062

For my wife Barbara,
my daughters Carolyn
and Meredith

CONTENTS

Preface   ix

Introduction   xi

Lucretia Smith's Soldier   1

Aurelia's Unfortunate Young Man   9

A Mediæval Romance   15

The Esquimau Maiden's Romance   25

Hellfire Hotchkiss   43

A Story without an End   71

Wapping Alice   81

How Nancy Jackson Married
Kate Wilson   105

A Horse's Tale   125

Eve's Diary   181

Saint Joan of Arc   199

Little Bessie   215

Mark Twain, Rebellious Girls, and
Daring Young Women   229

Works Cited   251

Suggestions for Further Reading   253

Sources   255

Preface

This edition brings together for the first time Mark Twain's stories that feature girls and independent, unmarried young women. Although Twain wrote adolescent female fiction principally between 1895 and 1905, his earliest piece of that genre was published in 1864 and his last was written in 1908. Not only do these stories reflect Twain's changing representation of young women over forty years (essentially his entire writing career), they reflect changing ideas in his culture about gender and the rapidly evolving roles of women in American society at the time.

During the last decade Mark Twain scholarship has focused extensively on his representation of race and gender. Recent feminist and gender-related contributions to Twain scholarship include: Susan Gillman's *Dark Twins: Imposture and Identity in Mark Twain's America*, Peter Stoneley's *Mark Twain and the Feminine Aesthetic*, Laura Skandera-Trombley's *Mark Twain in the Company of Women*, and J. D. Stahl's *Mark Twain, Culture, and Gender*, as well as important essays by Shelly Fisher Fishkin and Vic Doyno, among others. The presence of teenaged girls in Twain's life and writing has been an important subject of inquiry in these studies.

Like many Victorian men, Clemens struggled to accept changing concepts of sexual identity and gender roles, yet simultaneously held reservations about the strides women were making toward greater independence at the end of the nineteenth century. The stories assembled in this edition should be both entertaining and insightful to those interested in late-Victorian gender conflicts and the evolving roles of girls and women in American society.

I wish to acknowledge the valuable contributions made by the scholars mentioned above in furthering our understanding of the important roles women played in Samuel Clemens's personal and artistic life, and of the varied and significant presence of girls and women in Mark Twain's writing. This edition owes its measure of success, in significant part, to their revelations and insights. I wish in particular to thank Laura Skandera-Tromley and Michael Kiskis for their support and encouragement. To Western Michigan University my thanks, as well, for the much-needed support of a sabbatical leave and a faculty research award.

Introduction

Until very recently Mark Twain's portraits of female characters have been dismissed as stereotypical. Critics have generally faulted him for neglecting to create authentic portraits
of young women, and in their place presenting colorful portraits of widows and elderly spinsters such as Miss Watson and
the widow Douglas from *Huckleberry Finn*. Similarly, the girls
Twain portrayed have been characterized as innocent, pure,
and narrowly limited in experience, even for his day. This collection of girl and young women stories should help remap
the female presence in Twain's literary landscape. In fact, the
dominant characteristics of the female protagonists in these
stories couldn't be further afield from those exemplars of Victorian middle-class girlhood: Becky Thatcher in *Tom Sawyer*
and Mary Jane Wilks in *Huckleberry Finn*.

Although Twain's interest in stories about girls and young
women spans his writing career, it intensified between the
years 1895 and 1908. He experimented boldly with a wide
range of unconventional, even socially unacceptable female
personalities, and he placed his girl characters in challenging
plots that required unexpected skills and daring actions. Unlike the helpless Becky Thatcher and the naive Mary Jane Wilks,
Twain's "new girls" fend capably for themselves. Not only do
they respond effectively to the challenges before them, their
male counterparts appear indecisive or incapable of effective
action. These stories give readers an opportunity to witness
the evolution of his female characters over four decades.

Even if Mark Twain had planned to write a collection of
stories featuring young female protagonists, it is doubtful he
would have presented a wider variety of plots, settings, and

characters than these possess. His girl and young women protagonists come from the widest possible social backgrounds;
their ages range from three to about twenty; some live at home
and others are without parents or living independently. Among
their common characteristics are that none are married, they
are intelligent and independent, and most possess bold, assertive personalities. Taken as a whole, these young women are
not waiting at home, polishing their domestic arts and hoping
for a marriage proposal. Instead, they are off riding stallions
and fighting battles, resisting traditional female roles and bat-
tling, each in her own way, for a new order of women's freedoms and rights.

Mark Twain's evolving feminine aesthetic came from the
daily influence of his wife, Olivia, from his three daughters,
and from the contributions of a wider circle of women, some
of whom gave valuable literary advice or were involved in the
revolution for women's rights. Thanks in large part to his
wife's influence, he became a supporter of the progressive
causes of his day. Clemens and all of Victorian society were exposed to and challenged by a succession of issues centering on
women's rights: suffrage, higher education, professional ca-
reers, changing gender roles and definitions, changing sexual
habits, and the accepted concepts of marriage and family life.

Toward the end of the century, as more and more women
attended college or received professional training, entered the
job market, and lived independent lives, gender roles were
being redefined (whether wished for or not), and the change
affected men as well as women. Male reaction to the "New
Woman" movement came in a variety of forms and responses.
For the most part, in Britain and America a counterattack of
manliness appeared in reaction to the rise of women and a perceived softening of men. New scrutiny was given to the education of boys, the publicly accepted images of men, the training
of military troops, and the belligerence of foreign policy.

Samuel Clemens was a product of his times, eventually becoming a divided character: partly embracing the views and
aspirations of the New Woman, partly resisting such radical
changes. Various biographers have surmised that in his per-

sonal interactions with adult women, Clemens admired a certain quality of innocence and girlish youthfulness, and he disliked and tended to keep his distance from powerful, highly successful women such as Mary Baker Eddy (*Complete Works,* 24:33). During his early adult years Clemens could not imagine a professional life for women, an attitude he shared with the majority of middle- and upper-class men.

Yet Clemens also pointed out on many occasions that since women were morally superior to men they should have the vote as a tempering and mitigating counterforce to the easily corruptible male voter. He preferred suffragettes who spoke only modestly in favor of women's rights, and found occasion to ridicule or satirize the pitched voices of the strident leaders of the movement. Joyce Warren has observed that Clemens came to believe justice would be served best when women won the right to vote, and on occasion he advocated sexual equality (196). Yet, despite his statements of public support, he appears to have had private reservations about suffrage and found it difficult to imagine women (those "earthly angels") becoming politically active, let alone running for and holding public office. Interestingly, his series of stories of girls and young women showcases characters who more closely resemble strident suffragettes and vociferous campaigners for public office than homebound angels-in-training.

Many women writers emerged during the 1880s and 1890s, and they generally expressed the dynamics of change in women's lives. New freedoms, possibilities, and dangers for women appear in the fiction of writers such as Kate Chopin, Charlotte Perkins Gilman, and Susan Glaspell. Chopin and Gilman frequently portrayed women as willing or driven to risk their marriages, families, and personal security for their visions of a freer, more independent life. Although Twain drew on many of these strong qualities and strategies in his fictional portraits of girls and young women, he hesitated to write about adult New Women, perhaps to avoid threats to the institution of marriage, including his own. As a humorist he comically dealt with the serious subject of gender conflict, humorously capturing its symptoms during a tumultuous era of transition.

In one of his letters to Olivia before their marriage, Clemens revealed his ideas about the kind of woman he saw in her—or wished her to be: "You are as pure as the driven snow, & I would have you always so—untainted, untouched by the impure thoughts of others" (*Love Letters*, 76). After their marriage he adored and worshiped her for her purity and beauty, but his expectations and demands were sometimes difficult for Olivia to fulfill. She nonetheless accepted the role of being his "darling little mentor" and before long his "faithful, judicious, and painstaking editor."

Regarding his wife's influence on his writing, Twain said she taught him "the only right thing was to get into my serious meaning always, to treat my audience fairly, to let them really feel the underlying moral that gave body and essence to my jest" (Henderson, 183). Twain had been writing mainly burlesques, satires, and humorous sketches before his marriage in 1870, but thanks partly to his young wife's influence he raised his sights from being a regional humorist to becoming a successful national writer. Twain also relied on the advice of his daughters as they became teenagers, and of women outside the family circle such as Mary Mason Fairbanks. Women were the primary buyers of books during the latter third of the nineteenth century, and Twain realized his success as a writer was increasingly tied to a female and family-oriented readership. In the view of Shelly Fisher Fishkin, "Women, it turns out, far from being detrimental to Twain's work, were key to his creative process during his most productive and successful periods as a writer" (54).

During their childhood years Clemens's daughters Susy, Clara, and Jean romped about in their large Hartford house and each summer scampered about the lawn and fields of the family summer retreat at Quarry Farm. When he was not writing or away on business, Clemens was quick to join in the fun, including card games, charades, and home theatricals. One of Clemens's favorite games involved telling an extemporaneous story around a name, word, or picture supplied by his daughters. As he describes the challenge, "Once Clara required me to build a sudden tale of a plumber and a 'bawgun strictor,' and I had to do it" (Neider, 204). At the age of fourteen Susy wrote, "we are a very happy family," a statement that reflected her father's views as well.

As they became teenagers the girls began to render opinions about his works in progress and even to provide some editing. After dinner at Quarry Farm Twain would read aloud from his day's output and await the family's approval, indifference, or condemnation. Susy became an active "editor" at age eight, helping with *The Prince and the Pauper*, and Clara joined the family staff in time to help with the production of *Huckleberry Finn*. By all reports Susy was a precocious child: she read voraciously, adored her father (even wrote a biography of him), and wanted to become a writer herself. She was also, it seems clear, his favorite child, perhaps for the reasons already mentioned but also because of her untimely death in 1896. Twain began writing *The Personal Recollections of Joan of Arc* at Susy's bidding, he read passages from the manuscript for her editorial suggestions, and he viewed the finished novel as a tribute to her. Later, while Twain was working on *A Horse's Tale* he came to the realization that he was fashioning the character of Cathy Alison around his memories of Susy at the same age.

In 1906 at the age of seventy-two, perhaps because he missed the youth of his own daughters (who were now grown) Clemens began seeking surrogate granddaughters. He was so successful at befriending girls that within a year or two his friendships numbered a dozen girls he called his "Angel-Fish." He wrote over three hundred letters to these young ladies between 1905 and 1910 and enjoyed the pleasure of their company on many occasions. Several of the Angel-Fish were so precocious and "electric" that they reminded him of Susy, especially Carlotta Welles and Dorothy Quick. He carefully selected his Angel-Fish, probably because they were polite, well mannered, and perfectly adjusted to the traditional role of girls and women at the turn of the century.

The traditional Angel-Fish stand in dramatic contrast to the rebellious, unconventional "new girls" in Twain's short stories of roughly the same period. Twain's girl protagonists are notable for their qualities of superior intellect, strength of character, self-assurance, and physical daring. In fact, the assertive, heroic, and sometimes tragic roles lived by his young protagonists and the frequency with which they turn to gender strategies such as cross-dressing and transvestism in order to achieve their goals in a male-dominated society are causing scholars to revise previous assessments that Twain was ineffective in representing women and unreceptive to women's rights.

Lucretia Smith's Soldier

Twain completed "Lucretia Smith's Soldier" in 1864 and published it that year in the 3 December issue of the *Californian*, a San Francisco literary magazine edited by Bret Hart and Charles Henry Webb. Like "Aurelia's Unfortunate Young Man," this story is a product of Twain's San Francisco bohemian period of apprenticeship as a writer (1863–71). It follows the format of the "condensed novel," a story style popular at the time. According to James Wilson, Twain was influenced here by popular Civil War romances, particularly the novels of Pierce Egan and Mary Elizabeth Braddon (LeMaster and Wilson, 195).

Twain revised the story and published it in *The Celebrated Jumping Frog of Calaveras County and Other Sketches* in 1867. Satires of romantic love and sentimentality were popular among Twain's contemporaries, and satire was also the basis for much of the comedy in his fiction. Wilson points out that Twain worked with the condensed novel form and burlesque effects that had been popularized by Bret Hart in this country and perfected by William Makepeace Thackeray in England (LeMaster and Wilson, 193–94).

Twain mentions Lucretia's full name, Lucretia Borgia Smith, just after she has accused her sweetheart of cowardice for not enlisting in the Union army. He may have been thinking of Lucrezia Borgia, the powerful and calculating fifteenth-century duchess of Ferrara. In her anger and in her parting words, Twain's Lucretia reveals both her temper and her ambition, giving us a very early hint of the assertive and controlling girl and young women protagonists who later emerged from his mature pen.

1

I am an ardent admirer of those nice, sickly war stories which have lately been so popular, and for the last three months I have been at work upon one of that character, which is now completed. It can be relied upon as true in every particular, inasmuch as the facts it contains were compiled from the official records in the War Department at Washington. It is but just, also, that I should confess that I have drawn largely on *Jomini's Art of War*, the *Message of the President and Accompanying Documents*, and sundry maps and military works, so necessary for reference in building a novel like this. To the accommodating Directors of the Overland Telegraph Company I take pleasure in returning my thanks for tendering me the use of their wires at the customary rates. And finally, to all those kind friends who have, by good deeds or encouraging words, assisted me in my labors upon this story of "Lucretia Smith's Soldier," during the past three months, and whose names are too numerous for special mention, I take this method of tendering my sincerest gratitude.

CHAPTER I

On a balmy May morning in 1861, the little village of Bluemass, in Massachusetts, lay wrapped in the splendor of the newly-risen sun. Reginald de Whittaker, confidential and only clerk in the house of Bushrod & Ferguson, general drygoods and grocery dealers and keepers of the post-office, rose from his bunk under the counter, and shook himself. After yawning and stretching comfortably, he sprinkled the floor and proceeded to sweep it. He had only half finished his task, however, when he sat down on a keg of nails and fell into a reverie. "This is my

3

last day in this shanty," said he. "How it will surprise Lucretia when she hears I am going for a soldier! How proud she will be, the little darling!" He pictured himself in all manner of warlike situations; the hero of a thousand extraordinary adventures; the man of rising fame; the pet of Fortune at last; and beheld himself, finally, returning to his own home, a bronzed and scarred brigadier-general, to cast his honors and his matured and perfect love at the feet of his Lucretia Borgia Smith.

At this point a thrill of joy and pride suffused his system; but he looked down and saw his broom, and blushed. He came toppling down from the clouds he had been soaring among, and was an obscure clerk again, on a salary of two dollars and a half a week.

CHAPTER II

At eight o'clock that evening, with a heart palpitating with the proud news he had brought for his beloved, Reginald sat in Mr. Smith's parlor awaiting Lucretia's appearance. The moment she entered, he sprang to meet her, his face lighted by the torch of love that was blazing in his head somewhere and shining through, and ejaculated, "Mine own!" as he opened his arms to receive her.

"Sir!" said she, and drew herself up like an offended queen.

Poor Reginald was stricken dumb with astonishment. This chilling demeanor, this angry rebuff, where he had expected the old, tender welcome, banished the gladness from his heart as the cheerful brightness is swept from the landscape when a dark cloud drifts athwart the face of the sun. He stood bewildered a moment, with a sense of goneness on him like one who finds himself suddenly overboard upon a midnight sea, and beholds the ship pass into shrouding gloom, while the dreadful conviction falls upon his soul that he has not been missed. He tried to speak, but his pallid lips refused their office. At last he murmured:

"O Lucretia! what have I done; what is the matter; why this cruel coldness? Don't you love your Reginald any more?"

Her lips curled in bitter scorn, and she replied, in mocking tones:

"Don't I love my Reginald any more? No, I *don't* love my Reginald any more! Go back to your pitiful junk-shop and grab your pitiful yard-stick, and stuff cotton in your ears, so that you can't hear your country shout to you to fall in and shoulder arms. Go!" And then, unheeding the new light that flashed from his eyes, she fled from the room and slammed the door behind her.

Only a moment more! Only a single moment more, he thought, and he could have told her how he had already answered the summons and signed his name to the muster-roll, and all would have been well; his lost bride would have come back to his arms with words of praise and thanksgiving upon her lips. He made a step forward, once, to recall her, but he remembered that he was no longer an effeminate drygoods student, and his warrior soul scorned to sue for quarter. He strode from the place with martial firmness, and never looked behind him.

CHAPTER III

When Lucretia awoke next morning, the faint music of fife and the roll of a distant drum came floating upon the soft spring breeze, and as she listened the sounds grew more subdued, and finally passed out of hearing. She lay absorbed in thought for many minutes, and then she sighed and said: "Oh! if he were only with that band of fellows, how I could love him!"

In the course of the day a neighbor dropped in, and when the conversation turned upon the soldiers, the visitor said:

"Reginald de Whittaker looked rather down-hearted, and didn't shout when he marched along with the other boys this morning. I expect it's owing to you, Miss Loo, though when I met him coming here yesterday evening to tell you he'd enlisted, he thought you'd like it and be proud of—Mercy! what in the nation's the matter with the girl?"

Nothing, only a sudden misery had fallen like a blight upon her heart, and a deadly pallor telegraphed it to her countenance. She rose up without a word and walked with a firm step out of the room; but once within the sacred seclusion of her own chamber, her strong will gave way and she burst into a flood of passionate tears. Bitterly she upbraided herself for her foolish haste of the night before, and her harsh treatment of

5

her lover at the very moment that he had come to anticipate the proudest wish of her heart, and to tell her that he had enrolled himself under the battle-flag, and was going forth to fight as *her* soldier. Alas! other maidens would have soldiers in those glorious fields, and be entitled to the sweet pain of feeling a tender solicitude for them, but she would be unrepresented. No soldier in all the vast armies would breathe her name as he breasted the crimson tide of war! She wept again— or, rather, she went on weeping where she left off a moment before. In her bitterness of spirit she almost cursed the precipitancy that had brought all this sorrow upon her young life. "Drat it!" The words were in her bosom, but she locked them there, and closed her lips against their utterance.

For weeks she nursed her grief in silence, while the roses faded from her cheeks. And through it all she clung to the hope that some day the old love would bloom again in Reginald's heart, and he would write to her; but the long summer days dragged wearily along, and still no letter came. The newspapers teemed with stories of battle and carnage, and eagerly she read them, but always with the same result: the tears welled up and blurred the closing lines—the name she sought was looked for in vain, and the dull aching returned to her sinking heart. Letters to the other girls sometimes contained brief mention of him, and presented always the same picture of him—a morose, unsmiling, desperate man, always in the thickest of the fight, begrimed with powder, and moving calm and unscathed through tempests of shot and shell, as if he bore a charmed life.

But at last, in a long list of maimed and killed, poor Lucretia read these terrible words, and fell fainting to the floor: "R. D. *Whittaker, private soldier, desperately wounded!*"

CHAPTER IV

On a couch in one of the wards of a hospital at Washington lay a wounded soldier; his head was so profusely bandaged that his features were not visible; but there was no mistaking the happy face of the young girl who sat beside him—it was Lucretia Borgia Smith's. She had hunted him out several weeks before, and since that time she had patiently watched by him and nursed him, coming in the morning as soon as the surgeon had finished dressing his wounds, and never leaving him until relieved at nightfall. A ball had shattered his lower jaw, and he could not utter a syllable; through all her weary vigils she had never once been blessed with a grateful word from his dear lips; yet she stood to her post bravely and without a murmur, feeling that when he did get well again she would hear that which would more than reward her for all her devotion.

At the hour we have chosen for the opening of this chapter, Lucretia was in a tumult of happy excitement; for the surgeon had told her that at last her Whittaker had recovered sufficiently to admit of the removal of the bandages from his head, and she was now waiting with feverish impatience for the doctor to come and disclose the loved features to her view. At last he came, and Lucretia, with beaming eyes and fluttering heart, bent over the couch with anxious expectancy. One bandage was removed, then another and another, and lo! the poor wounded face was revealed to the light of day.

"O my own dar—"

What have we here! What is the matter! Alas! it was the face of a stranger!

Poor Lucretia! With one hand covering her upturned eyes, she staggered back with a moan of anguish. Then a spasm of fury distorted her countenance as she brought her fist down with a crash that made the medicine bottles on the table dance again, and exclaimed:

"Oh! confound my cats, if I haven't gone and fooled away three mortal weeks here, snuffling and slobbering over the wrong soldier!"

It was a sad, sad truth. The wretched but innocent and unwitting impostor was R. D., or Richard Dilworthy Whittaker, of Wisconsin, the soldier of dear little Eugenie Le Mulligan, of that State, and utterly unknown to our unhappy Lucretia B. Smith.

Such is life, and the tail of the serpent is over us all. Let us draw the curtain over this melancholy history—for melancholy it must still remain, during a season at least, for the real Reginald de Whittaker has not turned up yet.

Aurelia's Unfortunate Young Man

"Aurelia's Unfortunate Young Man" was first published under the title "Whereas" in the San Francisco *Californian* on 22 October 1864. Twain later shortened this initial newspaper version and included it in the British edition of *The Celebrated Jumping Frog of Calaveras County and Other Sketches*, published by George Routledge and Sons in 1872.

This satirical sketch, with its burlesque elements, pokes fun at sentimental portrayals of romantic love, a frequent target of the San Francisco literary bohemians with whom Twain was then associated, while simultaneously parodying newspaper advice columns of the time (LeMaster and Wilson, 46–47). The original context for this sketch was a mock-serious response to "letters from lovelorn seeking advice" from Twain and other columnists at the *Californian*.

As a "professional columnist" Twain presents the facts of the case and then his personal recommendation to the unfortunate Aurelia (who has written him), while at the same time avoiding any suggestion that he might find this woeful tale of romantic fidelity bordering on the absurd. He experiments here with the "deadpan" style he so masterfully deployed in his classic stories of the Bohemian period, including "The Celebrated Jumping Frog" and "Jim Blaine and His Grandfather's Ram." "Aurelia's Unfortunate Young Man" also bears a resemblance to "Lucretia Smith's Soldier": in both stories a young female character is the passive witness to absurd male action (war, accident, and tongue-in-cheek advice from a "Miss Lonelyhearts"). In his early stories Twain explored a major theme and stylistic strategies that lasted a lifetime as

9

he continued to satirize romantic sensitivities and genteel expectations.

The gender implications are also interesting and anticipate Twain's later "new girl" stories. Aurelia's hapless fiancé, Caruthers, is an early version of the inept and bumbling male, a type more fully developed in the characters John Brown (from "A Story without an End") and Oscar Carpenter (in "Hellfire Hotchkiss").

The facts in the following case came to me by letter from a young lady who lives in the beautiful city of San José; she is perfectly unknown to me, and simply signs herself "Aurelia Maria," which may possibly be a fictitious name. But no matter, the poor girl is almost heart-broken by the misfortunes she has undergone, and so confused by the conflicting counsels of misguided friends and insidious enemies, that she does not know what course to pursue in order to extricate herself from the web of difficulties in which she seems almost hopelessly involved. In this dilemma she turns to me for help, and supplicates for my guidance and instruction with a moving eloquence that would touch the heart of a statue. Hear her sad story:

She says that when she was sixteen years old she met and loved, with all the devotion of a passionate nature, a young man from New Jersey, named Williamson Breckinridge Caruthers, who was some six years her senior. They were engaged, with the free consent of their friends and relatives, and for a time it seemed as if their career was destined to be characterized by an immunity from sorrow beyond the usual lot of humanity. But at last the tide of fortune turned; young Caruthers became infected with small-pox of the most virulent type, and when he recovered from his illness his face was pitted like a waffle-mould, and his comeliness gone for ever. Aurelia thought to break off the engagement at first, but pity for her unfortunate lover caused her to postpone the marriage-day for a season, and give him another trial.

The very day before the wedding was to have taken place, Breckinridge, while absorbed in watching the flight of a balloon, walked into a well and fractured one of his legs, and it had to be taken off above the knee. Again Aurelia was moved to break the engagement, but again love triumphed, and she set the day forward and gave him another chance to reform.

And again misfortune overtook the unhappy youth. He lost one arm by the premature discharge of a Fourth-of-July cannon, and within three months he got the other pulled out by a carding-machine. Aurelia's heart was almost crushed by these latter calamities. She could not but be deeply grieved to see her lover passing from her by piecemeal, feeling, as she did, that he could not last for ever under this disastrous process of reduction, yet knowing of no way to stop its dreadful career, and in her tearful despair she almost regretted, like brokers who hold on and lose, that she had not taken him at first, before he had suffered such an alarming depreciation. Still, her brave soul bore her up, and she resolved to bear with her friend's unnatural disposition yet a little longer.

Again the wedding-day approached, and again disappointment overshadowed it: Caruthers fell ill with the erysipelas, and lost the use of one his eyes entirely. The friends and relatives of the bride, considering that she had already put up with more than could reasonably be expected of her, now came forward and insisted that the match should be broken off, but after wavering awhile, Aurelia, with a generous spirit which did her credit, said she had reflected calmly upon the matter, and could not discover that Breckinridge was to blame.

So she extended the time once more, and he broke his other leg.

It was a sad day for the poor girl when she saw the surgeons reverently bearing away the sack whose uses she had learned by previous experience, and her heart told her the bitter truth that some more of her lover was gone. She felt that the field of her affections was growing more and more circumscribed every day, but once more she frowned down her relatives and renewed her betrothal.

Shortly before the time set for the nuptials another disaster occurred. There was but one man scalped by the Owens River Indians last year. That man was Williamson Breckinridge

Caruthers, of New Jersey. He was hurrying home with happiness in his heart, when he lost his hair for ever, and in that hour of bitterness he almost cursed the mistaken mercy that had spared his head.

At last Aurelia is in serious perplexity as to what she ought to do. She still loves her Breckinridge, she writes, with truly womanly feeling—she still loves what is left of him—but her parents are bitterly opposed to the match, because he has no property and is disabled from working, and she has not sufficient means to support both comfortably. "Now, what should she do?" she asks with painful and anxious solicitude.

It is a delicate question; it is one which involves the life-long happiness of a woman, and that of nearly two-thirds of a man, and I feel that it would be assuming too great a responsibility to do more than make a mere suggestion in the case. How would it do to build to him? If Aurelia can afford the expense, let her furnish her mutilated lover with wooden arms and wooden legs, and a glass eye and a wig, and give him another show; give him ninety days, without grace, and if he does not break his neck in the meantime, marry him and take the chances. It does not seem to me that there is much risk, any way, Aurelia, because if he sticks to his singular propensity for damaging himself every time he sees a good opportunity, his next experiment is bound to finish him, and then you are safe, married or single. If married, the wooden legs and such other valuables as he may possess revert to the widow, and you see you sustain no actual loss save the cherished fragment of a noble but most unfortunate husband, who honestly strove to do right, but whose extraordinary instincts were against him. Try it, Maria. I have thought the matter over carefully and well, and it is the only chance I see for you. It would have been a happy conceit on the part of Caruthers if he had started with his neck and broken that first; but since he has seen fit to choose a different policy and string himself out as long as possible, I do not think we ought to upbraid him for it if he has enjoyed it. We must do the best we can under the circumstances, and try not to feel exasperated at him.

A Mediæval Romance

This condensed novel of five chapters was written in 1869 and published in 1870 in the *Buffalo Express* as "An Awful Terrible Mediæval Romance." The story first appeared under its present title in *Mark Twain's Sketches, Old and New* (1875).

Charles L. Crowe considers "A Mediæval Romance" a burlesque that indulges the Victorian attraction to manipulative plots and historical romances in the tradition of Sir Walter Scott (LeMaster and Wilson, 505). To these popular conventions, Twain adds a literary hoax (imposing an unsolvable dilemma on the reader) and a transvestite theme by which the plot turns on the hidden sexual identity of the protagonist. Perhaps because this is the first of Twain's many transvestite female stories, he forces the plot into a corner that appears to signal the inevitable execution of two young women. Thirty years later, in the stories "How Nancy Jackson Married Kate Wilson" and *Wapping Alice*, Twain manipulates his same-sex protagonists into marriage—a solution that would also have saved the pretty necks of Conrad and Lady Constance, though he leaves no hint this might be their fateful salvation.

CHAPTER I: *The Secret Revealed*

It was night. Stillness reigned in the grand old feudal castle of Klugenstein. The year 1222 was drawing to a close. Far away up in the tallest of the castle's towers a single light glimmered. A secret council was being held there. The stern old lord of Klugenstein sat in a chair of state meditating. Presently he said, with a tender accent—"My daughter!"

A young man of noble presence, clad from head to heel in knightly mail, answered—"Speak, father!"

"My daughter, the time is come for the revealing of the mystery that hath puzzled all your young life. Know, then, that it had its birth in the matters which I shall now unfold. My brother Ulrich is the great Duke of Brandenburgh. Our father, on his deathbed, decreed that if no son were born to Ulrich the succession should pass to my house, provided a *son* were born to me. And further, in case no son were born to either, but only daughters, then the succession should pass to Ulrich's daughter if she proved stainless; if she did not, my daughter should succeed if she retained a blameless name. And so I and my old wife here prayed fervently for the good boon of a son, but the prayer was vain. You were born to us. I was in despair. I saw the mighty prize slipping from my grasp—the splendid dream vanishing away! And I had been so hopeful! Five years had Ulrich lived in wedlock, and yet his wife had borne no heir of either sex.

"'But hold,' I said, 'all is not lost.' A saving scheme had shot athwart my brain. You were born at midnight. Only the leech, the nurse, and six waiting-women knew your sex. I hanged them every one before an hour sped. Next morning all the bar-

17

ony went mad with rejoicing over the proclamation that a *son* was born to Klugenstein—an heir to mighty Brandenburgh! And well the secret has been kept. Your mother's own sister nursed your infancy, and from that time forward we feared nothing.

"When you were ten years old a daughter was born to Ulrich. We grieved, but hoped for good results from measles, or physicians, or other natural enemies of infancy, but were always disappointed. She lived, she throve—Heaven's malison upon her! But it is nothing. We are safe. For, ha! ha! have we not a son? And is not our son the future Duke? Our well-beloved Conrad, is it not so?—for woman of eight-and-twenty years as you are, my child, none other name than that hath ever fallen to *you*!

"Now it hath come to pass that age hath laid its hand upon my brother, and he waxes feeble. The cares of state do tax him sore, therefore he wills that you shall come to him and be already Duke in act, though not yet in name. Your servitors are ready—you journey forth to-night.

"Now listen well. Remember every word I say. There is a law as old as Germany, that if any woman sit for a single instant in the great ducal chair before she hath been absolutely crowned in presence of the people—SHE SHALL DIE! So heed my words. Pretend humility. Pronounce your judgments from the Premier's chair, which stands at the *foot* of the throne. Do this until you are crowned and safe. It is not likely that your sex will ever be discovered, but still it is the part of wisdom to make all things as safe as may be in this treacherous earthly life."

"O my father! is it for this my life hath been a lie? Was it that I might cheat my unoffending cousin of her rights? Spare me, father, spare your child!"

"What, hussy! Is this my reward for the august fortune my brain has wrought for thee? By the bones of my father, this puling sentiment of thine but ill accords with my humor. Betake thee to the Duke instantly, and beware how thou meddlest with my purpose!"

Let this suffice of the conversation. It is enough for us to know that the prayers, the entreaties, and the tears of the gentle-natured girl availed nothing. Neither they nor anything could move the stout old lord of Klugenstein. And so, at last, with a heavy heart, the daughter saw the castle gates close behind her, and found herself riding away in the darkness surrounded by a knightly array of armed vassals and a brave following of servants.

The old baron sat silent for many minutes after his daughter's departure, and then he turned to his sad wife, and said—

"Dame, our matters seem speeding fairly. It is full three months since I sent the shrewd and handsome Count Detzin on his devilish mission to my brother's daughter Constance. If he fail we are not wholly safe, but if he do succeed no power can bar our girl from being Duchess, e'en though ill fortune should decree she never should be Duke!"

"My heart is full of bodings; yet all may still be well."

"Tush, woman! Leave the owls to croak. To bed with ye, and dream of Brandenburgh and grandeur!"

CHAPTER II: Festivity and Tears

Six days after the occurrences related in the above chapter, the brilliant capital of the Duchy of Brandenburgh was resplendent with military pageantry, and noisy with the rejoicings of loyal multitudes, for Conrad, the young heir to the crown, was come. The old Duke's heart was full of happiness, for Conrad's handsome person and graceful bearing had won his love at once. The great halls of the palace were thronged with nobles, who welcomed Conrad bravely; and so bright and happy did all things seem, that he felt his fears and sorrows passing away, and giving place to a comforting contentment.

But in a remote apartment of the palace a scene of a different nature was transpiring. By a window stood the Duke's only child, the Lady Constance. Her eyes were red and swollen, and full of tears. She was alone. Presently she fell to weeping anew, and said aloud—

"The villain Detzin is gone—has fled the dukedom! I could not believe it at first, but, alas! it is too true. And I loved him so. I dared to love him though I knew the Duke my father would never let me wed him. I loved him—but now I hate him! With all my soul I hate him! Oh, what is to become of me? I am lost, lost, lost! I shall go mad!"

CHAPTER III: *The Plot Thickens*

A few months drifted by. All men published the praises of the young Conrad's government, and extolled the wisdom of his judgments, the mercifulness of his sentences, and the modesty with which he bore himself in his great office. The old Duke soon gave everything into his hands, and sat apart and listened with proud satisfaction while his heir delivered the decrees of the crown from the seat of the Premier. It seemed plain that one so loved and praised and honored of all men as Conrad was could not be otherwise than happy. But, strangely enough, he was not. For he saw with dismay that the Princess Constance had begun to love him! The love of the rest of the world was happy fortune for him, but this was freighted with danger! And he saw, moreover, that the delighted Duke had discovered his daughter's passion likewise, and was already dreaming of a marriage. Every day somewhat of the deep sadness that had been in the princess's face faded away; every day hope and animation beamed brighter from her eye; and by and by even vagrant smiles visited the face that had been so troubled.

Conrad was appalled. He bitterly cursed himself for having yielded to the instinct that had made him seek the companionship of one of his own sex when he was new and a stranger in the palace—when he was sorrowful and yearned for a sympathy such as only women can give or feel. He now began to avoid his cousin. But this only made matters worse, for naturally enough, the more he avoided her the more she cast herself in his way. He marvelled at this at first, and next it startled him. The girl haunted him; she hunted him; she happened upon him at all times and in all places, in the night as well as in the day. She seemed singularly anxious. There was surely a mystery somewhere.

This could not go on for ever. All the world was talking about it. The Duke was beginning to look perplexed. Poor

Conrad was becoming a very ghost through dread and dire distress. One day as he was emerging from a private ante-room attached to the picture gallery Constance confronted him, and seizing both his hands in hers, exclaimed—

"Oh, why do you avoid me? What have I done—what have I said, to lose your kind opinion of me—for surely I had it once? Conrad, do not despise me, but pity a tortured heart? I cannot, cannot hold the words unspoken longer, lest they kill me—I LOVE YOU, CONRAD! There, despise me if you must, but they *would* be uttered!"

Conrad was speechless. Constance hesitated a moment, and then, misinterpreting his silence, a wild gladness flamed in her eyes, and she flung her arms about his neck and said—

"You relent! you relent! You *can* love me—you *will* love me! Oh, say you will, my own, my worshipped Conrad!"

Conrad groaned aloud. A sickly pallor overspread his countenance, and he trembled like an aspen. Presently, in desperation, he thrust the poor girl from him, and cried—

"You know not what you ask! It is for ever and ever impossible!" And then he fled like a criminal, and left the princess stupefied with amazement. A minute afterward she was crying and sobbing there, and Conrad was crying and sobbing in his chamber. Both were in despair. Both saw ruin staring them in the face.

By and by Constance rose slowly to her feet and moved away, saying—

"To think that he was despising my love at the very moment that I thought it was melting his cruel heart! I hate him! He spurned me—did this man—he spurned me from him like a dog!"

CHAPTER IV: *The Awful Revelation*

Time passed on. A settled sadness rested once more upon the countenance of the good Duke's daughter. She and Conrad were seen together no more now. The Duke grieved at this. But as the weeks wore away Conrad's color came back to his cheeks, and his old-time vivacity to his eye, and he administered the government with a clear and steadily ripening wisdom.

Presently a strange whisper began to be heard about the palace. It grew louder; it spread farther. The gossips of the city got hold of it. It swept the dukedom. And this is what the whisper said —

"The Lady Constance hath given birth to a child!"

When the lord of Klugenstein heard it he swung his plumed helmet thrice around his head and shouted —

"Long live Duke Conrad! — for lo, his crown is sure from this day forward! Detzin has done his errand well, and the good scoundrel shall be rewarded!"

And he spread the tidings far and wide, and for eight-and-forty hours no soul in all the barony but did dance and sing, carouse and illuminate, to celebrate the great event, and all at proud and happy old Klugenstein's expense.

CHAPTER V: *The Frightful Catastrophe*

The trial was at hand. All the great lords and barons of Brandenburgh were assembled in the Hall of Justice in the ducal palace. No space was left unoccupied where there was room for a spectator to stand or sit. Conrad, clad in purple and ermine, sat in the Premier's chair, and on either side sat the great judges of the realm. The old Duke had sternly commanded that the trial of his daughter should proceed without favor, and then had taken to his bed broken-hearted. His days were numbered. Poor Conrad had begged, as for his very life, that he might be spared the misery of sitting in judgment upon his cousin's crime, but it did not avail.

The saddest heart in all that great assemblage was in Conrad's breast.

The gladdest was in his father's, for, unknown to his daughter "Conrad," the old Baron Klugenstein was come, and was among the crowd of nobles triumphant in the swelling fortunes of his house.

After the heralds had made due proclamation and the other preliminaries had followed, the venerable Lord Chief-Justice said — "Prisoner, stand forth!"

The unhappy princess rose, and stood unveiled before the vast multitude. The Lord Chief-Justice continued —

"Most noble lady, before the great judges of this realm it hath been charged and proven that out of holy wedlock your Grace hath given birth unto a child, and by our ancient law the penalty is death excepting in one sole contingency, whereof his Grace the acting Duke, our good Lord Conrad, will advertise you in his solemn sentence now; wherefore give heed."

Conrad stretched forth his reluctant sceptre, and in the self-same moment the womanly heart beneath his robe yearned pityingly toward the doomed prisoner, and the tears came into his eyes. He opened his lips to speak, but the Lord Chief-Justice said quickly—

"Not there, your Grace, not there! It is not lawful to pronounce judgment upon any of the ducal line SAVE FROM THE DUCAL THRONE!"

A shudder went to the heart of poor Conrad, and a tremor shook the iron frame of his old father likewise. CONRAD HAD NOT BEEN CROWNED—dared he profane the throne? He hesitated and turned pale with fear. But it must be done. Wondering eyes were already upon him. They would be suspicious eyes if he hesitated longer. He ascended the throne. Presently he stretched forth the sceptre again, and said—

"Prisoner, in the name of our sovereign Lord Ulrich, Duke of Brandenburgh, I proceed to the solemn duty that hath devolved upon me. Give heed to my words. By the ancient law of the land, except you produce the partner of your guilt and deliver him up to the executioner you must surely die. Embrace this opportunity—save yourself while yet you may. Name the father of your child!"

A solemn hush fell upon the great court—a silence so profound that men could hear their own hearts beat. Then the princess slowly turned, with eyes gleaming with hate, and pointing her finger straight at Conrad, said—

"Thou art the man!"

An appalling conviction of his helpless, hopeless peril struck a chill to Conrad's heart like the chill of death itself. What power on earth could save him! To disprove the charge he must reveal that he was a woman, and for an uncrowned woman to sit in the ducal chair was death! At one and the same moment he and his grim old father swooned and fell to the ground.

The remainder of this thrilling and eventful story will NOT be found in this or any other publication, either now or at any future time.

The truth is, I have got my hero (or heroine) into such a particularly close place that I do not see how I am ever going to get him (or her) out of it again, and therefore I will wash my hands of the whole business, and leave that person to get out the best way that offers — or else stay there. I thought it was going to be easy enough to straighten out that little difficulty, but it looks different now.

The Esquimau Maiden's Romance

First published in *Cosmopolitan Magazine* in 1893, "The Esquimau Maiden's Romance" was one of twelve original stories Twain wrote for that magazine while under a five-thousand-dollar contract. It was later reprinted in *The Man that Corrupted Hadleyburg and Other Stories and Essays* (1900).

Twain and his family were living near Florence, Italy, and elsewhere in Europe in 1893, and his writing during this period was driven by the need to maximize his income and avoid financial ruin as, one after another, his business investments turned unprofitable. Unfortunately, his failing investments led to bankruptcy a year later. During this period he also worked on the novels *Puddn'head Wilson* (published serially in *Century* magazine), and *Tom Sawyer Abroad* (which appeared serially in *St. Nicholas* magazine). Like "Aurelia's Unfortunate Young Man," this story is another burlesque of the ever-popular and conventional romantic love story of the era.

In this frame story, as in "The Celebrated Jumping Frog of Calaveras County," serious themes emerge from the frame more than from the story itself. The narrator's interview with Lasca, the Eskimo ("Esquimau") maiden, reveals the cultural contrast between two radically different societies. Lasca's culture had placed a grossly inflated value on iron fish-hooks, much the way Twain's had on pieces of paper called dollars, stocks, and bonds. Her society, like Twain's Gilded Age, willingly sacrificed honor, honesty, and community values in pursuit of wealth, as James Wilson points out (LeMaster and Wilson, 255–56).

Twain's portrait of Princess Lasca, a sad young woman who has inadvertently caused the death of her lover, departs from the "Becky Thatcher" tradition of the pretty and innocent teenaged girl. Although Twain parodies conventional love romances, he also suggests that beauty is, like gender, a cultural construction. Although Lasca is considered a great beauty by her culture, Twain's narrator struggles to find a trace of beauty in the very plump Lasca, who occupies herself "scraping blubber-grease from her cheeks." Beauty aside, Lasca demonstrates her skills at the manly art of hunting, placing her in the company of capable female protagonists such as Hellfire Hotchkiss and Cathy Alison. The poignancy of this story derives from the author's circumstances during its composition, as Twain battled desperately to avoid bankruptcy while Wall Street roller-coastered, then crashed.

"Yes, I will tell you anything about my life that you would like to know, Mr. Twain," she said, in her soft voice, and letting her honest eyes rest placidly upon my face, "for it is kind and good of you to like me and care to know about me."

She had been absently scraping blubber-grease from her cheeks with a small bone-knife and transferring it to her fur sleeve, while she watched the Aurora Borealis swing its flaming streamers out of the sky and wash the lonely snow-plain and the templed icebergs with the rich hues of the prism, a spectacle of almost intolerable splendor and beauty; but now she shook off her reverie and prepared to give me the humble little history I had asked for. She settled herself comfortably on the block of ice which we were using as a sofa, and I made ready to listen.

She was a beautiful creature. I speak from the Esquimaux point of view. Others would have thought her a trifle over-plump. She was just twenty years old, and was held to be by far the most bewitching girl in her tribe. Even now, in the open air, with her cumbersome and shapeless fur coat and trousers and boots and vast hood, the beauty of her face was at least apparent; but her figure had to be taken on trust. Among all the guests who came and went, I had seen no girl at her father's hospitable trough who could be called her equal. Yet she was not spoiled. She was sweet and natural and sincere, and if she was aware that she was a belle, there was nothing about her ways to show that she possessed that knowledge.

She had been my daily comrade for a week now, and the better I knew her the better I liked her. She had been tenderly and carefully brought up, in an atmosphere of singularly rare refinement for the polar regions, for her father was the most important man of his tribe and ranked at the top of Esquimau cultivation. I made long dog-sledge trips across the mighty ice-floes with Lasca—that was her name—and found her company always pleasant and her conversation agreeable. I went fishing with her, but not in her perilous boat: I merely followed along on the ice and watched her strike her game with her fatally accurate spear. We went sealing together; several times I stood by while she and the family dug blubber from a stranded whale, and once I went part of the way when she was hunting a bear, but turned back before the finish, because at bottom I am afraid of bears.

However, she was ready to begin her story, now, and this is what she said:

"Our tribe had always been used to wander about from place to place over the frozen seas, like the other tribes, but my father got tired of that, two years ago, and built this great mansion of frozen snow-blocks—look at it; it is seven feet high and three or four times as long as any of the others—and here we have stayed ever since. He was very proud of his house, and that was reasonable, for if you have examined it with care you must have noticed how much finer and completer it is than houses usually are. But if you have not, you must, for you will find it has luxurious appointments that are quite beyond the common. For instance, in that end of it which you have called the 'parlor,' the raised platform for the accommodation of guests and the family at meals is the largest you have ever seen in any house—is it not so?"

"Yes, you are quite right, Lasca; it is the largest; we have nothing resembling it in even the finest houses in the United States." This admission made her eyes sparkle with pride and pleasure. I noted that, and took my cue.

"I thought it must have surprised you," she said. "And another thing: it is bedded far deeper in furs than is usual; all kinds of furs—seal, sea-otter, silver-gray fox, bear, marten, sable—every kind of fur in profusion; and the same with the ice-block sleeping-benches along the walls, which you call 'beds.' Are your platforms and sleeping-benches better provided at home?"

"Indeed, they are not, Lasca—they do not begin to be." That pleased her again. All she was thinking of was the *number* of furs her æsthetic father took the trouble to keep on hand, not their value. I could have told her that those masses of rich furs constituted wealth—or would in my country—but she would not have understood that; those were not the kind of things that ranked as riches with her people. I could have told her that the clothes she had on, or the every-day clothes of the commonest person about her, were worth twelve or fifteen hundred dollars, and that I was not acquainted with anybody at home who wore twelve-hundred dollar toilets to go fishing in; but she would not have understood it, so I said nothing. She resumed:

"And then the slop-tubs. We have two in the parlor, and two in the rest of the house. It is very seldom that one has two in the parlor. Have you two in the parlor at home?"

The memory of those tubs made me gasp, but I recovered myself before she noticed, and said with effusion:

"Why, Lasca, it is a shame of me to expose my country, and you must not let it go further, for I am speaking to you in confidence; but I give you my word of honor that not even the richest man in the city of New York has two slop-tubs in his drawing-room."

She clapped her fur-clad hands in innocent delight, and exclaimed:

"Oh, but you cannot mean it, you cannot *mean* it!"

"Indeed, I am in earnest, dear. There is Vanderbilt. Vanderbilt is almost the richest man in the whole world. Now, if I were on my dying bed, I could say to you that not even he has two in his drawing-room. Why, he hasn't even *one*—I wish I may die in my tracks if it isn't true."

Her lovely eyes stood wide with amazement, and she said, slowly, and with a sort of awe in her voice:

"How strange—how incredible—one is not able to realize it. Is he penurious?"

"No—it isn't that. It isn't the expense he minds, but—er—well, you know, it would look like showing off. Yes, that is it, that is the idea; he is a plain man in his way, and shrinks from display."

"Why, that humility is right enough," said Lasca, "if one does not carry it too far—but what does the place look like?"

"Well, necessarily it looks pretty barren and unfinished, but—"

"I should think so! I never heard anything like it. Is it a fine house—that is, otherwise?"

"Pretty fine, yes. It is very well thought of."

The girl was silent awhile, and sat dreamily gnawing a candle-end, apparently trying to think the thing out. At last she gave her head a little toss and spoke out her opinion with decision:

"Well, to my mind there's a breed of humility which is *itself* a species of showing-off, when you get down to the marrow of it; and when a man is able to afford two slop-tubs in his parlor, and don't do it, it *may* be that he is truly humble-minded, but it's a hundred times more likely that he is just trying to strike the public eye. In my judgment, your Mr. Vanderbilt knows what he is about."

I tried to modify this verdict, feeling that a double slop-tub standard was not a fair one to try everybody by, although a sound enough one in its own habitat; but the girl's head was set, and she was not to be persuaded. Presently she said:

"Do the rich people, with you, have as good sleeping-benches as ours, and made out of as nice broad ice-blocks?"

"Well, they are pretty good—good enough—but they are not made of ice-blocks."

"I want to know! *Why* aren't they made of ice-blocks?"

I explained the difficulties in the way, and the expensiveness of ice in a country where you have to keep a sharp eye on your ice-man or your ice-bill will weigh more than your ice. Then she cried out:

"Dear me, do you *buy* your ice?"

"We most surely do, dear."

She burst into a gale of guileless laughter, and said:

"Oh, I *never* heard of anything so silly! My, there's plenty of it—it isn't worth anything. Why, there is a hundred miles of it in sight, right now. I wouldn't give a fish-bladder for the whole of it."

"Well, it's because you don't know how to value it, you little provincial muggins. If you had it in New York in midsummer, you could buy all the whales in the market with it."

She looked at me doubtfully, and said:

"Are you speaking true?"

"Absolutely. I take my oath to it."

This made her thoughtful. Presently she said, with a little sigh:

"I wish I could live there."

I had merely meant to furnish her a standard of values which she could understand; but my purpose had miscarried. I had only given her the impression that whales were cheap and plenty in New York, and set her mouth to watering for them. It seemed best to try to mitigate the evil which I had done, so I said:

"But you wouldn't care for whale-meat if you lived there. Nobody does."

"What!"

"Indeed they don't."

"*Why* don't they?"

"Wel-l-l, I hardly know. It's prejudice, I think. Yes, that is it—just prejudice. I reckon somebody that hadn't anything better to do started a prejudice against it, some time or other, and once you get a caprice like that fairly going, you know, it will last no end of time."

"That is true—*perfectly* true," said the girl, reflectively. "Like our prejudice against soap, here—our tribes had a prejudice against soap at first, you know."

I glanced at her to see if she was in earnest. Evidently she was. I hesitated, then said, cautiously:

"But pardon me. They *had* a prejudice against soap? Had?"—with falling inflection.

"Yes—but that was only at first; nobody would eat it."

"Oh—I understand. I didn't get your idea before."

She resumed:

"It was just a prejudice. The first time soap came here from the foreigners, nobody liked it; but as soon as it got to be fashionable, everybody liked it, and now everybody has it that can afford it. Are you fond of it?"

"Yes, indeed; I should die if I couldn't have it—especially here. Do you like it?"

"I just *adore* it! Do you like candles?"

"I regard them as an absolute necessity. Are you fond of them?"

Her eyes fairly danced, and she exclaimed:

"Oh! Don't mention it! Candles!—and soap!—"

"And fish-interiors!—"

"And train-oil!—"

"And slush!—"

"And whale-blubber!—"

"And carrion! and sour-krout! and beeswax! and tar! and turpentine! and molasses! and—"

"Don't—oh, don't—I shall expire with ecstasy!—"

"And then serve it all up in a slush-bucket, and invite the neighbors and sail in!"

But this vision of an ideal feast was too much for her, and she swooned away, poor thing. I rubbed snow in her face and brought her to, and after a while got her excitement cooled down. By-and-by she drifted into her story again:

"So we began to live here, in the fine house. But I was not happy. The reason was this: I was born for love; for me there could be no true happiness without it. I wanted to be loved for myself alone. I wanted an idol, and I wanted to be my idol's idol; nothing less than mutual idolatry would satisfy my fervent nature. I had suitors in plenty—in over-plenty, indeed—but in each and every case they had a fatal defect; sooner or later I discovered that defect—not one of them failed to betray it—it was not me they wanted, but my wealth."

"Your wealth?"

"Yes; for my father is much the richest man in this tribe—or in any tribe in these regions."

I wondered what her father's wealth consisted of. It couldn't be the house—anybody could build its mate. It couldn't be the furs—they were not valued. It couldn't be the sledge, the dogs, the harpoons, the boat, the bone fish-hooks and needles, and such things—no, these were not wealth. Then what could it be that made this man so rich and brought this swarm of sordid suitors to his house? It seemed to me, finally, that the best way to find out would be to ask. So I did it. The girl was so manifestly gratified by the question that I saw she had been aching to have me ask it. She was suffering fully as much to tell as I was to know. She snuggled confidentially up to me and said:

"Guess how much he is worth—you never can!"

I pretended to consider the matter deeply, she watching my anxious and laboring countenance with a devouring and delighted interest; and when, at last, I gave it up and begged her to appease my longing by telling me herself how much this polar Vanderbilt was worth, she put her mouth close to my ear and whispered, impressively:

"*Twenty-two fish-hooks*—not bone, but foreign—*made out of real iron!*"

Then she sprang back dramatically, to observe the effect. I did my level best not to disappoint her. I turned pale and murmured:

"Great Scott!"

"It's as true as you live, Mr. Twain!"

"Lasca, you are deceiving me—you cannot mean it."

She was frightened and troubled. She exclaimed:

"Mr. Twain, every word of it is true—every word. You believe me—you *do* believe me, now *don't* you? *Say* you believe me—*do* say you believe me!"

"I—well, yes, I do—I am *trying* to. But it was all so *sudden*. So sudden and prostrating. You shouldn't do such a thing in that sudden way. It—"

"Oh, I'm *so* sorry! If I had only thought—"

"Well, it's all right, and I don't blame you any more, for you are young and thoughtless, and of course you couldn't foresee what an effect—"

"But oh, dear, I ought certainly to have *known* better. Why—"

"You see, Lasca, if you had said five or six hooks, to start with, and then gradually—"

"Oh, I see, I see—then gradually added one, and then two, and then—ah, why couldn't I have thought of that!"

"Never mind, child, it's all right—I am better now—I shall be over it in a little while. But—to spring the whole twenty-two on a person unprepared and not very strong anyway—"

"Oh, it *was* a crime! But you forgive me—say you forgive me. Do!"

After harvesting a good deal of very pleasant coaxing and petting and persuading, I forgave her and she was happy again, and by-and-by she got under way with her narrative once more. I presently discovered that the family treasury contained still another feature—a jewel of some sort, apparently—and that she was trying to get around speaking squarely about it, lest I get paralyzed again. But I wanted to know about that thing, too, and urged her to tell me what it was. She was afraid. But I insisted, and said I would brace myself this time and be prepared, then the shock would not hurt me. She was full of misgivings, but the temptation to reveal that marvel to me and enjoy my astonishment and admiration was too strong for her, and she confessed that she had it on her person, and said that if I was *sure* I was prepared—and so on and so on—and with that she reached into her bosom and brought out a battered square of brass, watching my eye anxiously the while. I fell over against her in a quite well-acted faint, which delighted her heart and nearly frightened it out of her, too, at the same time. When I came to and got calm, she was eager to know what I thought of her jewel.

"What do I think of it? I think it is the most exquisite thing I ever saw."

"Do you really? How nice of you to say that! But it *is* a love, now isn't it?"

"Well, I should say so! I'd rather own it than the equator."

"I thought you would admire it," she said. "I think it is *so* lovely. And there isn't another one in all these latitudes. People have come all the way from the Open Polar Sea to look at it. Did you ever see one before?"

I said no, this was the first one I had ever seen. It cost me a pang to tell that generous lie, for I had seen a million of them in my time, this humble jewel of hers being nothing but a battered old New York Central baggage-check.

"Land!" said I, "you don't go about with it on your person this way, alone and with no protection, not even a dog?"

"Ssh! not so loud," she said. "Nobody knows I carry it with

34

me. They think it is in papa's treasury. That is where it generally is."

"Where is the treasury?"

It was a blunt question, and for a moment she looked startled and a little suspicious, but I said:

"Oh, come, don't you be afraid about me. At home we have
seventy millions of people, and although I say it myself that
shouldn't, there is not one person among them all but would
trust me with untold fish-hooks."

This reassured her, and she told me where the hooks were
hidden in the house. Then she wandered from her course to
brag a little about the size of the sheets of transparent ice that
formed the windows of the mansion, and asked me if I had
ever seen their like at home, and I came right out frankly and
confessed that I hadn't, which pleased her more than she could
find words to dress her gratification in. It was so easy to please
her, and such a pleasure to do it that I went on and said—

"Ah, Lasca, you *are* a fortunate girl!—this beautiful house,
this dainty jewel, that rich treasure, all this elegant snow, and
sumptuous icebergs and limitless sterility, and public bears
and walruses, and noble freedom and largeness, and everybody's admiring eyes upon you, and everybody's homage and
respect at your command without the asking; young, rich,
beautiful, sought, courted, envied, not a requirement unsat-
isfied, not a desire ungratified, nothing to wish for that you
cannot have—it is immeasurable good-fortune! I have seen
myriads of girls, but none of whom these extraordinary things
could be truthfully said but you alone. And you are worthy—
worthy of it all, Lasca—I believe it in my heart."

It made her infinitely proud and happy to hear me say this,
and she thanked me over and over again for that closing remark, and her voice and eyes showed that she was touched.
Presently she said:

"Still, it is not all sunshine—there is a cloudy side. The burden of wealth is a heavy one to bear. Sometimes I have doubted
if it were not better to be poor—at least not inordinately rich.
It pains me to see neighboring tribesmen stare as they pass
by, and overhear them say, reverently, one to another, 'There—

that is she—the millionaire's daughter!' And sometimes they say sorrowfully, 'She is rolling in fish-hooks, and I—I have nothing.' It breaks my heart. When I was a child and we were poor, we slept with the door open, if we chose, but now—now we have to have a night-watchman. In those days my father was gentle and courteous to all; but now he is austere and haughty, and cannot abide familiarity. Once his family were his sole thought, but now he goes about thinking of his fish-hooks all the time. And his wealth makes everybody cringing and obsequious to him. Formerly nobody laughed at his jokes, they being always stale and far-fetched and poor, and destitute of the one element that can really justify a joke—the element of humor; but now everybody laughs and cackles at those dismal things, and if any fails to do it my father is deeply displeased, and shows it. Formerly his opinion was not sought upon any matter and was not valuable when he volunteered it; it has that infirmity yet, but, nevertheless, it is sought by all and applauded by all—and he helps do the applauding himself, having no true delicacy and a plentiful want of tact. He has lowered the tone of all our tribe. Once they were a frank and manly race, now they are measly hypocrites, and sodden with servility. In my heart of hearts I hate all the ways of millionaires! Our tribe was once plain, simple folk, and content with the bone fish-hooks of their fathers; now they are eaten up with avarice and would sacrifice every sentiment of honor and honesty to possess themselves of the debasing iron fish-hooks of the foreigner. However, I must not dwell on these sad things. As I have said, it was my dream to be loved for myself alone.

"At last, this dream seemed about to be fulfilled. A stranger came by, one day, who said his name was Kalula. I told him my name, and he said he loved me. My heart gave a great bound of gratitude and pleasure, for I had loved him at sight, and now I said so. He took me to his breast and said he would not wish to be happier than he was now. We went strolling together far over the ice-floes, telling all about each other, and planning, oh, the loveliest future! When we were tired at last we sat down and ate, for he had soap and candles and I had brought along some blubber. We were hungry, and nothing was ever so good.

"He belonged to a tribe whose haunts were far to the north, and I found that he had never heard of my father, which rejoiced me exceedingly. I mean he had heard of the millionaire, but had never heard his name — so, you see, he could not know that I was the heiress. You may be sure that I did not tell him. I was loved for myself at last, and was satisfied. I was so happy — oh, happier than you can think!

"By-and-by it was toward supper time, and I led him home. As we approached our house he was amazed, and cried out:

"'How splendid! Is that your father's?'

"It gave me a pang to hear that tone and see that admiring light in his eye, but the feeling quickly passed away, for I loved him so, and he looked so handsome and noble. All my family of aunts and uncles and cousins were pleased with him, and many guests were called in, and the house was shut up tight and the rag lamps lighted, and when everything was hot and comfortable and suffocating, we began a joyous feast in celebration of my betrothal.

"When the feast was over, my father's vanity overcame him, and he could not resist the temptation to show off his riches and let Kalula see what grand good-fortune he had stumbled into — and mainly, of course, he wanted to enjoy the poor man's amazement. I could have cried — but it would have done no good to try to dissuade my father, so I said nothing, but merely sat there and suffered.

"My father went straight to the hiding-place, in full sight of everybody, and got out the fish-hooks and brought them and flung them scatteringly over my head, so that they fell in glittering confusion on the platform at my lover's knee.

"Of course, the astounding spectacle took the poor lad's breath away. He could only stare in stupid astonishment, and wonder how a single individual could possess such incredible riches. Then presently he glanced brilliantly up and exclaimed:

"'Ah, it is *you* who are the renowned millionaire!'

"My father and all the rest burst into shouts of happy laughter, and when my father gathered the treasure carelessly up as if it might be mere rubbish and of no consequence, and carried it back to its place, poor Kalula's surprise was a study. He said:

"'Is it possible that you put such things away without count-ing them?'

"My father delivered a vain-glorious horse-laugh, and said:

"'Well, truly, a body may know *you* have never been rich, since a mere matter of a fish-hook or two is such a mighty matter in your eyes.'

"Kalula was confused, and hung his head, but said:

"'Ah, indeed, sir, I was never worth the value of the barb of one of those precious things, and I have never seen any man before who was so rich in them as to render the counting of his hoard worthwhile, since the wealthiest man I have ever known, till now, was possessed of but three.'

"My foolish father roared again with jejune delight, and al-lowed the impression to remain that he was not accustomed to count his hooks and keep sharp watch over them. He was showing off, you see. Count them? Why, he counted them every day!

"I had met and got acquainted with my darling just at dawn; I had brought him home just at dark, three hours afterward — for the days were shortening toward the six-months night at that time. We kept up the festivities many hours; then, at last, the guests departed and the rest of us distributed our-selves along the walls on sleeping-benches, and soon all were steeped in dreams but me. I was too happy, too excited, to sleep. After I had lain quiet a long, long time, a dim form passed by me and was swallowed up in the gloom that per-vaded the farther end of the house. I could not make out who it was, or whether it was man or woman. Presently that figure or another one passed me going the other way. I wondered what it all meant, but wondering did no good; and while I was still wondering I fell asleep.

"I do not know how long I slept, but at last I came sud-denly broad awake and heard my father say in a terrible voice, 'By the great Snow God, there's a fish-hook gone!' Some-thing told me that that meant sorrow for me, and the blood in my veins turned cold. The presentiment was confirmed in the same instant: my father shouted, 'Up, everybody, and seize the stranger!' Then there was an outburst of cries and curses from

all sides, and a wild rush of dim forms through the obscurity.
I flew to my beloved's help, but what could I do but wait and
wring my hands?—he was already fenced away from me by a
living wall, he was being bound hand and foot. Not until he
was secured would they let me get to him. I flung myself upon
his poor insulted form and cried my grief out upon his breast
while my father and all my family scoffed at me and heaped
threats and shameful epithets upon him. He bore his ill usage
with a tranquil dignity which endeared him to me more than
ever and made me proud and happy to suffer with him and
for him. I heard my father order that the elders of the tribe be
called together to try my Kalula for his life.

"'What?' I said, 'before any search has been made for the
lost hook?'

"'Lost hook!' they all shouted, in derision; and my father
added, mockingly, 'Stand back, everybody, and be properly
serious—she is going to hunt up that *lost* hook; oh, without
doubt she will find it!'—whereat they all laughed again.

"I was not disturbed—I had no fears, no doubts. I said:

"'It is for you to laugh now; it is your turn. But ours is coming;
wait and see.'

"I got a rag-lamp. I thought I should find that miserable
thing in one little moment; and I set about the matter with
such confidence that those people grew grave, beginning to
suspect that perhaps they had been too hasty. But, alas and
alas!—oh, the bitterness of that search! There was deep silence
while one might count his fingers ten or twelve times, then
my heart began to sink, and around me the mockings began
again, and grew steadily louder and more assured, until at
last, when I gave up, they burst into volley after volley of cruel
laughter.

"None will ever know what I suffered then. But my love was
my support and my strength, and I took my rightful place at my
Kalula's side, and put my arm about his neck, and whispered
in his ear, saying:

"'You are innocent, my own—that I know; but say it to me
yourself, for my comfort, then I can bear whatever is in store
for us.'

"He answered:

"'As surely as I stand upon the brink of death at this moment, I am innocent. Be comforted, then, O bruised heart; be at peace, O thou breath of my nostrils, life of my life!'

"'Now, then, let the elders come!'—and as I said the words there was a gathering sound of crunching snow outside, and then a vision of stooping forms filing in at the door—the elders.

"My father formally accused the prisoner, and detailed the happenings of the night. He said that the watchman was outside the door, and that in the house were none but the family and the stranger. 'Would the family steal their own property?' He paused. The elders sat silent many minutes; at last, one after another said to his neighbor, 'This looks bad for the stranger'—sorrowful words for me to hear. Then my father sat down. O miserable, miserable me! at that very moment I could have proved my darling innocent, but I did not know it!

"The chief of the court asked:

"'Is there any here to defend the prisoner?'

"I rose and said:

"'Why should *he* steal that hook, or any or all of them? In another day he would have been heir to the whole!'

"I stood waiting. There was a long silence, the steam from the many breaths rising about me like a fog. At last, one elder after another nodded his head slowly several times, and muttered, 'There is force in what the child has said.' Oh, the heart-lift that was in those words!—so transient, but, oh, so precious! I sat down.

"'If any would say further, let him speak now, or after hold his peace,' said the chief of the court.

"My father rose and said:

"'In the night a form passed by me in the gloom, going toward the treasury, and presently returned. I think, now, it was the stranger.'

"Oh, I was like to swoon! I had supposed that that was my secret; not the grip of the great Ice God himself could have dragged it out of my heart. The chief of the court said sternly to my poor Kalula:

"'Speak!'

"Kalula hesitated, then answered:

"'It was I. I could not sleep for thinking of the beautiful hooks. I went there and kissed them and fondled them, to appease my spirit and drown it in a harmless joy, then I put them back. I may have dropped one, but I stole none.'

"Oh, a fatal admission to make in such a place! There was an awful hush. I knew he had pronounced his own doom, and that all was over. On every face you could see the words hieroglyphed: 'It is a confession!—and paltry, lame, and thin.'

"I sat drawing in my breath in faint gasps—and waiting. Presently, I heard the solemn words I knew were coming; and each word, as it came, was a knife in my heart:

"'It is the command of the court that the accused be subjected to the trial by water.'

"Oh, curses be upon the head of him who brought 'trial by water' to our land! It came, generations ago, from some far country that lies none knows where. Before that, our fathers used augury and other unsure methods of trial, and doubtless some poor, guilty creatures escaped with their lives sometimes; but it is not so with trial by water, which is an invention by wiser men than we poor, ignorant savages are. By it the innocent are proved innocent, without doubt or question, for they drown; and the guilty are proven guilty with the same certainty, for they do not drown. My heart was breaking in my bosom, for I said, 'He is innocent, and he will go down under the waves and I shall never see him more.'

"I never left his side after that. I mourned in his arms all the precious hours, and he poured out the deep stream of his love upon me, and oh, I was so miserable and so happy! At last, they tore him from me, and I followed sobbing after them, and saw them fling him into the sea—then I covered my face with my hands. Agony? Oh, I know the deepest deeps of that word!

"The next moment the people burst into a shout of malicious joy, and I took away my hands, startled. Oh, bitter sight—he was *swimming*! My heart turned instantly to stone, to ice. I said, 'He was guilty, and he lied to me!' I turned my back in scorn and went my way homeward.

"They took him far out to sea and set him on an iceberg that was drifting southward in the great waters. Then my family came home, and my father said to me:

"'Your thief sent his dying message to you, saying, "Tell her I am innocent, and that all the days and all the hours and all the minutes while I starve and perish I shall love her and think of her and bless the day that gave me sight of her sweet face." Quite pretty, even poetical!'

"I said, 'He is dirt—let me never hear mention of him again.' And oh, to think—he *was* innocent all the time!

"Nine months—nine dull, sad months—went by, and at last came the day of the Great Annual Sacrifice, when all the maidens of the tribe wash their faces and comb their hair. With the first sweep of my comb, out came the fatal fish-hook from where it had been all those months nestling, and I fell fainting into the arms of my remorseful father! Groaning, he said, 'We murdered him, and I shall never smile again!' He has kept his word. Listen: from that day to this not a month goes by that I do not comb my hair. But oh, where is the good of it all now!"

So ended the poor maid's humble little tale—whereby we learn that since a hundred million dollars in New York and twenty-two fish-hooks on the border of the Arctic Circle represent the same financial supremacy, a man in straitened circumstances is a fool to stay in New York when he can buy ten cents' worth of fish-hooks and emigrate.

Hellfire Hotchkiss

Twain wrote the opening three chapters of this unfinished manuscript circa 1897. It remained unpublished until 1967 when it appeared in *Mark Twain's Satires and Burlesques*. For his setting Twain returns to the familiar Mississippi River village of Dawson's Landing, the setting for *Pudd'nhead Wilson*, which also resembles his hometown of Hannibal, Missouri. According to Sandra Littleton-Uetz, Oscar Carpenter, the story's male counterpart to Hellfire Hotchkiss, is a comically exaggerated version of the weak and inconsistent character Twain saw in his own brother, Orion (LeMaster and Wilson, 355). Margaret Sanborn believes that the closest model for Hellfire comes from Lillie Hitchcock, a friend of Twain's from his San Francisco period. Ironically, the most dramatic episode of the manuscript comes when Hellfire rescues Oscar from an ice floe on the Mississippi River—an incident that actually happened to Twain, not his brother.

The manuscript was written soon after Twain completed work on *The Personal Recollections of Joan of Arc* in 1895, and Hellfire, its female protagonist, appears to represent an American application of the strong qualities and strength of character he found in the French heroine. As Joan acted in forceful contrast to an effete king and unyielding aristocracy, Hellfire's prowess in all her physical and intellectual pursuits renders Oscar and all other males of Dawson's Landing pathetically ineffectual. The unfinished "Hellfire Hotchkiss" may be the beginning chapters of what Twain conceived of as an American version of Joan of Arc, depicting in it a young woman with the qualities and strengths of Joan but struggling for women's rights and opportunities, a theme that surfaces in the first three chapters of the story. This is not the only girl or young woman story in which female ambition is threatened by male jealousy and revenge.

"But James, he is our son, and we must bear with him. If we cannot bear with him, how can we expect others to do it?"

"I have not said I expected it, Sarah. I am very far from expecting it. He is the most trying ass that was ever born."

"James! You forget that he is our son."

"That does not save him from being an ass. It does not even take the sting out of it."

"I do not see how you can be so hard toward your own flesh and blood. Mr. Rucker does not think of him as you do."

"And why should he? Mr. Rucker is an ass himself."

"James—do think what you are saying. Do you think it becoming to speak so of a minister—a person called of God?"

"Who said he was?"

"Who *said* he was? Now you are becoming blasphemous. His office is proof that he was called."

"Very well, then, perhaps he was. But it was an error of judgment."

"James, I might have known you would say some awful thing like that. Some day a judgment will overtake you when you least expect it. And after saying what you have said about Mr. Rucker, perhaps you will feel some natural shame when you learn what he has been saying to me about our Oscar."

"What was it? What did he say?"

"He said there was not another youth of seventeen in the Sunday School that was so bright."

"Bright. What of that? He is bright enough, but what is brightness worth when it is allied to constitutional and indestructible instability of character? Oscar's a fool."

45

"For pity's sake! And he your own son."

"It's what he is. He is a fool. And I can't help his being my son. It is one of those judgments that overtake a person when he is least expecting it."

"James, I wonder how you can say such things. The idea of calling your own son a judgment."

"Oh, call him a benefaction if you like."

"I do call him one, James; and I bless the day that God in his loving thoughtfulness gave him to us."

"That is pure flattery."

"James Carpenter!"

"That is what it is, and you know it. What is there about it to suggest loving thoughtfulness—or any kind of thoughtfulness? It was an inadvertence."

"James, such language is perfectly shocking. It is profanity."

"Profanity is better than flattery. The trouble with you Presbyterians and other church-people is that you exercise no discrimination. Whatever comes, you praise; you call it praise, and you think it praise; yet in the majority of cases it is flattery. Flattery, and undignified; undignified and unworthy. Your singular idea that Oscar was a result of thoughtfulness—"

"James, I won't listen to such talk! If you would go to church yourself, instead of finding fault with people who do, it would be better."

"But I don't find fault with people who do."

"Didn't you just say that they exercise no discrimination, and all that?"

"Certainly, but I did not say that that was an *effect* of going to church. It probably is; and now that you press me, I think it *is*; but I didn't quite say it."

"Well, James, you as good as said it; and now it comes out that at bottom you thought it. It shows how staying away from church makes a person uncharitable in his judgments and opinions."

"Oh, come!"

"But it does."

"I dissent—distinctly."

"Now James, how can you know? In the nineteen years that

we have been married, you have been to church only once, and that was nearly nineteen years ago. You have been uncharitable in your judgments ever since—more or less so."

"I do not quite catch your argument. Do you mean that going to church only once made me uncharitable for life?"

"James, you know very well that I meant nothing of the kind. You just said that to provoke me. You know perfectly well that I meant—I meant—now you have got me all confused, and I don't know what I did mean."

"Don't trouble about it, Sarah. It's not like having a new experience, you know. For—"

"That will do, James. I do not wish to hear anything more about it. And as for Oscar—"

"Good—let us have some more Oscar for a change. Is it true that he has resigned from the Cadets of Temperance?"

"Ye-s."

"I thought he would."

"Indeed? And what made you think it?"

"Because he has been a member three months."

"What has that to do with it?"

"It's his limit."

"What do you mean by that, James?"

"Three months is his limit—in most things. When it isn't three weeks or three days or three hours. You must have noticed that. He revolves in threes—it is his make. He is a creature of enthusiasms. Burning enthusiasms. They flare up, and light all the region round. For three months, or weeks, or days. Then they go out and he catches fire in another place. You remember he was the joy of the Methodist Sunday school at 7— for three months. Then he was the joy of the Campbellite Sunday school—for three months. Then of the Baptist—for three months. Then of the Presbyterian—for three months. Then he started over again with the Methodist contingent, and went through the list again; and yet again; and still again; and so on. He has been the hope and joy of each of those sources of spiritual supply nine times in nine years; and from Mr. Rucker's remark I gather that he is now booming the Presbyterian interest once more. As concerns the Cadets of Temperance, I was just thinking that his quarterly period—"

"James, it makes me sick to hear you talk like that. You have never loved your boy. And you never encourage him. You know how sensitive he is to slights and neglect, yet you have always neglected him. You know how quickly he responds to praise, and how necessary praise and commendation and encouragement are to him—indeed they are his very life—yet he gets none of these helps from you. How can you expect him to be steadfast; how can you expect him to keep up his heart in his little affairs and plans when you never show any interest in them and never applaud anything he does?"

"Applaud? What is there to applaud? It is just as you say: praise is his meat and bread—it is his life. And there never was such an unappeasable appetite. So long as you feed him praise, he gorges, gorges, gorges, and is obscenely happy; the moment you stop he is famished—famished and wretched; utterly miserable, despondent, despairing. You ought to know all about it. You have tried to keep him fed-up, all his life, and you know what a job it is. I detest that word—encouragement—where the male sex is concerned. The boy that needs much of it is a girl in disguise. He ought to put on petticoats. Praise has a value—when it is earned. When it isn't earned, the male creature receiving it ought to despise it; and will, when there is a proper degree of manliness in him. Sarah, if it is possible to make anything creditable out of the boy, only a strong hand can do it. Not yours, and not mine. You are all indulgence, I all indifference. The earlier the strong hand takes him in charge, the better. And not here in Dawson's Landing, where he can be always running home for sympathy and pettings, but in some other place—as far off as St Louis, say. You gasp!"

"Oh, James, James, you can't mean what you say! Oh, I never could bear it; oh, I know I never could."

"Now come, don't cry, Sarah. Be reasonable. You don't want the boy ruined. Now do you?"

"But oh, to have him away off there, and I not by if anything should happen."

"Nothing's going to happen. He—"

"James—he might get sick. And if I were not there—"

"But you can go there, if he gets sick. Let us not borrow

trouble—there is time enough. Other boys go from home—it is nothing new—and if Oscar doesn't, he will be ruined. Now you know Underwood—a good man, and an old and trusty friend of mine."

"The printer?"

"Yes. I have been corresponding with him. He is willing to take Oscar as an apprentice. Now doesn't that strike you pleasantly?"

"Why—yes. If he *must* go away from home—oh, dear, dear, dear!—why of course I would rather have him with Mr. Underwood than with anyone else. I want to see Oscar succeed in the world; I desire it as much as you can. But surely there are other ways than the one proposed; and ways more soothing to one's pride, too. Why should our son be a common mechanic—a printer? As far back as we can go there have been no mechanics in your family, and none in mine. In Virginia, for more than two centuries they have been as good as anybody about them; they have been slave-holding planters, professional men, politicians—now and then a merchant, but never a mechanic. They have always been gentlemen. And they were that in England before they came over. Isn't it so?"

"I am not denying it. Go on."

"Don't speak in that tired way, James. You always act annoyed when I speak of our ancestors, and once you said 'Damn the ancestors.' I remember it very well. I wonder you could say such a horrid thing about them, knowing, as you do, how brief this life is, and how soon you must be an ancestor yourself."

"God forgive me, I never thought of that."

"I *heard* that, James—heard every word of it; and you said it ironically, too, which is not good taste—no better taste than muttering it was—muttering to yourself like that when your wife is talking to you."

"Well, I'm sorry; go on, I won't do it again. But if the irony was the thing that pinched, that was a quite unnecessary unkindness; I could have said it seriously, and so saved you the hurt."

"Seriously? How do you mean?"

"Oh, sometimes I feel as if I could give anything to give it

49

all up and lie down in the peace and the quiet and be an ancestor, I do get so tired of being posterity. It is when things go wrong and I am low spirited that I feel like that. At such times—peculiarly dark times, times of deep depression, when the heart is bruised and sore and the light of life is veiled in shadows—it has seemed to me that I would rather be a dog's ancestor than a lieutenant governor's posterity."

"For shame! James, it is the same as saying I am a disappointment to you, and that you would be happier without me than with me. Oh, James, how could you say such a thing?"

"I didn't say it."

"What *did* you say?"

"I said that sometimes I would rather be an ancestor than posterity."

"Well, isn't that separating us?"

"No—for I included you."

"That is different. But James you didn't *say* so. It sounded as if you only wanted to be an ancestor by yourself, and of course that hurt me. Did you *always* think of me, James? Did you always include me? Did you wish I was an ancestor as often as you wished you were one?"

"Yes. Oftener. Twice as often."

"How good you are, James—when you *want* to be. But you are not always good; I wish you were. Still, I am satisfied with you, just as you are; I don't want you changed. You don't want me changed, do you, James?"

"No, I don't think of any change that I would want to risk."

"How lovely of you!"

"Don't mention it. Now, as I remember it, your argument had reached the point where—well, I think you had about finished with the ancestry, and—"

"Yes—and was coming to you. You are county judge—the position of highest dignity in the gift of the ballot—and yet you would see your son become a mechanic."

"I would see him become a *man*. He needn't remain a mechanic, if you think it would damage his chances for the peerage."

"The peerage! I never said anything about the peerage. He

50

would never get rid of the stain. It would always be remembered that he had been a mechanic."

"To his discredit? Nonsense. Who would remember it as a smirch?"

"Well, I would, for one. And so would the widow Buckner—"

"Grand-daughter of a Hessian corporal, whom she has painted up in a breastpin as an English general. *She* despise mechanics! Why, her ancestors were bought and sold in shoals in Cassel, at the price of a pound of candles apiece. And it was an overcharge."

"Well, there's Miss Rector—"

"Bosh!"

"It isn't bosh! She—"

"Oh, I know all about that old Tabby. She claims to be descended in an illegal and indelicate way from Charles II. That is no distinction; we are all that. Come, she is no aristocracy. Her opinion is of no consequence. That poor scraggy old thing— why, she is the descendant of an interminable line of Presbyterian Scotch fishermen, and is built, from the ground up, out of hereditary holiness and herring-bones."

"James, it is scandalous to talk so. She—"

"Get back on your course, Sarah. We can discuss the Hessian and the osteological remains another time. You were coming to some more reasons why Oscar should not be a printer."

"Yes. It is not a necessity—either moneywise or otherwise. You are comfortably off and need no help from earnings of his. By grace of his grandfather he has a permanent income of four hundred dollars a year, which makes him rich—at least for this town and region."

"Yes; and fortunately for him it is but a life-interest and he can never touch the principal; otherwise I would rather have a hatful of smoke than that property."

"Well, that is neither here nor there. He has that income; and has six hundred dollars saved from it and laid up."

"Don't let him find it out, Sarah."

"I—I—he already knows it, James. I did not mean to tell him; it escaped me when I wasn't thinking. I'm sorry."

"I am, too. But it is no matter—yet awhile. It is out of his reach until he is of age."

Sarah said nothing, but she was a little troubled. She had lent trifles of money to Oscar from time to time, against the day of his financial independence.

Judge Carpenter mused a while, then said —

"Sarah, I think your objections to my project are not very strong. I believe we must let it stand, unless you can suggest something better. What is your idea about the boy?"

"I think he ought to be trained to one of the professions, James."

"Um-m. Medicine and surgery?"

"Oh, dear no! not surgery. He is too kind-hearted to give pain, and the sight of blood distresses him. A physician has to turn out of his bed at all hours and expose himself to all weathers. I should be afraid of that — for his health, I mean. I should prefer the law. There is opportunity for advancement in that; such a long and grand line of promotions open to one who is diligent and has talent. James, only think of it — he could become Chief Justice of the Supreme Court of the United States!"

"*Could? Would*, you mean."

"Oh, James, do you think he would?"

"Undoubtedly."

"Oh, James, what makes you think so?"

"I don't know."

"You don't *know?*"

"No."

"Then what made you say so?"

"I don't know."

"James, I think you are the most provoking man that ever — James, are you trifling with me? But I know you are — I can see it. I don't see how you can act so. I think he would be a great lawyer. If you have doubts —"

"Well, Sarah, I have. He has a fair education; good enough for the business — here in a region where lawyers are hardly ever college-bred men; he has a brighter mind than the average, hereabouts — very much brighter than the average, indeed; he is honest, upright, honorable, his impulses are always high, never otherwise — but he would make a poor lawyer. He has no firmness, no steadfastness, he is as changeable as the wind. He will stick at a thing no longer than the novelty of it lasts, and the praises—then he is off again. When his whole heart is in something and all his fires blazing, anybody can squirt a discouraging word on them and put them out; and any wordy, half-clever person can talk him out of his dearest opinion and make him abandon it. This is not the stuff that good lawyers are made of."

"James, you *cannot* be right. It cannot be as bad as you think; you are prejudiced. You never would consent to see any but the most unfavorable side of Oscar. Do you believe he is unfitted for *all* the professions?"

"All but one."

"Which one?"

"The pulpit."

"James, I could hug you for that! It was the secret wish of my heart—my day-dream all these years; but I never dared to speak of it to *you*, of all creatures. Oh, James, do you think, do you really and seriously think that he would make a name for himself in the pulpit—be spoken of, written about?"

"I *know* it."

"Oh, it is *too* good, too lovely! Think of it—our Oscar famous! You really believe he would be famous!"

"No. Notorious."

"Well—what is the difference?"

"There is a good deal."

"Well, what *is* it?"

"Why, fame is a great and noble thing—and permanent. Notoriety is a noise—just a noise, and doesn't last."

"So *that* is what you think our Oscar would reach. Then pray, why do you think him suited for the pulpit?"

"The law is a narrow field, Sarah; in fact it is merely a groove. Or, you may call it a house with only one room in it. But in religion there are a hundred sects. It is a hotel. Oscar could move from room to room, you know."

"James!"

"Yes, he could. He could move every quarter, and take a fresh start. And every time he moved, there would be a grand to-do about it. The newspapers would be full of it. That would make him happy. It is my opinion that he ought to be dedicated to this career of sparkling holiness, usefulness and health-giving theological travel."

Sarah's face flushed and all her frame quivered with anger. Her breath came in gasps; for the moment she could not get her voice. Then she got it, but before she could use it the thin pipe of a boy calling to a mate pierced to her ear through the still and murky air—

"Thug Carpenter's got drownded!"

"Oh, James, our Oscar—drowned!" She sank into a chair, pallid and faint, and muttered, "The judgment—I warned you."

CHAPTER II

"Drownded, you say?" This from another boy.

"Well, not just entirely, but he's goin' to be. The ice is break-ing up, and he's got caught all by himself on t'other side of the split, about a half a mile from shore. He's a goner!"

Sarah Carpenter was on her feet in a moment, and fumbling with bonnet and shawl with quaking hands. "Quick, James, there's hope yet!" The Judge was getting into his overcoat with all haste. Outside, the patter of hurrying footsteps was heard, and a confusion of excited voices; through the window one could see the village population pouring out upon the white surface of the vast Mississippi in a ragged long stream, the further end of it, away toward the middle of the river, reduced by distance to a creeping swarm of black ants.

Now arose the ringing sound of flying hoofs, and a trim and fair young girl, bareheaded and riding bareback and astride, went thundering by on a great black horse.

"There goes Hellfire Hotchkiss! Oh, James, he's saved, if any-body can save him!"

"You've said the truth, Sarah. She has saved him before, and she will do it again. Keep up your heart, it will all come right."

By this time the couple had crossed the river road and were starting down the ice-paved slope of the bank. Ahead, on the level white plain, the black horse was speeding past detach-ment after detachment of plodding citizens; and all along the route hats and handkerchiefs went up in welcome as the young girl swept by, and burst after burst of cheers rose and floated back, fainter and fainter, as the distance grew.

Far out toward the middle of the river the early arrivals were massed together on the border of a wide rift of indeterminable length. They could get no further. In front of them was the water; beyond it, clear to the Illinois shore, a moaning and grinding drift and turmoil of monster ice-cakes, which wandered apart at times, by compulsion of the swirling currents, then crashed thunderously together again, piling one upon another and rising for a moment into rugged hillocks, then falling to ruin and sagging apart once more. It was an impressive spectacle, and the people were awed by the sight and by the brooding spirit of danger and death that was in the air, and they spoke but little, and then in low voices. Most of them said nothing at all, but gazed fixedly out over the drifting plain, searching it for the missing boy. Now and then, through the vague steam that rose from the thawing ice they caught sight of a black speck away out among the recurrent up-bursting hillocks under the lowering sky, and then there would be a stir among the crowd, and eager questions of "Where? which is it? where do you see it?" and answers of "There—more to the right—still more—look where I am pointing—further out—away out—just a black speck—don't you see it now?" But the speck would turn out to be a log or some such thing, and the crowd would fall silent again.

By and by distant cheering was heard, and all turned to listen. The sound grew and grew, approached nearer and nearer, the black horse was sighted, the people fell apart, and down the lane the young girl came flying, with her welcome roaring about her. Evidently she was a favorite. All along, from the beginning of her flight, as soon as she was recognised the cry went up—

"It's Hellfire Hotchkiss—stand back and give her the road!" and then the cheers broke out.

She reined up, now, and spoke—

"Where is he?"

"Nobody knows. Him and the other boys were skating, along

about yonder, somewheres, and they heard a rip, and the first they knew their side of the river begun to break up. They made a rush, and got through all right; but he was behind, and by the time he got here the split was too wide for him—for *him*, you understand—so they flew home to tell, and get help, and he broke for up the river to hunt a better place, and—"

The girl did not wait for the rest, but rode off up stream, peering across the chasm as she went, the people following her with their eyes, and commenting.

"She's the only person that had enough presence of mind to come fixed to *do* something in case there was a chance. She's got a life-preserver along." It was Miss Hepworth, the milliner, that said that. Peter Jones, the blacksmith, said—

"It ought to do some good, seeing she took the trouble and had the thoughtfulness to fetch it, but there's never any telling which way Thug Carpenter is going to act. Take him as a rule, he is afraid of his shadow; and then again, after a mighty long spell, he'll up and do a thing which is brave enough for most anybody to be proud of. If he is just his ordinary natural self to-day, the life-preserver ain't going to be any good; he won't dare use it when Hellfire throws it to him."

"That's about the size of it," said Jake Thompson, the baker. "There's considerable difference betwixt them two—Thug and her. Pudd'nhead Wilson says Hellfire Hotchkiss is the only genuwyne male man in this town and Thug Carpenter's the only genuwyne female girl, if you leave out sex and just consider the business facts; and says her pap used to—hey, she's stopped."

"So she has. Maybe she's found him."

"No, only thought she had. She's moving on, again. Pudd'nhead Wilson says Thug's got the rightest heart and the best disposition of any person in this town, and pretty near the quickest brains, too, but is a most noble derned fool just the same. And *he* says Hellfire's a long sight the prettiest human creature that ever lived, and the trimmest built, too, and as graceful as a fish; and says he'd druther see her eyes snap when she's mad, or water up when she's touched than—'y George, she's stopped again. Say—she's faced around; she's coming this way."

"It's so. Stopped again. She's found him, sure. Seems to be talking across the rift—don't you see? Got her hand up to her mouth for a trumpet. Ain't it so?"

"Oh, yes, there ain't any doubt. She's got off of her horse. Hi!—come along, everybody. Hellfire's found him!"

The crowd set out at a pace which soon brought them to the girl; then they faced about and walked along with her. Oscar was abreast, prisoner on a detached and independent great square of ice, with a couple of hundred yards of water and scattered ice-cakes between him and the people. His case had a bad look. Oscar's parents arrived, now, and when his mother realized the situation she put out her hands toward him and began to wail and sob, and call him by endearing names, and implore him not to leave her, not to take away the light of her life and make it desolate; and then she looked beseechingly into the faces about her, and said, "Oh, will nobody save him? he is all the world to me; oh, I cannot give him up." She caught sight of the young girl, now, and ran to her and said, "Oh, Rachel, dear, dear Rachel, you saved him before, you'll not let him die now, *will* you?"

"No."

"Oh, you precious child! if ever—"

"'Sh! What is he saying? Listen."

Oscar was shouting something, but the words could not be made out with certainty.

"Wasn't it something about snags?" asked the girl. "Are there snags down yonder?"

"Snags? Yes," said the baker, "there's a whole rack-heap of them. That is what he's talking about, sure. He knows they are there, and he knows they'll wreck him."

"Then it won't do to wait any longer for the rift to get narrower," said Rachel. "He must be helped now or it will be too late."

She threw off her winter wrap, and began to take off her shoes.

"What are you going to do?" said old Uncle Benny Stimson, Indian doctor and tavern keeper.

"Take him the preserver. He isn't much of a swimmer, and couldn't ever make the trip without it."

"You little fool, you'll freeze to death."

"Freeze to death—the idea!"

"Well, you will. You let some of these young fellows do it."

"When I want anybody's help, I'll ask for it, Uncle Benny. I am one of the young fellows myself, I'll let you know."

"Right you are. The pig-headedest little devil, for a parson's daughter, I ever saw. But a brick just the same; I'll say that for you, H. H.,—every time."

"Thank you, dear. Please lead my horse and carry my things, and go along down yonder and stand by. Thug is pretty well chilled by this time; somebody please lend me a whisky-flask."

Thirty-five were offered. She took one, and put it in her bosom. Uncle Benny said—

"No use in that, he's teetotal—he won't touch it, girly."

"That was last week. He has reformed by this time."

She plunged in and struck out. Somebody said "Let us pray," but no one heard; all were absorbed in watching. The girl made good progress both ways—forward, by her own strength, and down-stream by the force of the current. She made her goal, and got a cheer when she climbed out of the water. Oscar had been in a state of exhausting fright for an hour and more, and he said he was weak and chilled and helpless and unmanned, and would rather die where he was than chance the desperate swim—he knew he couldn't make it.

"Yes you can. I'll help you, Thug, and the preserver will keep you up. Here, take some of this—it will hearten you."

"What is it?"

"Milk."

He took a drain.

"Good milk, too," he said. "It is so comforting, and I was so cold. I will take some more. How thoughtful it was of you to bring the flask; but you always think of everything."

"Hurry. Get off your overcoat, Thug."

But he glanced at the water and the wide distance, and said, "Oh, I don't dare to venture it. I never could make it."

"Yes you can. Trust to me. I'll help you with the coat. There, it's off. Now the boots. Sit down—I'll help. Now the preserver; hold still, I'll strap it around you. We are ready, now. Come—you are not afraid to trust to me, Thug?"

"I am going to do it, if I die—but I wouldn't risk it with any other person. You'll go through safe, I know that; and you'll fetch me through if anybody can." He added, tearfully, "But it may be that I'll never get across; I don't feel that I shall. And if these are my last words, I want to say this. If I go down, you must tell my mother that I loved her and thought of her to the last; and I want you to remember always that I was grateful to you. I think you are the best, best girl that ever lived; and if I pass from this troubled life this day, I shall enter heaven with a prayer on my lips for you, Hellfire. I am ready."

"You are a dear good boy, Thug, but it is not wise to be thinking about death at such a time as this. Come along, and don't be afraid; your mother is yonder, and you will be with her in a very little while. Quick, here are the snags."

They were away in time; in a few moments more their late refuge went to wreck and ruin with a crash.

"Rest your right hand on my shoulder, Thug, and keep the same stroke with me. And no matter what happens, don't get rattled. Slack up a little—we mustn't hurry." After a little she said, "We are half way, now—are you getting tired?"

"Yes, and oh, so cold! I can't hold out, Rachel."

"Yes you can. You must. We are doing well; we are going to make it. Turn on your back and float a little—two minutes. There, that will do; you mustn't get cramps."

"Rachel, they are cheering us. How that warms a person up! If they'll keep that up, I believe I can make it."

"They'll do it—hear that!"

"Rachel—"

"What?"

"I'm afraid there's a cramp coming."

"Hush—put it out of your mind!"

"I can't, Rachel—it's coming."

"Thug, you must put it out of your mind. Brace up—we are almost there. It is no distance at all, now. Two minutes more. Brace up. Don't give in—I know we are safe."

Both were well spent when they were hauled out on the ice, and also fairly well frozen; but a warm welcome and good whisky refreshed them and made them comfortable; and the attentions and congratulations and interest and sympathy and admiration lavished upon them deeply gratified Oscar's love of distinction and made him glad the catastrophe had happened to him.

CHAPTER III

Vesuvius, isolated, conspicuous, graceful of contour, is lovely when it is at peace, with the sunshine pouring upon its rich vineyards and its embowered homes and hamlets drowsing in the drift of the cloud-shadows; but it is subject to irruptions. Rachel was a Vesuvius, seen through the butt-end of the telescope. She was largely made up of feeling. She had a tropically warm heart, a right spirit and a good disposition; but under resentment her weather could change with remarkable promptness, and break into tempests of a surprising sort. Still, while the bulk of her was heart and impulse, the rest of her was mental, and good in quality. She had a business head, and practical sense, and it had been believed from the first, by Judge Carpenter and other thoughtful people, that she would be a valuable person when she got tame.

Part of what she was was born to her, the rest was due to environment and to her up-bringing. She had had neither brothers nor sisters; there was no young society for her in the house. Her mother was an invalid and kept her room most of the time. She could not endure noise, nor tempers, nor restless activities; and from the cradle her child was a master hand in these matters. So, in her first years she was deprived of the society of her mother. The young slave woman, Martha, was superstitious about her, thinking at first that she was possessed of a devil, and later that he had found the accommodations to his mind and had brought his family. She petted and spoiled the child, partly out of her race's natural fondness for children of any sort or kind, and partly to placate and pacify the devils; but she had a world of work to do and could give but little time to play, so the child would soon find the kitchen a dull place and seek elsewhere for amusement.

The father was sweetness and amiability itself, and greatly loved the child, but he was no company for the volatile creature, nor she for him. He was always musing, dreaming, absorbing himself in his books, or grinding out sermons, and while the child was present these industries suffered considerable interruption. There was conversation—abundance of it—but it was of a wearing and nerve-racking kind.

"Can I have this, fa'r?" (father.)

"No, dear, that is not for lit—"

"Could I have that?"

"No, dear, please don't handle it. It is very frail and you might—"

"What is this for, fa'r? Can Wildcat have it?" This was Martha's love-name for Rachel.

"Oh, *dear* no! My child, you must *not* put your hands on things without asking *beforehand* whether you may or—"

"Ain't there anything for me to play with?—and it's so lonesome; and there isn't any place to go."

"Ah, poor child, I wish—there! Oh, I knew you would; the whole inkstand emptied onto your nice clean clothes. Run along, dear, and tell Martha to attend to you—quick, before you smear it over everything."

There was no one to govern Rachel, no one to train her, so she drifted along without these aids; and such rearing as she got was her own handiwork and was not according to any familiar pattern. She was never still when awake, she was stored to the eyelids with energies and enthusiasms, her mind, her hands, her feet, her body, were in a state of constant and tireless activity, and her weather was about equally divided between brilliant and happy sunshine and devastating tempests of wrath. Martha said she was a "sudden" child—the suddenest she had ever seen; that when anything went wrong with her there was no time to provide against consequences: she had smashed every breakable thing she could get her hands on before a body could say a word; and then as suddenly her fury was over and she was gathering up the wreckage and mourning over it remorsefully.

By the law of her nature she had to have society; and as she could not get it in the house she forsook that desert early and found it outside. And so while she was as yet a toddling little thing it became a peaceful house—a home of deep and slumberous tranquillity, and for a good while perhaps forgot that it had ever been harassed and harried and terrorised by her family of uneasy devils.

She was a stranger outside, but that was nothing; she soon had a reputation there. She laid its foundations in her first week at Miss Roper's school, when she was six years old and a little past. At first she took up with the little girls, but they were a disappointment; she found their society a weariness. They played with dolls; she found that dull. They cried for a pin-scratch: she did not like that. When they quarreled, they took it out in calling each other names; according to her ideas, this was inadequate. They would not jump from high places; they would not climb high trees; they were afraid of the thunder; and of the water; and of cows; and would take no perilous risks; and had no love of danger for its own sake. She tried to reform them, but it failed. So she went over to the boys.

They would have none of her, and told her so. They said they were not going to play with girls—they despised them. Shad Stover threatened her with a stout hickory, and told her to move along or she would catch it. She perceived, now, that she could be happy, here, and was sorry she had wasted so much time with the little girls. She did not say anything to the boy, but snatched his switch away and wore it out on him. She made him beg. He was nearly twice her own age and size, and as he was the bully of the small-fry side of the school, she had established her ability to whip the whole of his following by whipping him—and if she had been a boy this would have been conceded and she would have succeeded to the bully's captainship without further balloting; but she was a girl, and boys have no manly sense of fairness and justice where girls are concerned; so she had to whip two or three of the others before opposition was quenched and her wish to play with the gang granted. Shad Stover withdrew and took a minor place in a group of somewhat larger boys.

Thenceforth Rachel trained with the boys altogether, and found in their rough play and tough combats and dangerous enterprises the contentment and joy for which she long had hungered. She took her full share in all their sports,

and was a happy child. All through the summer she was en-
countering perils, but she had luck, and disappointed all the
prophets. They all said she would get herself killed, but in no
instance did her damages reach quite to that, though several
times there were good hopes. She was a hardy and determined
fighter, and attacked anything that came along, if it offended.
By and by when the cool October came and the news went
about that the circus was coming, on its way to the South, she
was on hand outside the village, with many others, at sunrise,
to get a look at the elephant free of charge. With a cake in her
hand for the animal, she sat with the crowd on the grass by the
country road. When the elephant was passing by, he scooped
up a snoutful of dust and flung it over his back, then scooped
up another and discharged it into the faces of the audience.
They were astonished and frightened, and all except Rachel
flitted promptly over the rail fence with a rush, gasping and
coughing; but the child was not moved to run away. The little
creature was in a towering rage; for she had come to offer hos-
pitality, and this was the thanks she got. She sprang into the
road with the first stick that came handy and began to fiercely
bang and hammer the elephant's hind legs and scream at him
all the injurious epithets she could think of. But the elephant
swayed along, and was not aware of what was happening. This
offensive indifference set fire to all the child's reserves of temper, and she ran forward to see if she could get any attention
at that end. She gave the trunk a cordial bang, saying, "Now
let *that* learn you!" and raised her stick for another stroke;
but before she could deliver it the elephant, without changing
his gait, gathered her gently up and tossed her over the fence
among the crowd. She was beside herself at this new affront,
and was for clearing out after him again; and struggled to get
free, but the people held her. They reasoned with her, and said
it was no use to fight the elephant, for he didn't mind a stick.
"I know it," she said, "but I've got a pin, now, and if I can get
to him I will stick it in him."

A few months later her mother died. Rachel was then seven
years old. During the next three years she went on playing with
the boys, and gradually building up a perfect conflagration of

a reputation, as far as unusual enterprises and unsafe exploits went. Then at last arguments and reasonings began to have an effect upon her, and she presently stopped training with the boys.

She played with the girls six months, and tried to get used to it and fond of it, but finally had to give it up. The amusements were not rugged enough; they were much too tame, not to say drowsy. Kissing parties and candy pullings in the winter, and picnics in the summer: these were good romps and lively, but they did not happen often enough, and the intermediate dissipations seemed wholly colorless to Rachel.

She withdrew. She did not go back to the boys at once, but tried to get along by herself. But nature was too strong for her; she had to have company; within two months she was a tomboy again, and her life was once more a satisfaction to her, a worry to her friends, and a marvel to the rest of the community.

Before the next four and a half years were out she had learned many masculine arts, and was more competent in them than any boy of her age in the town. All alone she learned how to swim, and with the boys she learned to skate. She was the only person of her sex in the country who had these accomplishments—they were taboo. She fished, boated, hunted, trapped, played "shinny" on the ice and ball on the land, and ran foot races. She broke horses for pastime, and for the risk there was in it. At fifteen she ranked as the strongest "boy" in the town, the smartest boxer, a willing and fearless fighter, and good to win any fight that her heart was in. The firemen conferred an honorary membership upon her, and allowed her to scale the roofs of burning houses and help handle the hose; for she liked that sort of employment, she had good judgment and coolness in danger, she was spry and active, and she attended strictly to business when on the roof. Whenever there was a fire she and her official belt and helmet were a part of the spectacle—sometimes lit up with the red flush of the flames, sometimes dimly glimpsed through the tumbling volumes of smoke, sometimes helping to get out the inmates, sometimes being helped out herself in a suffocated condition. Several times she saved lives, several times her own life was saved by her mates; and once when she was overcome by the smoke they penetrated to her and rescued her when the chance of success was so slender that they would not have taken the risk for another.

She kept the community in an unrestful state; it could settle to no permanent conclusion about her. She was always rousing its resentment by her wild unfeminine ways, and always winning back its forgiveness again by some act or other of an undeniably creditable sort.

By the time she was ten she had begun to help about the house, and before she was thirteen she was become in effect its mistress—mistress and assistant housekeeper. She kept the accounts, checked wastage, and was useful in other ways. But she had earned her picturesque nickname, and it stayed by her. It was a country where nicknames were common; and once acquired, they were a life-property, and inalienable. Rachel might develop into a saint, but that would not matter: the village would acknowledge the saintship and revere the saint, but it would still call her Hellfire Hotchkiss. Old use and habit would take care of that.

Along in her sixteenth year she accidentally crossed the orbit of her early antagonist, Shad Stover, and this had good results for her; or rather it led up to something which did her that service. Shad Stover was now twenty, and had gone to the dogs, along with his brother Hal, who was twenty-one. They were dissipated young loafers, and had gotten the reputation of being desperadoes, also. They were as vain of this dark name as if they had legitimately earned it—which they hadn't. They went armed—which was not the custom of the town—and every now and then they pulled their pepper-box revolvers and made some one beg for his life. They traveled in a pair—two on one—and they always selected their man with good discretion, and no bloodshed followed. It was a cheap way to build up a reputation, but it was effective. About once a month they added something to it in an inexpensive way: they got drunk and rode the streets firing their revolvers in the air and scaring the people out of their wits. They had become the terror of the town. There was a sheriff, and there was also a constable, but they could never be found when these things were going on. Warrants were not sued out by witnesses, for no one wanted to get into trouble with the Stovers.

One day there was a commotion in the streets, and the cry went about that the Stovers had picked a quarrel with a stranger and were killing him. Rachel was on her way home from a ball-game, and had her bat in her hand. She turned a corner, and came upon the three men struggling together; at a little distance was gathered a crowd of citizens, gazing spell-bound and paralyzed. The Stovers had the stranger down, and he had a grip upon each of them and was shouting wildly for help. Just as Rachel arrived Shad snatched himself free and drew his revolver and bent over and thrust it in the man's face and pulled the trigger. It missed fire, and Rachel's bat fell before he could pull again. Then she struck the other brother senseless, and the stranger jumped up and ran away, grateful but not stopping to say so.

A few days later old Aunt Betsy Davis paid Rachel a visit. She was no one's aunt in particular, but just the town's. The title indicated that she was kind and good and wise, well beloved, and in age. She said—

"I want to have a little talk with you, dear. I was your mother's friend, and I am yours, although you are so headstrong and have never done as I've tried to get you to do. But I've got to try again, and you must let me; for at last the thing has happened that I was afraid might happen: you are being talked about."

Rachel's expression had been hardening for battle; but she broke into a little laugh, now, and said—

"Talked about? Why, Aunt Betsy, I was always talked about."

"Yes, dear, but not in this new way."

"New way?"

"Yes. There is one kind of gossip that this town has never dealt in before, in the fifty-two years that I've lived in it—and has never had any occasion to. Not in one single case, if you leave out the town drunkard's girls; and even that turned out to be a lie, and was stopped."

"Aunt Betsy!" Rachel's face was crimson, and an angry light rose in her eyes.

"There—now don't lose your temper, child. Keep calm, and let us have a good sensible talk, and talk it out. Take it all around, this is a fair town, and a just town, and has been good to you—very good to you, everything considered, for you *have* led it a dance, and you know it. Now ain't that so?"

"Ye-s, but—"

"Never mind the buts. Leave it just so. The town has been quite reasonably good to you, everything considered. Partly it was on account of your poor mother, partly on your father's account and your own, and partly because it's its natural and honorable disposition to stand by all its old families the best it can. Now then, haven't you got your share to do by it? Of course you have. Have you done it? In some ways you haven't, and I'm going to tell you about it. You've always preferred to play with the boys. Well, that's all right, up to a certain limit; but you've gone away beyond the limit. You ought to have stopped long ago—oh, long ago. And stopped being fireman, too. Then there's another thing. It's all right for you to break all the wild horses in the county, as long as you like it and are the best hand at it; and it's all right for you to keep a wild horse of your own and tear around the country everywhere on it all alone; but you are fifteen years old, now, and in many ways you are seventeen and could pass for a woman, and so the time has gone by for you to be riding astraddle."

"Why, I've not done it once since I was twelve, Aunt Betsy."

"Is that so? Well, I'm glad of it; I hadn't noticed. I'll set that down to your credit. Now there's another thing. If you *must* go boating, and shooting, and skating, and all that—however, let that go. I reckon you couldn't break yourself. But anyway, you don't need the boys' company—you can go alone. You see, if you had let the boys alone, why then these reports wouldn't ever—"

"Aunt Betsy, does anybody *believe* those reports?"

"Believe them? Why, how you talk! Of course they don't. Our people don't believe such things about our old families so easy as all that. They don't believe it *now*, but if a thing goes on, and on, and on, being talked about, why that's another matter. The thing to do is to stop it in time, and that is what I've come to plead with you to do, child, for your own sake and your father's, and for the sake of your mother who is in her grave—a good friend to me she was, and I'm trying to be hers, now."

She closed with a trembling lip and an unsteady voice. Rachel was not hearing; she was lost in a reverie. Presently a flush crept into her face, and she muttered—

"And they are talking about me—like that!" After a little she glanced up suddenly and said, "You spoke of it as new talk; how new is it?"

"Two or three days old."

"Two or three days. Who started it?"

"Can't you guess?"

"I think I can. The Stovers."

"Yes."

"I'll horsewhip them both."

The old lady said with simplicity—

"I was afraid you would. You are a dear good child, and your heart is always in the right place. And so like your grandfather. Dear me but he was a topper! And just as splendid as he could be."

After Aunt Betsy took her leave, Rachel sat a long time silent and thinking. In the end, she arrived at a conclusion, apparently.

"And they are talking about me—like that. Who would ever have dreamed it? Aunt Betsy is right. It *is* time to call a halt. It is a pity, too. The boys are such good company, and it is going to be so dull without them. Oh, everything seems to be made wrong, nothing seems to be the way it ought to be. Thug Carpenter is out of his sphere, I am out of mine. Neither of us can arrive at any success in life, we shall always be hampered and fretted and kept back by our misplaced sexes, and in the end defeated by them, whereas if we could change we should stand as good a chance as any of the young people in the town. I wonder which case is the hardest. I am sorry for him, and yet I do not see that he is any more entitled to pity than I am."

She went on thinking at random for a while longer, then her thoughts began to settle and take form and shape, and she ended by making a definite plan.

"I will change my way of life. I will begin now, and stick to it. I will not train with the boys any more, nor do ungirlish things except when it is a duty and I ought to do them. I mean, I will not do them for mere pleasure. Before this I would have horsewhipped the Stovers just as a pleasure; but now it will be for a higher motive—a higher motive, and in every way a worthier one.

"That is for Monday. Tomorrow I will go to church. I will go every Sunday. I do not want to, but it must be done. It is a duty.

"Withdraw from the boys. The Stovers. Church. That makes three. Three in three days. It is enough to begin with; I suppose I have never done three in three weeks before—just *as* duties."

And being refreshed and contented by this wholesale purification, she went to bed.

A Story without an End

Sometimes referred to as "John Brown and Mary Taylor," this "storiette" was probably written in 1896 and was published without title in *Following the Equator* (1897). In the opening paragraphs Twain challenges his readers to participate in a contest, the goal of which is to engineer a satisfactory conclusion (from a male point of view) for this comic tale that he has left dangling. The story has similarities to "A Mediæval Romance," which also asks the reader to imagine a happy or even satisfactory ending when none is apparent. Unlike the earlier story, which delivered no overt warnings that the protagonist and the reader were being led into a life-or-death dilemma, here readers are asked to consider "how the thing will turn out" from the outset. As in "Hellfire Hochkiss," Twain intentionally weakens the male role in order to emphasize the intelligence and capability of the female. Although male stupidity and nudity remain barely covered in the final scene, both are about to be exposed as Mary Taylor reaches out her hand to grasp the lap robe from John Brown. Twain merges satire, joke, sexual innuendo, and male embarrassment in this exquisitely paced and well-crafted storiette. He also captures here, as succinctly and poignantly as in any of his writing, the challenge posed to traditional males by the ill winds of changing gender fortunes—by capable, clear-thinking young women who are prepared to "grasp" new situations and act decisively in them.

We had one game in the ship which was a good time-passer—
at least it was at night in the smoking-room when the men
were getting freshened up from the day's monotonies and
dullnesses. It was the completing of non-complete stories.
That is to say, a man would tell all of a story except the finish,
then the others would try to supply the ending out of their own
invention. When every one who wanted a chance had had it,
the man who had introduced the story would give it its original ending—then you could take your choice. Sometimes the
new endings turned out to be better than the old one. But the
story which called out the most persistent and determined and
ambitious effort was one which had no ending, and so there
was nothing to compare the new-made endings with. The man
who told it said he could furnish the particulars up to a certain
point only, because that was as much of the tale as he knew.
He had read it in a volume of sketches twenty-five years ago,
and was interrupted before the end was reached. He would
give any one fifty dollars who would finish the story to the satisfaction of a jury to be appointed by ourselves. We appointed
a jury and wrestled with the tale. We invented plenty of endings, but the jury voted them all down. The jury was right. It
was a tale which the author of it may possibly have completed
satisfactorily, and if he really had that good fortune I would
like to know what the ending was. Any ordinary man will find
that the story's strength is in its middle, and that there is apparently no way to transfer it to the close, where of course it
ought to be. In substance the storiette was as follows:

John Brown, aged thirty-one, good, gentle, bashful, timid,
lived in a quiet village in Missouri. He was superintendent of

the Presbyterian Sunday-school. It was but a humble distinction; still, it was his only official one, and he was modestly proud of it and was devoted to its work and its interests. The extreme kindliness of his nature was recognized by all; in fact, people said that he was made entirely out of good impulses and bashfulness; that he could always be counted upon for help when it was needed, and for bashfulness both when it was needed, and when it wasn't.

Mary Taylor, twenty-three, modest, sweet, winning, and in character and person beautiful, was all in all to him. And he was very nearly all in all to her. She was wavering, his hopes were high. Her mother had been in opposition from the first. But she was wavering, too; he could see it. She was being touched by his warm interest in her two charity protégés and by his contributions toward their support. These were two forlorn and aged sisters who lived in a log hut in a lonely place up a cross-road four miles from Mrs. Taylor's farm. One of the sisters was crazy, and sometimes a little violent, but not often.

At last the time seemed ripe for a final advance, and Brown gathered his courage together and resolved to make it. He would take along a contribution of double the usual size, and win the mother over; with her opposition annulled, the rest of the conquest would be sure and prompt.

He took to the road in the middle of a placid Sunday afternoon in the soft Missourian summer, and he was equipped properly for his mission. He was clothed all in white linen, with a blue ribbon for a necktie, and he had on dressy tight boots. His horse and buggy were the finest that the livery-stable could furnish. The lap-robe was of white linen, it was new, and it had a hand-worked border that could not be rivaled in that region for beauty and elaboration.

When he was four miles out on the lonely road and was walking his horse over a wooden bridge, his straw hat blew off and fell in the creek, and floated down and lodged against a bar. He did not quite know what to do. He must have the hat, that was manifest; but how was he to get it?

Then he had an idea. The roads were empty, nobody was stirring. Yes, he would risk it. He led the horse to the roadside and set it to cropping the grass; then he undressed and put his clothes in the buggy, petted the horse a moment to secure its compassion and its loyalty, then hurried to the stream. He swam out and soon had the hat. When he got to the top of the bank the horse was gone!

His legs almost gave way under him. The horse was walking leisurely along the road. Brown trotted after it, saying, "Whoa, whoa, there's a good fellow"; but whenever he got near enough to chance a jump for the buggy, the horse quickened its pace a little and defeated him. And so this went on, the naked man perishing with anxiety, and expecting every moment to see people come in sight. He tagged on and on, imploring the horse, beseeching the horse, till he had left a mile behind him, and was closing up on the Taylor premises; then at last he was successful, and got into the buggy. He flung on his shirt, his necktie, and his coat; then reached for—but he was too late; he sat suddenly down and pulled up the lap-robe, for he saw some one coming out of the gate—a woman, he thought. He wheeled the horse to the left, and struck briskly up the cross-road. It was perfectly straight, and exposed on both sides; but there were woods and a sharp turn three miles ahead, and he was very grateful when he got there. As he passed around the turn he slowed down to a walk, and reached for his tr—too late again.

He had come upon Mrs. Enderby, Mrs. Glossop, Mrs. Taylor, and Mary. They were on foot, and seemed tired and excited. They came at once to the buggy and shook hands, and all spoke at once, and said, eagerly and earnestly, how glad they were that he was come, and how fortunate it was. And Mrs. Enderby said, impressively:

"It *looks* like an accident, his coming at such a time; but let no one profane it with such a name; he was sent—sent from on high."

They were all moved, and Mrs. Glossop said in an awed voice:

"Sarah Enderby, you never said a truer word in your life. This is no accident, it is a special Providence. He *was* sent. He is an angel—an angel as truly as ever angel was—an angel of deliverance. I say *angel*, Sarah Enderby, and will have no other word. Don't let any one ever say to me again, that there's no such thing as special Providences; for if this isn't one, let them account for it that can."

"I know it's so," said Mrs. Taylor, fervently. "John Brown, I could worship you; I could go down on my knees to you. Didn't something tell you—didn't you *feel* that you were sent? I could kiss the hem of your lap-robe."

He was not able to speak; he was helpless with shame and fright. Mrs. Taylor went on:

"Why, just look at it all around, Julia Glossop. Any person can see the hand of Providence in it. Here at noon what do we see? We see the smoke rising. I speak up and say, 'That's the Old People's cabin afire.' Didn't I, Julia Glossop?"

"The very words you said, Nancy Taylor. I was as close to you as I am now, and I heard them. You may have said hut instead of cabin, but in substance it's the same. And you were looking pale, too."

"Pale? I was that pale that if—why, you just compare it with this lap-robe. Then the next thing I said was, 'Mary Taylor, tell the hired man to rig up the team—we'll go to the rescue.' And she said, 'Mother, don't you know you told him he could drive to see his people, and stay over Sunday?' And it was just so. I declare for it, I had forgotten it. 'Then,' said I, 'we'll go afoot.' And go we did. And found Sarah Enderby on the road."

"And we all went together," said Mrs. Enderby. "And found the cabin set fire and burnt down by the crazy one, and the poor old things so old and feeble that they couldn't go afoot. And we got them to a shady place and made them as comfortable as we could, and began to wonder which way to turn to find some way to get them conveyed to Nancy Taylor's house. And I spoke up and said—now what did I say? Didn't I say, 'Providence will provide'?"

"Why sure as you live, so you did! I had forgotten it."

"So had I," said Mrs. Glossop and Mrs. Taylor; "but you certainly *said* it. Now wasn't that remarkable?"

"Yes, I said it. And then we went to Mr. Moseley's, two miles, and all of them were gone to the camp-meeting over on Stony Fork; and then we came all the way back, two miles, and then here, another mile—and Providence *has* provided. You see it yourselves."

They gazed at each other awe-struck, and lifted their hands and said in unison:

"It's per-fectly wonderful."

"And then," said Mrs. Glossop, "what do you think we had better do—let Mr. Brown drive the Old People to Nancy Taylor's one at a time, or put both of them in the buggy, and him lead the horse?"

Brown gasped.

"Now, then, that's a question," said Mrs. Enderby. "You see, we are all tired out, and any way we fix it it's going to be difficult. For if Mr. Brown takes both of them, at least one of us must go back to help him, for he can't load them into the buggy by himself, and they so helpless."

"That is so," said Mrs. Taylor. "It doesn't look—oh, how would this do!—one of us drive there *with* Mr. Brown, and the rest of you go along to my house and get things ready. I'll go with him. He and I together can lift one of the Old People into the buggy; then drive her to my house and—"

"But who will take care of the other one?" said Mrs. Enderby. "We mustn't leave her there in the woods alone, you know—especially the crazy one. There and back is eight miles, you see."

They had all been sitting on the grass beside the buggy for a while, now, trying to rest their weary bodies. They fell silent a moment or two, and struggled in thought over the baffling situation; then Mrs. Enderby brightened and said:

"I think I've got the idea, now. You see, we can't *walk* any more. Think what we've done; four miles there, two to Moseley's, is six, then back to here—nine miles since noon, and not a bite to eat; I declare I don't see how we've done it; and as for me, I am just famishing. Now, somebody's got to go back, to help Mr. Brown—there's no getting around that; but whoever goes has got to ride, not walk. So my idea is this: one of us to ride back with Mr. Brown, then ride to Nancy Taylor's house with one of the Old People, leaving Mr. Brown to keep the other old one company, you all to go now to Nancy's and rest and wait; then one of you drive back and get the other one and drive *her* to Nancy's, and Mr. Brown walk."

"Splendid!" they all cried. "Oh, that will do—that will answer perfectly." And they all said that Mrs. Enderby had the best head for planning in the company; and they said that they wondered that they hadn't thought of this simple plan themselves. They hadn't meant to take back the compliment, good simple souls, and didn't know they had done it. After a consultation it was decided that Mrs. Enderby should drive back with Brown, she being entitled to the distinction because she had invented the plan. Everything now being satisfactorily arranged and settled, the ladies rose, relieved and happy, and brushed down their gowns, and three of them started homeward; Mrs. Enderby set her foot on the buggy step and was about to climb in, when Brown found a remnant of his voice and gasped out—

"Please, Mrs. Enderby, call them back—I am very weak; I can't walk, I can't indeed."

"Why, dear Mr. Brown! You *do* look pale; I am ashamed of myself that I didn't notice it sooner. Come back—all of you! Mr. Brown is not well. Is there anything I can do for you, Mr. Brown—I'm real sorry. Are you in pain?"

"No, madam, only weak; I am not sick, but only just weak—lately; not long, but just lately."

The others came back, and poured out their sympathies and commiserations, and were full of self-reproaches for not having noticed how pale he was. And they at once struck out a new plan, and soon agreed that it was by far the best of all. They would all go to Nancy Taylor's house and see to Brown's needs first. He could lie on the sofa in the parlor, and while Mrs. Taylor and Mary took care of him the other two ladies would take the buggy and go and get one of the Old People, and leave one of themselves with the other one, and—

By this time, without any solicitation, they were at the horse's head and were beginning to turn him around. The danger was imminent, but Brown found his voice again and saved himself. He said—

"But, ladies, you are overlooking something which makes the plan impracticable. You see, if you bring *one* of them home, and one remains behind with the other, there will be three persons there when one of you comes back for that other, for some one must drive the buggy back, and *three* can't come home in it."

They all exclaimed, "Why, sure-ly, that is so!" and they were all perplexed again.

"Dear, dear, what *can* we do?" said Mrs. Glossop; "it is the most mixed-up thing that ever was. The fox and the goose and the corn and things—oh, dear, they are nothing to it."

They sat wearily down once more, to further torture their tormented heads for a plan that would work. Presently Mary offered a plan; it was her first effort. She said:

"I am young and strong, and am refreshed, now. Take Mr. Brown to our house, and give him help—you see how plainly he needs it. I will go back and take care of the Old People; I can be there in twenty minutes. You can go on and do what you first started to do—wait on the main road at our house until somebody comes along with a wagon; then send and bring away the three of us. You won't have to wait long; the farmers will soon be coming back from town now. I will keep old Polly patient and cheered up—the crazy one doesn't need it."

This plan was discussed and accepted; it seemed the best that could be done, in the circumstances, and the Old People must be getting discouraged by this time.

Brown felt relieved, and was deeply thankful. Let him once get to the main road and he would find a way to escape.

Then Mrs. Taylor said:

"The evening chill will be coming on, pretty soon, and those poor old burnt-out things will need some kind of covering. Take the lap-robe with you, dear."

"Very well, Mother, I will." She stepped to the buggy and put out her hand to take it—

That was the end of the tale. The passenger who told it said that when he read the story twenty-five years ago in a train he was interrupted at that point—the train jumped off a bridge.

At first we thought we could finish the story quite easily, and we set to work with confidence; but it soon began to appear that it was not a simple thing, but difficult and baffling. This was on account of Brown's character—great generosity and kindliness, but complicated with unusual shyness and diffidence, particularly in the presence of ladies. There was his love for Mary, in a hopeful state but not yet secure—just in a condition, indeed, where its affair must be handled with great tact, and no mistakes made, no offense given. And there was the mother—wavering, half willing—by adroit and flawless diplomacy to be won over, now, or perhaps never at all. Also,

there were the helpless Old People yonder in the woods waiting—their fate and Brown's happiness to be determined by
what Brown should do within the next two seconds. Mary was
reaching for the lap-robe; Brown must decide—there was no
time to be lost.

Of course none but a happy ending of the story would be
accepted by the jury; the finish must find Brown in high credit
with the ladies, his behavior without blemish, his modesty un-
wounded, his character for self-sacrifice maintained, the Old
People rescued through him, their benefactor, all the party
proud of him, happy in him, his praises on all their tongues.

We tried to arrange this, but it was beset with persistent and
irreconcilable difficulties. We saw that Brown's shyness would
not allow him to give up the lape-robe. This would offend Mary
and her mother; and it would surprise the other ladies, partly
because this stinginess toward the suffering Old People would
be out of character with Brown, and partly because he was a
special Providence and could not properly act so. If asked to
explain his conduct, his shyness would not allow him to tell
the truth, and lack of invention and practice would find him
incapable of contriving a lie that would wash. We worked at
the troublesome problem until three in the morning.

Meantime Mary was still reaching for the lap-robe. We gave
it up, and decided to let her continue to reach. It is the reader's
privilege to determine for himself how the thing came out.

Wapping Alice

This unconventional "girl" story began in 1877 with a malfunctioning burglar alarm. When the Clemenses built their lavish Victorian residence in Hartford, Connecticut, three years earlier, they had a burglar alarm installed that connected all the windows and doors of the large residence to a central switchbox. Ahead of its time and with its technology far from perfected, the system frustrated the family for more than a decade. Even with its problems, however, it did work well enough in mid-July of 1877 to indicate that the Clemenses' English maid, Lizzy Wells, had been opening an outside door from the servants' quarters late at night. Confronted with the evidence from Twain's alarm system, Lizzy blushingly admitted the intruder was not a burglar gaining entrance, but rather her gentleman friend, a young mechanic named Willie Taylor. Once her folly had been exposed, Lizzy also reported that she had been "ruined" by him. Tearfully, she placed her reputation and her fate in her employer's hands.

The steadily malfunctioning alarm system gave Twain sufficient satiric fodder for notebook entries and autobiographical dictations. It also gave him material for the story, "The McWilliamses and the Burglar Alarm," which he completed in 1882.

In 1897 Twain returned to the story of Lizzy and Willie, and, although he changed names and locations to distance his family from the incident, he retained much of the story's original material. What emerged is *Wapping Alice*, a transvestite farce in which Lizzy becomes converted into a young man named Alice from the Wapping district of London, and Willie appears as a virile young Swede named Bjurnsen Bjuggersen Bjorgensen. Initially Twain retained his first-person involvement in the story, but later changed the narrator's name to "Mr. Jackson" and shifted the location to the Deep South. This distancing probably occurred when Twain realized he was writing a gay transvestite story that would culminate in a "shotgun" same-sex marriage. Although the intent is clearly humorous, Alice takes Twain's long-standing fascination with cross-dressing and cross-acting into new territory. As an explorer in a strange, newly gendered landscape, Twain seems to recognize that a "girl" story could also represent the desires and aspirations of an effeminate male.

Two efforts to market *Wapping Alice* were rejected, probably because publishers surmised their audiences were not sufficiently prepared for a gay transvestite farce with suggestions of sodomy and culminating in a forced marriage. In 1907 Twain wrote in his "Autobiographical Dictations" that the transvestite element of the story was a "non-essential detail" designed to make it more marketable. A close textual reading, however, makes it difficult to consider these remarks as anything other than posturing by the aging author in order to maintain a comfortable distance from a highly controversial topic.

I

I will try to tell this story about as Jackson told it to me. We had been sailing the summer seas for many weeks, now, and the shell-removing influences had been putting in their work all that time. We had walked the decks together before meals, according to sea custom; played horse-billiards in the same team; dozed in company in the shade of the awnings; been partners at whist in the smoking-room, nights—and so-on and so-on; and now at last it was recognizable that the shell had wholly wasted away and disappeared. We knew it by this sign: the autobiographical stage had been reached.

We were in the Indian Ocean. It was past midnight, the promenade deck was a solitude; the weather was soft and balmy; the sea was silver under the moon, there was not a ripple on it. The wise could not leave this heaven for bed; so we were still there, lounging in the rich passengers' wonderful chairs, smoking the pipe of peace and contentment, and talking.

Jackson was telling me his history. He was a southerner. His people had been planters, away back to Pocahontas's time; their old plantation mansion was on the edge of a considerable town; their family had always occupied it, and had always kept it up to date in the matter of improvements and conveniences, whatever the date might chance to be.

When Jackson had gotten pretty well along in his autobiographical sketch, he said: "And now I come to the incident of Wapping Alice." Then he went on with his talk—about like this:

It was on the 2d of January of that year that we added Wap-

83

ping Alice to our household staff. According to her story she was born and reared in that part of London which is called Wapping, and the other servants soon got to calling her Wapping Alice to distinguish her from our other Alice, the colored cook. She came to us fresh from England; she brought no recommendations, but we took her on her face. She soon made her way. She was good-hearted and willing, she fitted neatly into her place, the children grew fond of her, everybody on the place had a good word for her, and we were glad of the luck that threw her in our way. She was a little frisky with her h's, but that was nothing.

Some of the ridiculous features of the incident which I am going to speak of presently will be better understood if I expose Wapping Alice's secret here and now, in the beginning — for she had a secret. It was this: she was not a woman at all, but a *man*.

It is very creditable to his ingenuity that he was able to masquerade as a girl seven months and a half under all our eyes and never awake in us doubt or suspicion. It must not be charged that a part of the credit is due to our dulness; for no one can say that our friends and neighbors were dull people, and they were deceived as completely as we were. They knew Alice almost as well as we knew him, yet no suspicion of the fraud he was playing ever crossed their minds. He must have had years of apprenticeship in his part, or he could not have been so competent in it. Why he unsexed himself was his own affair. In the excitement of the grand climax in August the matter was overlooked and he was not questioned about it.

For conveience, now, I will stop calling him "he." Indeed, with that fair and modest and comely young creature in blossomy hat and fluttering ribbons and flowing gown framed before me now in the mirror of my memory, it is awkward and unhandy to call it anything but "she."

Wapping Alice took up her abode with us on the 2d of January. The kitchen was an independent annex, built against the north side of the house; the house-entrance to it was from the dining room. It consisted of two stories and a cellar; this latter was a laundry, and communicated with the house-cellar. The laundry also had a door which opened upon the steep hillside, above the brook. All about our house was open ground; so it stood by itself. When it was locked up for the night, communication with the kitchen-annex was shut off, and the annex became in effect an independent establishment. After that, if the occupants of it wished to indulge in privacies of their own they had their opportunity: we should know nothing about it.

Wapping Alice and the cook had adjoining bedrooms on the second floor of the annex, over the kitchen. At 5 in the morning, February 2d, the burglar-alarm let go with an urgent clatter, and I was out on the floor before I was awake. Before I was fairly into the bathroom the clatter stopped. I turned up the gas and looked at the annunciator. One of the metal tabs was down, and was still wagging with excitement. The number exposed by it indicated the laundry door which opened upon the hillside. That was a curious thing. What was there in the annex that a burglar might want? And why should he want it so early in the morning? And the weather so bitter cold, too. Ought I to go all the way down there and inquire? My curiosity was strong, but not strong enough for that. I went back to bed, and reported progress. I said there was no present danger. We could wait, and listen for the alarm again. In case it should indicate that the burglar was breaking into the dining room, we could collect the children and climb out of the front window. Then we went to sleep.

At 5 the next morning the alarm rang again. I went in the bathroom and looked, and it was the laundry door once more. At breakfast I told George about it. He could not account for it, but thought maybe Dennis had taken a notion to come at that strange hour and fertilize the furnace because of the exceeding sharpness of the weather. It turned out that Dennis had better sense. All the same the laundry rang us up at 5 on the succeeding morning. The mystery was not wasted on the family; it made plenty of good talk for us at breakfast. And for George, too, of course; for whatever interested the rest of the family interested him, for that is the way with the colored brother when he is built in the right and usual way. Let me explain George—with just a word or two; otherwise you may presently think that my ways with him and his ways with me were not ceremonious enough, not distant enough. Put that all out of your mind, in justice to us both. Each of us knew his place quite well, and was in no danger of forgetting it. Let me throw some light—then you will understand: he was a hereditary servant—he was an institution—he was a part of us, not an excrescence—we had a great affection for him, and he for us—when he said to people "my family" are well, or "my family" are away, now, and so-on, he meant *my* family, not his. Consider this further light: my grandfather owned George's grand-father, my father owned George's father, and George owned *me*—at any rate that is what the family said. But to go back to the breakfast-table discussion of that burglar-alarm matter. Wapping Alice was in the room during this discussion. After breakfast she asked George what a burglar-alarm might be. George explained it to her, and showed her how the opening of a door or a window would set it off.

The laundry door troubled us no more. For a while we wondered at that; then the matter dropped out of our minds. The ninth of June we went away for the summer. Something more than two months afterward I happened to be within a hundred miles of home, and I thought I would run up and see how things were getting along there. I arrived in the gloaming and walked out from the station. On the way, a horse-car came loafing by, and a friend hailed me from its rear platform—

"I thought that would fetch you. How much did they get?"

"What do you mean?"

"Don't you know your house has been burglarized?"

"No."

"George wanted it kept out of the papers—so it didn't get in; but I supposed he telegraphed you."

"No, I haven't heard of it."

The house and the grounds had a lonesome and forsaken look. I rang, and got no answer. I walked all about the place, but found no one. The horses were in the stable, but Dennis and his family were gone. I went back and was going to open the front door with a latch-key, but concluded to try the knob first. The door swung open! It seemed an odd state of things

86

for a house that had so lately had experience of burglars. I went all over the house and the annex. Everything was in good order, but there were no human beings anywhere. So I lit up, in the library, and sat down to read and smoke, and wait.

I waited until ten at night, then George arrived. When he opened the door and saw me and the other lights, he was astonished.

"Why, when did you come, sir!"

I answered with austerity—meaning to impress George—

"More than three hours ago—and found the house absolutely unprotected. The whole tribe away; no one left to take care of the place. What do you think of that kind of conduct? A burglar could have emptied the house, unmolested."

George was not impressed. He laughed a comfortable, carefree laugh, and said—

"This house ain't in no danger, Mr. Jackson, don't you worry. There ain't a burglar that don't know there's a burglar alarm in this house. It's business for them to know where there's alarms, and they know it, you can 'pend upon that. No, sir, they don't tetch no house that's got a—"

"Do you mean to say that you keep the alarm on, day and night both?"

"No, sir, don't keep it on at all, generally. Just the *fact* is a plenty. They ain't going to meddle here."

"You think so, do you? Where have you all been?"

"Been down the river on the excursion boat."

"All of you?"

"Yes, sir, the whole bilin'."

"I think it's scandalous. Even if there is a burglar alarm, I think you might at least lock the front door when you desert the house."

George smiled a placid smile, and said—

"Well, now, we ain't quite so far gone as all that, Mr. Jackson. Whenever we go we always lock the front door, and—"

"George, I came in without a latch-key."

George caught his breath with a gasp, and reeled in his tracks. The next moment he was flying up stairs like a rocket. I was almost as much startled as he was. He was gone five minutes, then he came drooping into the room, limp and weak, and swabbing his face, which had paled to the hue of old amber. He came and leaned against the book shelves near me, and waited a little to get his breath, his breast rising and falling with his pantings. Then he gave his face a final wipe, and said—

"My souls, Mr. Jackson, what a turn you did gimme! The front door not even on the latch, and fifteen hundred dollars hard-earned money up there betwixt my mattrasses!"

"Oh," I said, "I see. To leave my things unprotected is a small thing; but when it imperils yours it's quite another matter. I'm ashamed of you, George."

"Well, now I come to look at it, I dunno but I feel mostly the same way, sir."

"How did you come to have all that money in the house?—you that let on to be so careful about always banking the results of your pious robberies. Have you been betting on the revival-catch again? Is there another religious epidemic in your African church?"

I could see that that wounded him—poor old George. I knew it would, for it was probably true. It had been charged against him by the brother whom he supplanted as deacon of the church, and it was a sore spot with George, who always said it was a slander; but as he never went quite far enough to say it was a lie, and as he was something of a purist in language, this subtle discrimination was noticed by the family, to his damage. Out of love, they did not twit him with it; but out of love, I did—and rubbed it in, sometimes.

"Mr. Jackson you oughtn't to talk so—because I never done it. I do bet on horse-races, and elections, and sprints, and base ball, and foot ball, and everything that ain't sinful and got money in it, but I never done that."

"You didn't, didn't you? Well, let it go, for this time—though I suppose you did. Where did you get this fifteen hundred?"

"At the Nashville races, day before yistiddy."

"George! do you mean to say that you have been five hundred miles from home and left nobody but women in the house all that time?"

But George was not much troubled. He said—

"I only went for three or four days, and it ain't likely that anybody would break into the house in that little time. Especially where there's an alarm. And Dennis was right there in his house, anyway, and nothing to do but ring him up."

I had now artfully worked George up to the right place to spring my surprise upon him, and I touched it off:

"George, you haven't telegraphed anything to me lately; through your happy relations with the press, the papers have been muzzled. And so you think you have managed to hide something away which you didn't want me to find out. But your hand was not well played. George, I know everything. This house has been burglarized! And on top of this, you all go off larking and leave it to be burglarized again. Now what do you think of yourself!"

It didn't phaze him. It didn't start a hair. It left him as serene as a summer morning. He was the most provoking creature about making a person's calculations all go for nothing. A pleasant smile allowed a wink of his white teeth to show for a moment, and he said, comfortably—

"There hain't been no burglars here, Mr. Jackson. Nary a burglar."

"Now you know better. Mr. —— told me, as I came up from the station."

"Yes, sir. Well, he done right. I put that up on him. I done it for a purpose."

"You did, did you? Well, what was your purpose?"

"I'm going to tell you all about it, Mr. Jackson. You see, there was something happened here in the house, and it was a mystery. Yes, sir, that is what it was; it was a mystery. I reckoned it would get out, and get in the papers, and then the family would be worried, and you would come flying here, four hundred miles, and no use in it. Fact is, I knowed the other servants couldn't keep it, and I knowed they would ruther have something big to tell than something little, so I come flat out and told them to say it was a burglar. That pleased them, of course, and they done it. Then the rest of it was easy for me. I went down to the papers and told them a noble good lie—be-

cause that ain't no sin when you are trying to do good by it—
and asked them to keep still and not scare the burglars out of
town, for I was right on their track; and so they done it. Now
then, the thing that *did* happen was like this. Last Sunday we
all went up to Hopkinsville on a little excursion—"

"Well, by gracious! The whole tribe, of course."

"No, sir, not all, that time. Three or four of Dennis's children
warn't very well, but most of the others went, and Bridget and
Dennis. And the rest of us went, except Wapping Alice. She
allowed she'd stay at home and take care of the house, and she
done it."

"She shall have a monument."

"Yes, sir. Well, we missed the connection at Wildcat, so we
come back home. We got here about three in the afternoon,
and there warn't nobody in sight anywhere in these regions—
just the way it always is out here Sunday afternoons in the summer time—lonesome; perfectly gashly. It was awful hot. So we
come in by the ground-floor bedroom window, because it was
handier than the annex, and come in here where it was cool.
We set down here and begun to chat along. Now I had put the
front door on the alarm that morning, and didn't say anything
about it. I most always done so when we went on excursions—
sometimes, anyway, if I thought of it. So we was setting here
chatting, and the doors into the dining room was spread apart
a piece—about a foot. I was setting just where you are now,
and could see that crack. All of a sudden I see a man go past it.
It give me such a start I couldn't get my breath for as much as
ten seconds; then I sung out 'By Jimminy, there's a man!' and
we jumped for the hall door. Just then, zzzzzip! went the alarm,
then the front door banged to, and it stopped. I was there in a
second, and out; and see a young man sailing over the sward
like a deer. Now whatever went with him I couldn't make out;
but when I got to the upper gate he warn't anywhere in sight.

"So then we come back, and looked the house over, and nothing was gone. That is, I told them to search the house and I
would search the annex. We set here and talked it over, and
over, and over, and *over*. Couldn't seem to get enough of it. I
told them everything was all right, in the annex, and Wapping

Alice sleeping like a graveyard; nothing hadn't disturbed her. So then we agreed on burglary, and they said they would go out and take a walk. I judged they would. And I judged it would be a long one, if they met up with a good many friends that was interested in burglaries.

"I had a chance to set down and think, now. I turned this and that and 'tother thing over in my head for about an hour, and pieced them together, and when I was done I had made up my mind. What do you reckon it was, Mr. Jackson?"

"I don't know. What was it, George?"

"Well, sir, this was it. I says to myself, I don't want to wrong nobody, and anybody that knows me knows it ain't my disposition; but it's my opinion that Wapping Alice ain't what she ought to be."

"Oh, nonsense!"

"I hope it is, Mr. Jackson; there wouldn't be anybody gladder than me; for I am like the rest—I like Wapping Alice, and wouldn't hurt a hair of her head for the world. And she's far from her home and her people, too, poor thing, and I ain't no dog, and can feel for that."

"What things did you piece together, George, to build up that wild idea?"

"Well, it's curious. The first thing that come into my head didn't seem to have any business there, and took me by surprise. Do you remember, sir, the time the alarm went off three mornings last February, long before daylight? That was it. You know it warn't ever accounted for."

"I know, but how does that connect itself with this remote matter?"

"Well, the third morning, Wapping Alice was in the breakfast room when we was all talking about it; and she asked me what a burglar alarm was, and I told her. Now, Mr. Jackson, the landry didn't wake you up any more after that."

"Come, that was well thought out. Go on."

"The next thing that come into my head was this. Last January the plumbers ripped out some woodwork to get at a leaky pipe, and a young carpenter was here a couple of days putting it back. A young Swede he was, by the name of Budjurnsen Budjuggersen Budjorgensen. Turrible name, and oversized him considerable, so it seemed to me, but that was it. He set around in the kitchen a good deal, chatting, because he was working by the day and that always makes a person tireder than the other kind, and so we all got to know him pretty well, and liked him. About the first of June I went into Wapping Alice's room one morning, and there was a suit of men's clothes laying there, and she was half-soling the seat of the pants. I asked her about it and she said she was mending them up for the young carpenter—he asked her to do it. So that come into my head, now, I didn't know why.

"Thinking it over, I remembered another thing. When I was telling her about the burglar alarm that morning, I smelt her breath, and there was liquor on it. That was curious, because there ain't any but locked-up liquor in this house, and I keep the key. She got that liquor outside. I never thought any more about it then; but this time when it come up in my mind, I reckoned maybe she turned out at 5 in the morning, being dry, which is natural to the English, and tramped down to the Union bar and moistened up. Well, it would have made a fine stir if she had done it in women's clothes. So I judged maybe she disguised herself as a man and done it. How does that seem to strike you, sir?"

"Pretty thin, George. Still, it will do for a link if you can't find anything better."

"But I reckon I can. I told the girls I found Wapping Alice sleeping like a graveyard. It warn't strictly true, Mr. Jackson. She warn't in her room; she warn't in the house at all."

"Is that so?"

"She warn't in the house at all. Now, then, when I had thought out my think, I says to myself, it stands like this: Wapping Alice knowed we was to be off on the excursion two days—"

"Two days! Well, I'll be—"

"Mr. Jackson, you oughtn't to swear."

"I *didn't* swear, and I wasn't even thinking of it. But a person could be forgiven for it if he did, considering the way things go on in this house the minute we turn our backs. Go on!"

"Well, as I was saying, sir, I says to myself it stands like this: Wapping Alice couldn't know we were back and down there chatting in the library, and so, being dry, she reckoned she was perfectly safe to slip on her breeches and things and go out and oil up. If it *was* her, she heard me shout, and knowed she was out of luck this time. And if it was her, she would know we wouldn't be in the house long, but would go out excursioning around somewhere and passing the time, then she could slide back and get into her own clothes again. So I just set still and waited. Well, sir, sure enough, just as it was getting 'most dark, here she comes stretching and yawning into the library in her own clothes, and let on to be astonished to see me back from Hopkinsville, and said she had most slept her head off, and I said, pretty sharp, 'Blame your cats you ought to slept it *clear* off; it ain't any good to you in a time of trouble; there's been a man in the house, and if we had all been as sleepy-headed as you he would have got away with the whole place.' She pretended to be ever so sorry she was asleep, but I reckoned she got considerable comfort out of the notion that she hadn't been found out. Now, then, Mr. Jackson, that is the case the way it stands. You see, yourself, that it warn't of any importance, and not worth disturbing the family about. And so I put it up on the papers for a burglary, and got them to keep still and give it a chance to blow over and pass away. I warn't thinking about myself, I done it for the family's sake, to save them from worry. Wasn't I right?"

"George, you are *always* right. Half the time I don't believe it, but to keep peace in the family it is safest to let on to. It's an idiotic family, and thinks you know more than the dictionary. You have figured this matter out pretty well, for an unprofessional, but it is pretty hard on Wapping Alice, George. To sum up, what do you think of her now?"

"Well, Mr. Jackson, I still think what I said before; she ain't what she ought to be."

"You don't think there is anything really bad about her, do you?"

"Yes, sir, I do. I think she drinks."

"Is that all?"

George, the rabid prohibitionist, was speechless for a moment, then he said, with deep solemnity—

"All? Mr. Jackson, ain't that enough?"

I had a reason for asking the next question.

"George, are you sure—I mean are you perfectly sure—that you aren't a little prejudiced against Alice?"

It made George uncomfortable. I was expecting it would. He coughed an embarrassed cough or two, loosened his collar with his fingers, and presently found speech.

"You mean the joke she played on me, Mr. Jackson?"

"Yes."

"Well, sir, I give you my word I done quit worrying 'bout it. It was scanlous—it was just scanlous—but she didn't mean no harm. There ain't no malice in her, she's the best-hearted girl there is; and if a person is poor or in trouble there ain't nothing she won't do for them. They can have everything she's got; and everything anybody else has got, too, if she can get aholt of it. But—when it comes to joking—oh, my land! Mr. Jackson, she can't help it; it's born in her. She ain't got no resisting power. If she see a chance to play a joke and couldn't play it, I believe it would kill her. She keeps the kitchen in a sweat; we don't ever know what's a coming next. Now then—"

"George, you are wandering from the subject. You always do, when I bring up that joke. I never can manage to pump your version of it out of you. You always go palavering off on side issues. Why is that?"

"Now, Mr. Jackson, I don't like to talk about that joke. It was just scanlous. Why, it went all over this country; yes, sir, and clean out to Gilroy. Everybody knows me in this town, little and big; and I hardly das't to show up anywheres for four weeks, they kept at me so. Now Major Archibald, and Mr. Dickson, and Mr. Rogers, and Mr. Hubbard, and Gen'l—"

"Well, never mind, George, let it go. I see I am never going to bring you to book. I think you would dodge around that joke a year and never step over the outside edge of it. Tell me—have you ever examined that laundry door?"

George cheered up and looked relieved.

"No, sir, not as I remember. What would I do it for?"

"Well, your tale makes me think it will bear it. I wonder at you, George. Such a good detective and not think of that."

We went down and examined; and sure enough the ends of the metal pegs which made the electric connection had been filed off till they no longer touched the plate when the door was swung open.

"George, you explained the function of these pegs to Wapping Alice?"

"Yes, sir; and of course she went and filed them off, and that door hain't been on the alarm since the first week of last February. I ain't got no more to say; I'm just a fool."

"No, you mustn't say that, because it includes me, and isn't respectful. I ought to have examined the door last February."

II

Up to this time this whole matter had seemed trifling to me, but it suddenly began to look cloudy, now. The laundry door had been tampered with for a purpose. George said—

"Yes sir; and it was done so as Wapping Alice could put on men's clothes and slide out whenever she wanted to, and liquor up. I am more set, now, than ever, that that girl ain't what she ought to be. Mr. Jackson, if I had my way, I'd make her take the pledge before she's a day older; I'd do it as shore as I'm a standing here."

Privately, I went further than that. I believed that Alice was harboring sneak-thieves. I felt sure that an exhaustive search of the house would show that a thousand little things had been carried off.

I resolved to hold a court in the morning, and fan out the evidence and get at the bottom facts of this dark episode. I woke refreshed, and ready for business. Eager to begin, too; all alive with the novelty and interest and mystery of the situation, and sure I could manage it in as imposing style as any detective in the land, except George. When George brought up my breakfast we discussed and matured the plans; then he went down and sent up the witnesses, one at a time, and I questioned them separately. Last of all came Wapping Alice. She had on a white summer gown, with a pink ribbon at the throat and another one around her waist, and looked very neat and comely and attractive and modest; also troubled and downcast. I questioned her gently, on this, that and the other point, and found her cautious, evasive and reluctant. She kept slipping through my fingers all the time; I never could quite catch her, anywhere. I was forced to admire her penetration and her ingenuity. I was not able to arrange any trap which she would walk into. Still I was making progress, and she could see it. She did not know what the previous witnesses had said, and this was a hindrance to her. Every now and then, consequently, I was able to drop a surprise on her which disordered her story and made difficulties for her. She was determined she wouldn't know that there had been a man in the house. No, it could be that there had been a man, and of course there *had* been, since the others said so, but she had no personal knowledge of it.

However, I gradually drove her into a corner; and at last when I thought the right time had come, I sprung my final surprise and showed all my cards. I wove the stories of the servants into a clear and compact narrative, and reeled it off like a person who had been behind the door and seen it all. The astonishment that rose in her face, and grew, and grew, as I went along—ah, well, it was an inspiration to me! It was as if I was plucking the secretest privacies out of her heart, one by one, and displaying them before her amazed eyes. When I had finished she seemed dazed, and said humbly—

"I see it is no use, sir; you know all. I am a poor girl. I do not know what to do," and she stood there pitifully twining and untwining her fingers and gazing down at the carpet. To tell the truth, it brought the moisture to my eyes.

"Make a clean breast, Alice; it is the only wise and honest thing to do."

After a struggle she said she would do it, and she began. This is the substance of her story:

That young Swede, Bjurnsen Bjuggersen Bjorgensen did some joiner-work in the house in January, and when it was finished he was out of work and remained so. In the kitchen they all liked him and were sorry for him. Presently he had nowhere to sleep and nothing to eat. She took pity on him and secretly allowed him to sleep in our main cellar—in a part of it which had been walled off for a bowling alley and afterwards neglected and never used, and never visited. She made a pallet for him there. Also she carried food there for him. She warned him to enter, nights, before Dennis went his final rounds—ten o'clock—and get out before he came in the morning to replenish the furnace. There was a lock on the laundry door, but it was never used; the burglar alarm was protection enough. She knew the lock was not used, but she knew nothing about the burglar alarm. She learned about it the third time that it raised me out of bed. George explained the thing to her; then Bjurnsen Bjorgensen filed off the ends of the metal pegs, and after that he came and went at any hour he pleased.

"Ever since?"

"Yes sir; he has slept in the cellar all these months. When there was excursions he would come daytimes. He was free of the whole house, then. But he never took anything, sir. He was perfectly honest. I mended his clothes for him, I made that pallet for him, I fed him all these months. I hope you will forgive me, sir; I'm but a poor girl and I never meant any harm."

"Forgive you? Why, hang it, you poor good-hearted thing, you haven't done anything to forgive. I was afraid he was a thief, that's all. And so there's been all this pow-wow about just nothing. I thought there was going to be something dramatic, something theatrical, and now it's all spoilt; it's enough to make a man swear. You ought to be taken out and drowned for it. But never mind, let it go; there's nothing but disappointments in this world, anyhow. Go along about your work, and leave me to my sorrows. But there's one thing—that young fellow ought to be very grateful to you; you've been a good friend to him, Alice."

She suddenly broke down and burst out sobbing as if her heart would break.

"Grateful? Him? Oh, sir, he— he—" Through the breaks in her sobs words escaped which conveyed a paralyzing revelation.

"What!"

"Oh, dear-dear, it is too true, sir—and now he won't marry me! And I a poor friendless girl in a strange land."

"Won't marry you! Oh, he won't, won't he? We'll see about that!"

The rage I was in—well, a rage like that exhausts a person more in half an hour than a forty-mile walk. I sent the girl away, with instructions to keep her secret to herself and tell George I wanted to see him. When he came I spread the ghastly facts before him, and they nearly straightened his wool with horror and indignation. And he was astonished and grieved at young Bjorgensen's conduct. He said he was as nice and good-hearted and manly a young fellow as he ever saw, and he couldn't ever have dreamed such things of him.

First, we telephoned for Rev. Thomas X.; next, we laid plans for the marriage of that couple. I said I would teach that young scamp a lesson that he wouldn't forget till he was a widower. By the time the plans were completed, Mr. X. was with us. The Reverend Joe was off on his vacation, and Tom was supplying his pulpit. Next to Joe, he was the choicest man in the world for this kind of a circus. He was lovely, all through, like Joe, and he had Joe's luxuriant passion for adventure and doing good. He was fatter than Joe; a good deal fatter, and the hot weather made a kind of perennial water-works of him; but no matter, his good heart was touched by the tale we told him, and he was ready to shed his last drop of perspiration in the cause, for he knew our Alice well, and liked her, and was outraged by her pitiful fate. He took the names and ages of the couple, and went off down to the town clerk's to get the licence. He was to arrive at our house at 7 sharp, in the evening, and shut himself up in the bathroom attached to what we called the schoolroom, and sweat there till he was wanted; it was on the second floor, over the library.

Wapping Alice was to send a note by hand to her unintending intended, and invite him to come out at 8 o'clock sharp, and spend the evening.

George was to telephone the chief of police and ask him to furnish me an officer in plain clothes, and have him at the house at sharp 7.30, where George would be on the lookout for him and shut him up in the library. He was to stay there until I should ring a bell—one stroke.

I was to be alone in the schoolroom at 8; Wapping Alice was to receive Bjuggersen Bjorgensen at the front door, betray him into the schoolroom, and then glide into the nursery, adjoining, and leave him to me.

At 6 in the evening the servants were to be let into the secret. They were then to dress in gala; then shut themselves up in the kitchen and stay there until I rang three bells—the signal that the wedding was ready to begin, and witnesses wanted.

On the dining-room table there was to be moisture for the crowd, to finish up the wedding with, and no charge for corkage.

My native appetite for doing things in a theatrical way feasted itself with a relish on this spectacular program. George admired the arrangement, too, and was proud of his share in contriving it. He said it was one of the showiest things he had ever helped to put together. Then we fidgeted around and waited. It was a feverish long afternoon for us, but it dragged itself through, and the twilight began to gather and deepen at last.

No hitch occurred anywhere. Each actor was in his place at his appointed time. At 7 the Reverend Tom arrived, and was shown up stairs and shut into the bathroom; at 7.30 the policeman arrived and was shut up in the library; at 7.45 I was in the schoolroom; at 8 the bridegroom was with me, and the bride had taken post in the nursery. The curtain was up, the performance ready to begin.

Bjorgensen was startled when he saw me, and began to apologize, supposing there had been a mistake; but I said it was all right, I was expecting him. He did not want to sit down, and said he should feel more comfortable standing; but I insisted persuasively, and presently he yielded and took a chair—the edge of it. He seemed a good deal perplexed, and a trifle uneasy.

He was a handsome young fellow, with a good face and a clear eye, and I noticed with some concern that he was able to throw me out of the window in case he should want to. His Alice had fed him well. I opened up the conversation with ordinary topics, for it was my purpose to thaw him out and get him into a comfortable and persuadable frame of mind before I should enter upon the main business. I meant to keep at him until I made him laugh, if it took all night. It was hard work, and long; but it won. At the end of half an hour he let go a hearty and unconstrained laugh, and I recognized that things were in shape now to call game.

So then I drifted along gradually into a revealment of the fact that I knew he had been sleeping in our cellar for months; that he had been seen to pass through the house; and that he had destroyed the electric connection which guarded the laundry and indeed the whole establishment. I told the story sorrowfully, and in a reproachful voice, and the cheerfulness gradually faded out of his face, and his head drooped in shame.

There was a painful silence now, for some moments, for I paused to let the effects work up; then I said—

"Alice was your benefactor—your *benefactor*, do you understand? She saved you, she nourished you, she protected you when you were friendless. And for reward—you take away her purity!"

He jumped as if he had been shot, and his face was transfigured with fury.

"I? Who says I did!"

"She says so."

"She lies! To the bottom of her soul she lies!"

Confound him, he almost convinced me. He went raging up and down the room, denying, protesting, almost crying; and really it was pitiful to see. But I had my duty to perform for that poor girl, and I hardened my heart and held to my purpose. Now and then I said a soothing word, and urged him to tranquilize himself and sit down and let us have a quiet, reasonable talk over the matter and see if we could not arrive at an adjustment that would be fair and satisfactory to both parties. And I said—

"You see, there is really only one right and honorable thing for you to do—only one—you must marry her."

It warmed his fury up to boiling-point again.

"Marry her! I'd see her hanged a hundred times, first, and then I wouldn't. Marry her! Why in the nation should I marry her?"

"Why, what objection have you?"

"Objection! Oh, great guns! Why I don't care anything for her beyond warm friendship—there's no love. Why in the world should I marry her?—I don't want a wife."

I said, coaxingly—

"Ah, but consider the hard circumstances. Here she is, a poor girl far from home, and her good name gone; surely you will have pity on her. Think—to you is granted a gracious and noble privilege: you can make an honest woman of her."

"But I don't *want* the privilege; and I won't *have* it! If her character needs coopering up, I can't help that. It isn't any affair of mine. Why am I selected out for the job. *Privilege*, you call it! It just makes me want to rip and curse—that's what it does."

I soothed him further. At least I meant it for that.

"Mind, Bjorgensen, I am not blaming you for denying it—far from it. Anybody would—first off; I would myself. For when we are excited we say things which we are not really responsible for. I am not blaming you. You are excited, now; but when you get cool, and are your own honest, honorable self again—"

He threw up his hands in a sort of agony of despair, and said—

"Ah, how did I ever get into this awful mess! Mr. Jackson, *don't* you believe me?—*can't* you believe me?"

Hang it, I was touched; but I had a duty to perform, and I put my weakness aside and kept my grip. By gentle persuasions I at last got the young fellow to come and sit down again; and with a proper delicacy I turned my head away, for the tears were running down his face. I said—

"Well, you know, Bjorgensen, that I haven't merely Alice's testimony. It is formidably backed up—*more* than that—convincingly backed up—made unshakable—"

"How?"

"By circumstantial evidence. You spent a hundred and fifty nights in our cellar; your presence was known to only one person; that person secretly fed and bedded you there; that person was a simple, confiding, unprotected girl. Answer me, now, out of your own common sense: with these facts back of Alice's testimony, what would a jury say?"

It wrung a groan from him.

"Lord help me!" he said. "I never thought of that; never thought how it would look." He sat silent a while—hunting for a straw to catch at. Then he said, in an aggressive tone, "But it wouldn't be *proof*, say what you may; a court would have to admit that I could have been there for—for—"

"Burglary, for instance?"

It made him jump.

"Mr. Jackson, I make solemn oath that I never took even so much as a straw; I swear that I—"

"Yes—but that is not to the purpose. And it is not important. Quite aside from that, you were guilty,—by your own admission five minutes ago—of a crime which can send you to State prison for ten years."

"Who? I?"

"You."

"What was it?"

"House-breaking. You entered by unlawful means. You destroyed the safeguard of the laundry door."

He was quaking all over, now, and his breath was coming and going in gasps.

"Mr. Jackson, is that a penitentiary offence? Oh, take it back, take it back! *Don't* say it!"

"But I must. It is only the truth."

He dropped his elbows on the table, and his head in his hands, and moaned and grieved. Presently, all of a sudden he looked up and set his eyes on mine with such a fierce light in them that it gave me a start.

"This is a game!" he shouted, and brought his fist down on the table with a crash. "It's a game that you've put up on me; that's what it is—a game to force me to marry that lying baggage. I see it all. Now deny it if you can!"

"I am not denying it. It *is* a game; and I am playing this end of it."

"You mean you *have* played it. And you've lost, too. I'll *never* marry that girl—no, not if I live a thousand years! *Now*, then, what are you going to do about it!"

"You will be a married man inside of an hour, or—"

"Or *what?*" he scoffed.

"Go to jail. Take your choice."

That warmed up his scorn. He rose, took his hat, and made a fine and rather elaborate bow, and said—

"I wish you a very good evening, sir. When you start out another time to play a game, you want to look at your cards, first, and see how much they are worth. And next time you start in to scare a man, you want to select better. Pleasant evening, to you, dear sir. Good-bye."

"Good-bye. Pleasant evening. Allow me—I will touch the bell. You will find a policeman down stairs who will help you out."

I put my finger on the button, and waited. The color went out of the young fellow's face, and he said, with a rather dubious attempt at bluster—

"*That* don't scare, either."

"All right. Shall I ring?"

He hesitated, then his confidence forsook him, and he said—

"No. Wait." He came and sat down. He mused a moment or two, then said,—

"Mr. Jackson, I put you on your honor: is there an officer down there?"

"There is. Your time is short. Look at the clock. It is five minutes to ten. You may have the lacking five to make up your mind in. At ten you marry, or go to jail."

It was time to walk the floor again. Any person in his circumstances would know that. He got up and did it. Sometimes moaning, sometime swearing; always trying to find some way out of his bitter toils, and not succeeding. At last I put my finger on the button, and began to count, solemnly—

"One—two—three—"

"Damn her eyes, I'll marry her! Oh, it's awful—awful. But I've got to do it, and I will. I'll marry her next winter, I give you my word."

"Why not now?"

"*Now?* I reckon you are forgetting one or two details?"

"Which ones?"

"License—preacher—witnesses—and so-on."

"Oh, you think so! Tom! Alice!" They entered. I touched the bell—three times, then once—to fetch the others. The whole gang burst in on the instant, policeman and all; they had been listening at the door.

Alice was dressed to kill; so were her mates. The Reverend Tom was melted away to half his size, and had hardly strength enough to get about. It must have been a frightful three hours in that little blistering bathroom for a fat man like that. In my time I have seen millions of astonished carpenters, but not all of them put together were as astonished as our bridegroom. It knocked him groggy; and he was a married man before he knew what he was about. At the preacher's suggestion he kissed the bride—it didn't seem to taste over-good to him—and said to me, with a sigh—

"It's your game, sir. What a hand you held!"

Then they all cleared for the dining room below and the refreshments, and Tom and I sat down, I to smoke and he to fan; and we talked the whole grand thing over, and were very, very happy and content. And he put his hand in blessing on my head, and said, with tears in his voice—

"Jackson, dear boy, you will be forgiven many a sin for the good deed you have done this night."

I was touched, myself. Just then George staggered in, looking stunned and weak, and said—

"That Wapping Alice—blame her skin, she's a *man!*"

And so it turned out. She explained that it had never occurred to her to make that dire charge against poor Bjorgensen till I complained that the outcome of the original episode wasn't theatrical enough. She thought she could mend that defect. Well, her effort wasn't bad—you see it, yourself. I keep calling her *she*—I can't help it; I mean *he.*

A quartermaster came along, and said it had just gone six bells. It was time to forsake the moonlit sea and turn in; so we did it.

How Nancy Jackson Married
Kate Wilson

Almost nothing is known about the composition of this story. Twain probably worked on "Nancy Jackson" circa 1902, but never attempted to publish the controversial tale (which is also known as "Feud Story and the Girl Who Was Ostensibly a Man"). It was first published by the *Missouri Review* in March 1987. The story may reflect Twain's troubled mind regarding his daughter Susy's lesbian relationship with Louise Brownell, a college classmate.

The conflict in this story springs from Nancy Jackson's revenge for her brother's murder, an act that renders her a wanted criminal running from the law, the fate of any male who had committed a similar crime. This story departs, however, from Twain's usual presentation of cross-dressers: Nancy's male clothing and behavior are forced upon her as a condition for her safety and survival. Like Conrad in "A Mediæval Romance," Nancy makes a flawless transition, becoming a young man named Robert Finlay. The same-sex solution that Twain concocts for Nancy Jackson and Kate Wilson would also have given him the satisfactory ending he searched for in the problematic conclusion of "Mediæval Romance." In addition to the themes of survival and imposture, Twain develops male revenge in the character of Thomas Furlong, who both helps Nancy in her quest for a new life and exacts a private revenge. See *Wapping Alice* for a surprising twist in Twain's development of same-sex relationships.

Thomas Furlong was a grizzled and sour bachelor of fifty who lived solitary and alone in a log house which stood remote and lonely in the middle of a great cornfield at the base of the rising spurs of the mountains. At two o'clock on a certain morning he came in out of a drizzling rain, lit his tallow dip, pulled down the cheap oiled shade of the single window, punched up his fire, took off his steaming coat, hung it before the fire to dry, sat down, spread his damp hands in front of the blaze, and said to himself—

"It's a puzzle. I wonder what ever did become of her. Seven hours. Maybe she ain't as much of a fool as people think." He sat silently considering the puzzle for some moments, then added, with energy, "Damn her! damn her whole tribe!"

The wooden latch clicked, the door opened and closed softly, and a fresh and comely young girl, clothed in the sunbonnet and the linsey woolsey of the region, stood before him. The man exhibited amazement. He bent a hostile eye upon her and said—

"You here! I just this minute said you warn't a fool. I take it back."

He rose and made [a] step toward the door. The girl motioned him back.

"Leave it alone," she said, "I'm not going to run away."

She sat down and put her feet to the fire. The man hesitated a moment, then resumed his seat with the air of one who has encountered another puzzle.

"You never had much sense, Nancy Jackson," he growled; "I reckon you've lost what you had."

"You think so, do you? What makes you think so?"

"What makes me?" He flung it out with vexed impatience. "Would anybody but a goose come to a sworn enemy's house when he is being hunted for his life?"

The girl did not seem overcome by the argument.

"Did they go to our house?"

"Of course."

"And didn't find me. Are they hiding around it, waiting to catch me when I come?"

"Of course—any fool could guess that."

"I am one of the fools; I guessed it. Have they hunted all the farmsteads for me for miles around—you and the others?"

"For seven hours. Yes. We've searched every one of them."

"Every one?"

"Yes, every one."

The girl gave a satisfied toss of the head and said—

"No you haven't. You didn't search this one."

The man seemed puzzled again, and said—

"I don't get your idea. Would anybody in his right mind ever think of coming *here* to find a cussed Jackson?"

Nancy laughed.

"I judged you'd all be in your right minds," she said; "so I came straight here."

"Great Scott, you can't mean it!"

"I've been sitting safe and comfortable by the embers in the dark of your kitchen six hours and a half."

Furlong gazed at her in silence a while, then shook his head and said—

"Well, it beats me. Of course it *was* the only place they wouldn't search, come to think." He turned the matter over in his mind a moment or two, then said, reluctantly, "You ain't the fool you look."

"Thanks," she said. "I can return the compliment."

"Er—what do you mean by that?"

"Oh, take it as you please—you people. My idea was, that you are not just the kind of fools you look."

Furlong started an angry sentence or two, dropped them in the middle, then brushed the dispute aside with a wave of his hand, and said—

"Come down to business. What are you here for? What's your game?"

The girl's face grew grave. She did not answer at once; after a little she began to word it, carefully, heedfully, and she seemed to watch for effects as the words fell.

"No one—saw me—shoot him—but you." The man's face betrayed nothing. If the girl was fishing for a confirmation of this statement, the project failed. She paused a moment, and seemed a trifle fluttered; then she pulled herself together and began to speak with what looked like good confidence. "Maybe one witness can hang me—I don't know, but I reckon not—it can't be law." A pause; no response from the man. She resumed. "Well, let that be as may be. If I hang, I hang; but I want my chance—I don't want to be lynched. That is why I took the risk and came here, where they'll never look for me. You hate me, and you hate all of my name, Thomas Furlong, but a man that's a man couldn't turn a dog out that fled to him for help when it was hunted for its life—hide me three days till the lynching fever's over, and I'll go and stand my trial!"

There was no change in Furlong's face. It had been implacably resentful before; it remained so.

"Did you kill Jim Bradley in self-defence?"

"Ye—s," hesitatingly.

"You did, did you?"

A nod of the head.

"It'll get you off unhung, you think?"

"I—I—it is my hope."

The man slowly crushed a dried tobacco leaf in his hand, loaded his pipe, emptied some embers on it with the shovel, gave a whiff or two, then said with calm conviction—

"Drop the idea. You'll hang, for sure."

"Why?" and the girl shrunk together and her face paled.

"I'll tell you, when I come to it. Didn't you know there'd be blood when Jim Bradley and your brother Floyd met?"

"Why—yes, I believed so."

"Quite likely. Everybody knew it, you knew it, your mother knew it. How did *you* come to be at the cross roads with Floyd just as dark was coming on and Jim was likely to come by?"

No answer.

"You was there to help. You can't deny it. And when Jim got the drop of Floyd and killed him and broke for the woods, you grabbed Floyd's gun and chased him a hundred yards and sent a bullet through his temple when he turned to look back. He shot Floyd when Floyd stepped from behind the tree raising his gun—and it was self-defence. Yourn *wasn't*, my girl. What do you say to that?"

Nancy was very white. She put up her hands appealingly, and said—

"Oh, oh, have some pity, Mr. Furlong! You can save me—you are the only witness—"

"There was two others!"

"Two? Oh—"

"And they don't love the Jacksons. I name no names, but when the trial comes off I can't save you—couldn't if I wanted to."

Nancy was sobbing now, and wringing her hands miserably.

"Oh, what shall I do! what shall I do!" she said. "My mother's heart will be broken."

At the mention of the mother the anger in Furlong's eyes blazed up fiercely, and he said—

"Let it break! let it break, I say! On the very morning of the day set for our wedding she flung me over and married that low-grade fool your father; humiliated me, made me the joke of the countryside; spoiled my life and made it bitter and lonely and a burden; and the children that should have been mine—but damn these histories, they—look here! Do you want to live?"

"Oh, I do, I do. Let me live!"

"Then you shall! And I'll make it so hard for you, and for *her*, that—"

"Oh, make it anything you like, only let me live, and I will be thankful and she—"

"Then these are the terms. Now listen. You will leave this region, and go far away—for good and all."

"I shall be glad to, God knows. And she may go with me?"

"No."

The word smote like a blow. The girl said faintly—

"Not go with me?"

"I said it."

Nancy rocked her head from side to side, as one in physical pain, and said—

"Oh, it is hard—never to see her again—she never to see me again—oh, she could not bear it, it would kill her—I will not go!"

"As you please. Stay here and hang, if that would suit her better."

"Oh, no, no, no!—I didn't mean it, I didn't indeed; I will go! To know that I am alive will be a comfort to her. She *will* know it, won't she?"

"You will write her every week—in a disguised hand; and for your own safety, see to it that you send the letters under cover to me, who will not be suspected of corresponding with a Jackson. A letter every week, do you understand? If you fail once, I set the dogs of the law on your track."

"I will not fail; oh, I shall be glad to write her and take some of the aches out of her heart."

"Another detail. To-night you are wearing women's clothes for the last time in your life."

"What!"

"For the last time—it is what I said."

"Ah, be merciful; do not require this—say you will not, Mr. Furlong. I—"

"You can't get away from here without a disguise; you can't risk living where you are going without a disguise—"

"But I can dress as a—"

"You will dress as a *man*—that is what you will do. It suits my humor. Say no more about it. Do you agree?"

"I do. There is no help."

"On your honor, now: will you *never* leave off your male dress nor reveal your real sex under any pressure whatever? Promise."

"Oh, must it be—be—always?"

"Absolutely. Promise!"

"Oh, if any other—if—."

"Promise! If in ten seconds you have not pr—"

"I promise! On my honor I promise!"

"Very well, then. Go up in the garret and go to bed. The clothes of the young negro I used to have three years ago before they lynched him on suspicion of stealing two dollars from Jake Carter, who never had two dollars that he got honestly, are up there, and they'll fit you. Put them on in the morning, and hide your own or burn them; you won't need that kind anymore. I'll trim your head and make a young fellow of you. Every day you'll practice, and I'll help you; and by and by when you're letter perfect and can walk and act like a male person and the lynch-fever has blown over, I'll take you out of this region some night and see you safe over the border and on your way. You will call yourself Robert Finlay."

After the girl was gone to the garret, Furlong smoked and thought, and listened to the peaceful patter of the rain on the shingles for half an hour; then he muttered—

"Two of them are dead, two of them are miserable from this out. My chance was a long time coming, but it was worth waiting for. I've drunk a lot of bitter in these twenty years, but there's sugar in this."

He was very happy, and smiled the smile of a contented fiend.

Roughly stated, it was like this.

Jacob Wilson was a farmer who owned a hundred acres of good land, and raised hogs, mules and corn for the southern market. He lived half a mile from the village of Hackley, which had a population of three hundred persons, young and old, and had also a store, a blacksmith shop and a small square church which was without steeple or other gaud. Wilson was of middle age, and had a wife and three children—two young boys and a girl. The girl was well along in her eighteenth year, and was trim and pretty, and carried herself in an independent fashion and upon occasion exhibited a masterful spirit. Her name was Catherine, and she was called Kate. For more than two years, now, she had been of marriageable age, and the young fellows of the farmsteads and the village had been paying awkward court to her, but her heart was still untouched.

She was quite willing to flirt with them, and she did it, and got great pleasure out of it, encouraging each of the youths in turn to think she was taking him seriously, then discarding him and laughing at him when she was tired of him. She made some sore hearts, and for it she got many reproaches, from her mother, and from other mothers concerned; but she was not troubled, she only tossed her head and curled her lip and baited her traps again. Her mother tried to warn her, tried to reason with her, and feared that a judgment would overtake her; but she laughed a gay laugh and said that on the contrary the judgments seemed to be overtaking those others. The mother was grieved, and asked her if she had no heart. The girl said maybe she had, maybe she hadn't; but if she had, it was her intention to market it to her satisfaction or not at all; meantime perhaps there was no great harm in amusing herself with it.

Then came a stranger along, in the early June days, and he had fine manners, and eastern ways, and tailor-made clothes, and was easy, and at home, and bright in his talk, and the village took him to its heart and was happy in his possession. He soon found his way to the Wilson farm; and Kate rejoiced, and straightway she set a trap for him. He came often, then oftener, and he and the girl roamed the primeval woods and the hills hour by hour in the soft gloaming and the moonlight.

If there had been a doubt as to whether Catherine Wilson had a heart or not, that doubt had now vanished. She had one, and she gave it in its absolute entirety to this young stranger, Alfred Hamilton, and was deeply, passionately, unspeakably happy. She walked on air, she thought herself in heaven. There was a week of this delicious trance, this delirium, then Hamilton bade the family good-bye and left for the east to richly prepare and make beautiful a home for his back-settlements bride. He would telegraph, every day, on his journey, to keep his Kate comforted and enable her to bear the separation, and with every opportunity he would write a letter.

All the countryside were talking about the engagement. The Wilsons did not deny it, but that was as far as they went. However, they looked happy, and that was considered equivalent to a confession.

That first telegram did not come!

Had Hamilton met with an accident? was he sick? The family were in great tribulation, Kate was in a state of pitiable terror. She could not sleep that night, but counted the slow hours and waited for next day's news.

It did not come. There was no telegram.

The third day the same.

Kate could not endure the heart-breaking suspense. Should she telegraph Mr. Hamilton's family for tidings? There was a family consultation over this question. It was finally judged best not to indulge in privacies over the wire; to write would be more judicious. So the letter went, to the Hamilton family's Boston address.

A blank week followed—a wretched week for the Wilsons. No answer came. What did the silence mean? Suspicions began to rise in the minds of those poor people. They did not voice them; out of charity for each other each kept his own counsel and suffered in silence.

But this could not go on so; something must be done. What should it be? Apparently there was no choice, there was but one thing to do. Mr. Wilson did it. He wrote the Boston police.

There was another blank week. Then came news which the sufferers had been trying hard not to expect: no Hamiltons had ever lived at that address. Kate Wilson swooned away and was carried to her bed. The mother went to the village and visited among her friends, and talked as pleasantly and cheerfully as she could about all sorts of things, waiting meanwhile for the topic of supreme interest to drift into the conversation; then she smiled and said—

"Oh, that girl, she is incurable! We did hope, for a while, that this time she would stick; but no, what's bred in the bone will come out in the flesh, as the saying is. She's flung him over, just as usual."

"It's too bad."

"Yes, it is. She made him promise to keep still and wait a month for his answer, and now she's sent it ahead of time. I've told her time and again she'll bring a judgment on herself some day, but she always laughs and says the judgments seem to fall to the others. What nice weather we're having. Well, good-bye, I must be going."

So, with a shamed spirit and an aching heart she went her rounds under a cheery mask and distributed her pride-saving and excusable lie.

Kate Wilson kept her bed only a day; then she pulled her courage together and went about her affairs as in former days. Exteriorly she seemed unchanged, but her gayeties were not real; she was entertaining a volcano inside. She wanted revenge for the insult which had been put upon her; she had taken a medicine which she had often administered, and had not found it to her taste. Had the others found it to their taste? That was a question of no importance; it did not interest her, perhaps it did not even suggest itself. She wanted revenge. How could she get it? Well, on the whole the old way was good enough. She would resume, at the old stand. She would never marry, for she could not love again, but she would break every heart that came in her way, and try to imagine it was Hamilton's.

When she had been out of bed a couple of days her father brought home at eventide a waif whom he had found wandering the country roads a mile from the house—a comely young fellow of nineteen or twenty. He said his name was Robert Finlay. He was worn out and famishing. They fed him to his stomach's content, then he was palleted for the night on the floor, and promised a home if he was willing to work for it. He was very grateful, and said he would prove himself worthy.

There was an unoccupied log cabin in the edge of the forest a half mile from the house, and next day the Wilsons fitted this up and installed him in it. As the days went by he won his way with the family and they all liked him and were glad he fell to their share. He was not good for very heavy work, but he did all kinds of light work well and handily, and was a willing and diligent soul.

He was very gentle, and very winning in his ways, but inclined to sadness. Mrs. Wilson pitied him, mothered him, loved him, and the gratefulness that shone in his kind eyes and fell caressingly from his tongue was her sufficient reward.

He seemed to shrink a little from talking about himself, but a fleeting word dropped here and there and now and then revealed in time a kind of outline of his history. Thus it was perceived that he had come from far away; that his liberty, if not his life, had been in danger because of a crime plausibly laid to his charge but which he said he had not committed; that he could never go back whence he came. If he could stay where he was now he should be safe, and in this house he could be happier than anywhere else in the world. Several times he said, pressing mother Wilson's hand and looking up worshipingly in her good face —

"You cannot know what you are doing for me; my life was a terror and a misery to me, and you have taken all that away and made it dear to me and beautiful. I kiss your hands — I could kiss your feet! Do you believe there is any sacrifice I would not make for you and yours? Any sacrifice! The harder the better. I wish I could show you. If a time ever comes you shall see, oh, you shall see!"

The only fault papa Wilson could find in him was these outbursts. He was a plain man and destitute of "gush," and these things discomforted him. He kept his thought to himself for a time, but at last, with caution — feeling that the ice was thin — he took a risk and privately suggested to his wife that the young fellow protested too much. It fired a mine! He did not make that venture a second time. He continued to hold his opinion, but he did not air it any more.

Before Robert had been on the place four days Kate had set her trap for him. But there was no result; Robert responded to her advances, and was evidently pleased by them, but he did not respond in the usual way; he radiated gratified friendliness, but nothing warmer. Kate was surprised, dissatisfied, and privately indignant. But she was not troubled; he was human; a few days would change the complexion of things — there was no hurry.

She was soon deeply interested in her enterprise, and found it unusually attractive because it was difficult; which was a new thing in her experience. She got to happening upon Robert accidentally in the fields and all about; she double-charged the batteries of her eyes and let him have the whole load; she sweetly weaned him from calling her Miss Wilson, and beguiled him to call her Kate; she rewarded him by calling him—timorously—Robert, then she watched for the effect—and was vexed to see that there wasn't any.

When Sunday came around she happened by his cabin and took him for a walk through the sweet solitudes of the wooded hills, and talked sentiment and romance and poetry to him; she allowed her elbow to touch his, but could not discover that it communicated a thrill; she gave a little scream at an imaginary snake, and put her hand upon his arm, and forgot it and left it there a while; then took it away with inviting reluctance and slowly, but he did not try to retain it. Finally she said she was weary, and he offered to turn back homeward, "like a fool," she said to herself; but she said a little rest would restore her; so they sat down on a mossy bank and she worked along up to the subject of love, and said, dreamily—

"It may be beautiful—it would be, no doubt—if one could find the right and loyal heart, a heart that could feel and return a deep and sincere affection—but I—I—something tells me I shall never find it."

She paused, to give Robert an opportunity. After reflection, he said, sympathetically—

"Do not say that. You will find it."

"Oh, do you think so—do you?"

"Why, yes—I think it must happen."

"How good of you! And you are *always* so good. So good and so—so—affectionate, if you will let me say it and not think me bold. You *have* an affectionate nature, *haven't* you?"

"Why—I hope I have—I—"

"Oh I *know* you have! It is in your eyes, Robert—I love to look in your eyes; do you love to have me?" She laid her warm soft hand upon his with a gentle pressure. "You do, don't you, Robert?"

"Why, yes, I—I'm sure I—"

Her pouting lips were near to his; languidly she whispered, "Kiss me, Robert," and closed her eyes.

She waited. Nothing happened. She unclosed her eyes; they

were spouting anger. He began to explain humbly that she had misunderstood him; that he liked her—liked her ever so much, but—

"I hate you!" she burst out, and gathered up her skirts and strode away without looking backward.

The next day she sat brooding over the humiliation which he had put upon her, and over her yesterday's failure to avenge that wrong upon another member of his detested sex. Was this defeat to stand? Well, no. Her resentment against Robert flamed up, and she said she would find a way somehow to make him sorry that he had ever crossed her path. She began to form a plan; as she proceeded with it she grew enamored of it. She finished it to her content, and said it would answer— now let him look to himself.

After a little a new thought came drifting into her brain— and it stopped her breath for a moment. Her lips fell apart; she moistened them with her tongue; her face blenched, her breath began to come in gasps; she muttered a frightened ejaculation, her head drooped, her chin sank upon her breast.

Two days later mother Wilson went to the village and made another house-to-house visitation with news to deliver. Happy news this time: her daughter was engaged to Robert Finlay. She was snowed under with enthusiastic congratulations everywhere she went, and as soon as her back was turned the friends discussed the matter and pitied the bridegroom. They agreed that although he was a tramp and unknown he was manifestly a simple and honest good creature and a better man than Kate Wilson deserved. In their opinion a judgment had fallen again—and on the wrong person, as usual. A few cautious conservatives said it was too early, as yet, to be locating the judgment; Kate could back out before the wedding day, and it was an even bet that she would do it. There was wisdom in this remark, and it sensibly cooled the general joy produced by the prospect of the exasperating flirt's early retirement from her professional industries.

There was a fortnight's suspense, then all doubts and all questionings were put to rest: Kate and Robert were married.

The wedding took place at the farm at noonday, and was followed by a barbecue and a dance. It was noticed that Robert, in his wedding clothes, was a surprisingly handsome person; also that fleeting glimpses of his accustomed sadness were catchable through chance rifts in his new happiness; also that Kate's exuberant joy seemed a little overdone, at times; also that there was a haunting and pathetic something in mother Wilson's face that took the strength out of one's congratulations and made them sound almost like words of comfort and compassion; also that papa Wilson's manner was grave, austere, almost gloomy; that when he gave his daughter a deed of half his farm as a wedding present from her parents he did not look at his son-in-law, and did not grace the gift with a speech of any kind; that he then excused himself and took his leave with a general bow and some mumbled words which nobody heard, and was seen no more.

The guests departed at six in the afternoon, observing privately to each other that there was "something wrong there — what can the matter be?" Arrived at their several homes, they reported to their households that they had been at a funeral, they didn't know whose — maybe Kate's, maybe Robert's, maybe the whole family's.

The company gone, the bride, the groom and the mother found themselves sitting together — with liberal spaces between — moody, distraught, silent, each waiting for the others to begin. It was the groom who began, finally. He said —

"You commanded, mother Wilson; I have obeyed. Against my will. I obeyed because I could not help myself; I obeyed because there was no possible way out, and I had to do it; if there had been a way out, I never would have obeyed. I — "

Mother Wilson interrupted him, in a tone of gentle reproach.

"Ah, Robert, you could not honorably and humanely do otherwise than obey. You denied the charge, but obeying was confession, Robert."

The young man rejoined, with almost a groan in his voice —

"Oh, the deadly logic of it! I *know* it looks like that, and there's no answering it; it is unanswerable, and yet I say again, the charge is not true. It is my misfortune that I cannot at this time explain why I was obliged to obey; and so—"

"Yes, it *is* unfortunate," the bride remarked, tauntingly; "shall you ever be able to explain?"

"That is the worst of it—no! But you! how do you dare to speak? You who sit smirking there—you, Catherine Wil—Finlay—you know I never did you harm. You—"

"I say it again. The charge I made was true."

Finlay tugged at his collar to loosen it; tried to retort; the words choked in his throat. Mother Wilson said, in gentle rebuke—

"You are a stranger, Robert; we love you, but we do not know you yet. It is not reasonable to expect us to believe you against our daughter's word."

"Oh, I know it, I know it! My case is weaker than water; and all because I cannot explain, I cannot *explain*! You believe her; papa Wilson believes her, and both of you are justified—I were a fool to deny it. Papa Wilson thinks me an ungrateful cur, and despises me—and in the circumstances he is right, though I have never done harm to any member of this family, nor meditated it."

"Ah well," said mother Wilson, soothingly, "things are as they are, and we must accept them; they may be blessings in disguise—we cannot know. Let us let bygones be bygones, and think no more about them, resolving to begin a new life and a happy and righteous one. Put your fault behind you, dear and beloved son; it is forgiven, it shall be forgotten. My child will make you a good and loving wife—"

"No—no—no! She is no wife of mine, and never shall be, except in name."

"My dear son! You—"

"You commanded, mother; I have obeyed—because I could not help myself. I have saved your daughter's good name from gossip and wreck—let the sacrifice stop there. I will never live with her—not even so much as a single day."

"My son, oh, my son! What are you saying! Oh—"

"Let him alone, mother," said the new wife, with a serene confidence born of old experience; "if I shall ever desire his society, trust me I shall know how to acquire it."

After supper the new husband betook himself at once to his lonely cabin and sat down and wrote a long letter; sealed it in an envelope directed to "Mrs. Sarah Jackson;" sealed that envelope in a larger one; directed this one to an obscure village in a distant State, and addressed it to "Mr. Thomas Furlong." Then he went to bed and to sleep.

The letter was several days on its road. Mr. Furlong took it from the village postoffice and carried it to his ancient log cabin three or four miles in the country. He was expecting the letter; one came from the same source punctually every week. Furlong stirred up his fire, lit his cob pipe, and made himself comfortable. He exhibited the strong and lively interest of a person who is expecting exhilarating tidings and is proposing to get a deal of enjoyment out of them. Yet he knew that the letter was not for him. He settled himself in his chair and opened both envelops. The letter began—

"DEAR MOTHER: To-day I was married to the girl I have already spoken of."

Furlong put down pipe and letter and threw back his head and delivered himself of crash after crash, gust after gust of delighted laughter; then, middle-aged man as he was, got up, mopping the happy tears from his leathery cheeks, and expended the remaining remnant of his strength in a breakdown of scandalous violence, and finally sank into his chair, heaving and panting, limp and exhausted, and said with what wind he had left—

"Lord, it's just good to be alive!"

He resumed his pipe and Mrs. Jackson's letter, now, and read the latter through to the end, making comments as he proceeded. The story of the marriage, and what brought it about, and what happened after it, was detailed and complete—all the facts, just as we already know them—and they gave Mr. Furlong high satisfaction and amusement, particularly where poor Finlay broke into pathetic lamentations over his miseries and wrongs and humiliations. At these places Furlong slapped his thigh and said with evil glee—

"It's great, it's grand, it's lovely! It couldn't suit me better if I had planned it myself."

The letter closed with—

"And so, as you see, I am married, yet have no wife; for, as I told them at the end of that wretched talk, I shall never live with her for even so much as a single day. Dear mother, pity your poor son. ROBERT FINLAY."

"He's keeping his word," was Furlong's comment. "And damn him he'd better, if he knows what's good for him!"

He put the letter in his pocket without re-enveloping it, and left his cabin, remarking to himself—

"His mamma must have it straight off. Her head's turning gray; I reckon this will help."

At the Wilson farm the months dragged drearily along. The four members of the family ate their meals together, and sometimes they took their food in silence, sometimes they talked, but it was in a constrained and colorless way, and papa Wilson's share in it was exceedingly small, and was confined to the two women as a rule; it was but rarely that he included "Mr. Finlay"—as he called him—in his remarks, and when he did it was not in order to pay him compliments. The young couple called each other "Mr." and "Mrs." Mother Wilson and Robert remained affectionate toward each other, and she continued to call him Robert and "son," and he continued to call her Mother Wilson. The good lady made many attempts to soften and sweeten this arid life, but she got no encouragement and had no success. She mourned much, and shed many tears.

After the free ways of the country, visitors came often—uninvited—and stopped to a meal, to spy out the conditions. On these occasions efforts were made by all the family to seem friendly and content, but those made by papa Wilson were so lame and poor that they spoiled the game and no visitor went away deceived.

Evenings at eight o'clock the family met at family worship for half an hour. Papa Wilson read and prayed, and he always wanted to ignore Robert, and would have done it but for his wife's anguished appeals. Through their influence a compromise was effected—such as it was—and nightly a prayer went up for "mercy" for "the stranger within our gates;" a prayer which always came from the cold-storage closet in the supplicant's heart and changed the temperature of the room. Mother Wilson tried hard to get a blessing put in the place of mercy, but the embittered old man would not have it so. He said—

"I loved this cur and was kind to him; and for pay he . . . . drop the subject, I will not listen to it!"

Nightly, after prayers, [Robert] withdrew promptly from the house's depressing atmosphere and betook him to the refuge of his cabin, and was not seen again until morning. Sundays he rode by his wife's side to the village, along with her parents, and by her side he sat through the forenoon service. The keeping up of appearances in public went little or no further than this. All the world knew that the pair did not live together; all the world wondered at it and discussed it, and tried to guess the reason; a former schoolmate of Kate's carried her curiosity so far as to leave hinting and boldly put the straight question—

"If the old friends ask me why things are as they are, what shall I say?"

Kate reflected; seemed to search warily for a safe and diplomatic answer, then laid her hand on the woman's knee, gazed into her face with yearning simplicity and said—

"How would it do to say it is none of their business?"

At last the child was born—a boy.

A Horse's Tale

In September 1905 Twain decided, after repeated requests by the actress and animal rights activist Minnie Maddern Fiske, to write a story exposing the cruelty and violence of bull-fighting. He became emotionally caught up in writing the tale, though it took him some time to realize the connection: his model for the precocious and rebellious young protagonist, Cathy Alison, was his recently deceased daughter, Susy Clemens. Twain published the completed manuscript serially in the 1906 summer issues of *Harper's Monthly*. He followed up on this success with a hardbound edition (illustrations by Lucius Hitchcock) published by Harper and Brothers in 1907.

Reviewers and scholars have found various structural and stylistic weaknesses in the story, but in the context of Ms. Fiske's request, his personal tribute to his lost daughter, and his intense interest in heroic girl protagonists, its sentimentality can be more easily understood. Cathy's military campaigns in the American West place this eleven-year-old in the reflected fire of Twain's tribute to Joan of Arc. Even though four or five of the girl and young women stories end just short of possibly tragic conclusions, Cathy and Joan represent, for Twain, the always-possible outcome when intelligent and spirited young women act independently, even defiantly, and ignore established male authority.

ACKNOWLEDGMENTS

Although I have had several opportunities to see a bull-fight, I have never seen one; but I needed a bull-fight in this book, and a trustworthy one will be found in it. I got it out of John Hay's *Castilian Days*, reducing and condensing it to fit the requirements of this small story. Mr. Hay and I were friends from early times, and if he were still with us he would not rebuke me for the liberty I have taken.

The knowledge of military minutiæ exhibited in this book will be found to be correct, but it is not mine; I took it from *Army Regulations*, ed. 1904; *Hardy's Tactics—Cavalry*, revised ed., 1861; and *Jomini's Handbook of Military Etiquette*, West Point ed., 1905.

It would not be honest in me to encourage by silence the inference that I composed the Horse's private bugle-call, for I did not. I lifted it, as Aristotle says. It is the opening strain in *The Pizzicato* in *Sylvia*, by Delibes. When that master was composing it he did not know it was a bugle-call, it was I that found it out.

Along through the book I have distributed a few anachronisms and unborn historical incidents and such things, so as to help the tale over the difficult places. This idea is not original with me; I got it out of Herodotus. Herodotus says, "Very few things happen at the right time, and the rest do not happen at all: the conscientious historian will correct these defects."

The cats in the chair do not belong to me, but to another.

These are all the exceptions. What is left of the book is mine.

MARK TWAIN.
Lone Tree Hill, Dublin, New Hampshire, October, 1905.

Part I

1 Soldier Boy—*Privately to Himself*

I am Buffalo Bill's horse. I have spent my life under his saddle
—with him in it, too, and he is good for two hundred pounds,
without his clothes; and there is no telling how much he does
weigh when he is out on the war-path and has his batteries
belted on. He is over six feet, is young, hasn't an ounce of waste
flesh, is straight, graceful, springy in his motions, quick as a
cat, and has a handsome face, and black hair dangling down
on his shoulders, and is beautiful to look at; and nobody is
braver than he is, and nobody is stronger, except myself. Yes,
a person that doubts that he is fine to see should see him in
his beaded buckskins, on my back and his rifle peeping above
his shoulder, chasing a hostile trail, with me going like the
wind and his hair streaming out behind from the shelter of his
broad slouch. Yes, he is a sight to look at then—and I'm part
of it myself.

I am his favorite horse, out of dozens. Big as he is, I have
carried him eighty-one miles between night-fall and sunrise
on the scout; and I am good for fifty, day in and day out, and
all the time. I am not large, but I am built on a business basis.
I have carried him thousands and thousands of miles on scout
duty for the army, and there's not a gorge, nor a pass, nor a
valley, nor a fort, nor a trading post, nor a buffalo-range in
the whole sweep of the Rocky Mountains and the Great Plains
that we don't know as well as we know the bugle-calls. He
is Chief of Scouts to the Army of the Frontier, and it makes
us very important. In such a position as I hold in the military
service one needs to be of good family and possess an education much above the common to be worthy of the place. I

am the best-educated horse outside of the hippodrome, everybody says, and the best-mannered. It may be so, it is not for me to say; modesty is the best policy, I think. Buffalo Bill taught me the most of what I know, my mother taught me much, and I taught myself the rest. Lay a row of moccasins before me—Pawnee, Sioux, Shoshone, Cheyenne, Blackfoot, and as many other tribes as you please—and I can name the tribe every moccasin belongs to by the make of it. Name it in horse-talk, and could do it in American if I had speech.

I know some of the Indian signs—the signs they make with their hands, and by signal-fires at night and columns of smoke by day. Buffalo Bill taught me how to drag wounded soldiers out of the line of fire with my teeth; and I've done it, too; at least I've dragged *him* out of the battle when he was wounded. And not just once, but twice. Yes, I know a lot of things. I remember forms, and gaits, and faces; and you can't disguise a person that's done me a kindness so that I won't know him thereafter wherever I find him. I know the art of searching for a trail, and I know the stale track from the fresh. I can keep a trail all by myself, with Buffalo Bill asleep in the saddle; ask him—he will tell you so. Many a time, when he has ridden all night, he has said to me at dawn, "Take the watch, Boy; if the trail freshens, call me." Then he goes to sleep. He knows he can trust me, because I have a reputation. A scout horse that has a reputation does not play with it.

My mother was all American—no alkali-spider about *her*, I can tell you; she was of the best blood of Kentucky, the bluest Blue-grass aristocracy, very proud and acrimonious—or maybe it is ceremonious. I don't know which it is. But it is no matter; size is the main thing about a word, and that one's up to standard. She spent her military life as colonel of the Tenth Dragoons, and saw a deal of rough service—distinguished service it was, too. I mean, she *carried* the Colonel; but it's all the same. Where would he be without his horse? He wouldn't arrive. It takes two to make a colonel of dragoons. She was a fine dragoon horse, but never got above that. She was strong enough for the scout service, and had the endurance, too, but she couldn't quite come up to the speed required; a scout horse has to have steel in his muscle and lightning in his blood.

My father was a bronco. Nothing as to lineage—that is, nothing as to recent lineage—but plenty good enough when you go a good way back. When Professor Marsh was out here hunting bones for the chapel of Yale University he found skeletons of horses no bigger than a fox, bedded in the rocks, and he said they were ancestors of my father. My mother heard him say it; and he said those skeletons were two million years old, which astonished her and made her Kentucky pretensions look small and pretty antiphonal, not to say oblique. Let me see. . . . I used to know the meaning of those words, but . . . well, it was years ago, and 'tisn't as vivid now as it was when they were fresh. That sort of words doesn't keep, in the kind of climate we have out here. Professor Marsh said those skeletons were fossils. So that makes me part blue grass and part fossil; if there is any older or better stock, you will have to look for it among the Four Hundred, I reckon. I am satisfied with it. And am a happy horse, too, though born out of wedlock.

And now we are back at Fort Paxton once more, after a forty-day scout, away up as far as the Big Horn. Everything quiet. Crows and Blackfeet squabbling—as usual—but no outbreaks, and settlers feeling fairly easy.

The Seventh Cavalry still in garrison, here; also the Ninth Dragoons, two artillery companies, and some infantry. All glad to see me, including General Alison, commandant. The officers' ladies and children well, and called upon me—with sugar. Colonel Drake, Seventh Cavalry, said some pleasant things; Mrs. Drake was very complimentary; also Captain and Mrs. Marsh, Company B, Seventh Cavalry; also the Chaplain, who is always kind and pleasant to me, because I kicked the lungs out of a trader once. It was Tommy Drake and Fanny Marsh that furnished the sugar—nice children, the nicest at the post, I think.

That poor orphan child is on her way from France—everybody is full of the subject. Her father was General Alison's brother; married a beautiful young Spanish lady ten years ago, and has never been in America since. They lived in Spain a year or two, then went to France. Both died some months ago. This little girl that is coming is the only child. General Alison is glad to have her. He has never seen her. He is a very nice old bachelor, but is an old bachelor just the same and isn't more than about a year this side of retirement by age limit; and so what does he know about taking care of a little maid nine years old? If I could have her it would be another matter, for I know all about children, and they adore me. Buffalo Bill will tell you so himself.

I have some of this news from overhearing the garrison-gossip, the rest of it I got from Potter, the General's dog. Potter is the great Dane. He is privileged, all over the post, like Shekels, the Seventh Cavalry's dog, and visits everybody's quarters and picks up everything that is going, in the way of news. Potter has no imagination, and no great deal of culture, perhaps, but he has a historical mind and a good memory, and so he is the person I depend upon mainly to post me up when I get back from a scout. That is, if Shekels is out on depredation and I can't get hold of him.

11 *Letter from Rouen—To General Alison*

My dear Brother-in-Law,—Please let me write again in Spanish, I cannot trust my English, and I am aware, from what your brother used to say, that army officers educated at the Military Academy of the United States are taught our tongue. It is as I told you in my other letter: both my poor sister and her husband, when they found they could not recover, expressed the wish that you should have their little Catherine—as knowing that you would presently be retired from the army—rather than that she should remain with me, who am broken in health, or go to your mother in California, whose health is also frail.

You do not know the child, therefore I must tell you something about her. You will not be ashamed of her looks, for she is a copy in little of her beautiful mother—and it is that Andalusian beauty which is not surpassable, even in your country. She has her mother's charm and grace and good heart and sense of justice, and she has her father's vivacity and cheerfulness and pluck and spirit of enterprise, with the affectionate disposition and sincerity of both parents.

My sister pined for her Spanish home all these years of exile;

she was always talking of Spain to the child, and tending and nourishing the love of Spain in the little thing's heart as a precious flower; and she died happy in the knowledge that the fruitage of her patriotic labors was as rich as even she could desire.

Cathy is a sufficiently good little scholar, for her nine years; her mother taught her Spanish herself, and kept it always fresh upon her ear and her tongue by hardly ever speaking with her in any other tongue; her father was her English teacher, and talked with her in that language almost exclusively; French has been her every-day speech for more than seven years among her playmates here; she has a good working use of governess—German and Italian. It is true that there is always a faint foreign fragrance about her speech, no matter what language she is talking, but it is only just noticeable, nothing more, and is rather a charm than a mar, I think. In the ordinary child-studies Cathy is neither before nor behind the average child of nine, I should say. But I can say this for her: in love for her friends and in high-mindedness and good-heartedness she has not many equals, and in my opinion no superiors. And I beg of you, let her have her way with the dumb animals—they are her worship. It is an inheritance from her mother. She knows but little of cruelties and oppressions—keep them from her sight if you can. She would flare up at them and make trouble, in her small but quite decided and resolute way; for she has a character of her own, and lacks neither promptness nor initiative. Sometimes her judgment is at fault, but I think her intentions are always right. Once when she was a little creature of three or four years she suddenly brought her tiny foot down upon the floor in an apparent outbreak of indignation, then fetched it a backward wipe, and stooped down to examine the result. Her mother said:

"Why, what is it, child? What has stirred you so?"

"Mamma, the big ant was trying to kill the little one."

"And so you protected the little one."

"Yes, mamma, because he had no friend, and I wouldn't let the big one kill him."

"But you have killed them both."

Cathy was distressed, and her lip trembled. She picked up the remains and laid them upon her palm, and said:

"Poor little anty, I'm so sorry; and I didn't mean to kill you, but there wasn't any other way to save you, it was such a hurry."

She is a dear and sweet little lady, and when she goes it will give me a sore heart. But she will be happy with you, and if your heart is old and tired, give it into her keeping; she will make it young again, she will refresh it, she will make it sing. Be good to her, for all our sakes!

My exile will soon be over now. As soon as I am a little stronger I shall see my Spain again; and that will make *me* young again!

MERCEDES.

III *General Alison to His Mother*

I am glad to know that you are all well, in San Bernardino.

. . . That grandchild of yours has been here—well, I do not quite know how many days it is; nobody can keep account of days or anything else where she is! Mother, she did what the Indians were never able to do. She took the Fort—took it the first day! Took me, too; took the colonels, the captains, the women, the children, and the dumb brutes; took Buffalo Bill, and all his scouts; took the garrison—to the last man; and in forty-eight hours the Indian encampment was hers, illustrious old Thunder-Bird and all. Do I seem to have lost my solemnity, my gravity, my poise, my dignity? You would lose your own, in my circumstances. Mother, you never saw such a winning little devil. She is all energy, and spirit, and sunshine, and interest in everybody and everything, and pours out her prodigal love upon every creature that will take it, high or low, Christian or pagan, feathered or furred; and none has declined it to date, and none ever will, I think. But she has a temper, and sometimes it catches fire and flames up, and is likely to burn whatever is near it; but it is soon over, the passion goes as quickly as it comes. Of course she has an Indian name already; Indians always rechristen a stranger early. Thunder-Bird attended to her case. He gave her the Indian equivalent for firebug, or fire-fly. He said:

"Times, ver' quiet, ver' soft, like summer night, but when she mad she blaze."

Isn't it good? Can't you see the flare? She's beautiful, mother, beautiful as a picture; and there is a touch of you in her face, and of her father—poor George! and in her unresting activities, and her fearless ways, and her sunbursts and cloud-bursts, she is always bringing George back to me. These impulsive natures are dramatic. George was dramatic, so is this Lightning-Bug, so is Buffalo Bill. When Cathy first arrived—it was in the forenoon—Buffalo Bill was away, carrying orders to Major Fuller, at Five Forks, up in the Clayton Hills. At midafternoon I was at my desk, trying to work, and this sprite had been making it impossible for half an hour. At last I said:

"Oh, you bewitching little scamp, *can't* you be quiet just a minute or two, and let your poor old uncle attend to a part of his duties?"

"I'll try, uncle; I will, indeed," she said.

"Well, then, that's a good child—kiss me. Now, then, sit up in that chair, and set your eye on that clock. There—that's right. If you stir—if you so much as wink—for four whole minutes, I'll bite you!"

It was very sweet and humble and obedient she looked, sitting there, still as a mouse; I could hardly keep from setting her free and telling her to make as much racket as she wanted to. During as much as two minutes there was a most unnatural and heavenly quiet and repose, then Buffalo Bill came thundering up to the door in all his scout finery, flung himself out of the saddle, said to his horse, "Wait for me, Boy," and stepped in, and stopped dead in his tracks—gazing at the child. She forgot orders, and was on the floor in a moment, saying:

"Oh, you are so beautiful! Do you like me?"

"No, I don't, I love you!" and he gathered her up with a hug, and then set her on his shoulder—apparently nine feet from the floor.

She was at home. She played with his long hair, and admired his big hands and his clothes and his carbine, and asked question after question, as fast as he could answer, until I excused them both for half an hour, in order to have a chance to finish my work. Then I heard Cathy exclaiming over Soldier Boy; and he was worthy of her raptures, for he is a wonder of a horse, and has a reputation which is as shining as his own silken hide.

IV Cathy to Her Aunt Mercedes

Oh, it is wonderful here, aunty dear, just paradise! Oh, if you could only see it! everything so wild and lovely; such grand plains, stretching such miles and miles and miles, all the most delicious velvety sand and sage-brush, and rabbits as big as a dog, and such tall and noble jackassful ears that that is what they name them by; and such vast mountains, and so rugged and craggy and lofty, with cloud-shawls wrapped around their shoulders, and looking so solemn and awful and satisfied; and the charming Indians, oh, how you would dote on them, aunty dear, and they would on you, too, and they would let you hold their babies, the way they do me, and they *are* the fattest, and brownest, and sweetest little things, and never cry, and wouldn't if they had pins sticking in them, which they haven't, because they are poor and can't afford it; and the horses and mules and cattle and dogs—hundreds and hundreds and hundreds, and not an animal that you can't do what you please with, except uncle Thomas, but I don't mind him, he's lovely; and oh, if you could hear the bugles: *too—too— too-too—too—too*, and so on—per-fectly beautiful! Do you recognize that one? It's the first toots of the *reveille*; it goes, dear me, *so* early in the morning!—then I and every other soldier on the whole place are up and out in a minute, except uncle Thomas, who is most unaccountably lazy, I don't know why, but I have talked to him about it, and I reckon it will be better, now. He hasn't any faults much, and is charming and sweet, like Buffalo Bill, and Thunder-Bird, and Mammy Dorcas, and Soldier Boy, and Shekels, and Potter, and Sour-Mash, and— well, they're *all* that, just angels, as you may say.

The very first day I came, I don't know how long ago it was, Buffalo Bill took me on Soldier Boy to Thunder-Bird's camp, not the big one which is out on the plain, which is White Cloud's, he took me to *that* one next day, but this one is four or five miles up in the hills and crags, where there is a great

shut-in meadow, full of Indian lodges and dogs and squaws
and everything that is interesting, and a brook of the clearest
water running through it, with white pebbles on the bottom
and trees all along the banks[,] cool and shady and good to
wade in, and as the sun goes down it is dimmish in there,
but away up against the sky you see the big peaks towering
up and shining bright and vivid in the sun, and sometimes an
eagle sailing by them, not flapping a wing, the same as if he
was asleep; and young Indians and girls romping and laughing and carrying on, around the spring and the pool, and not
much clothes on except the girls, and dogs fighting, and the
squaws busy at work, and the bucks busy resting, and the old
men sitting in a bunch smoking, and passing the pipe not to
the left but to the right, which means there's been a row in the
camp and they are settling it if they can, and children playing
just the same as any other children, and little boys shooting at
a mark with bows, and I cuffed one of them because he hit a
dog with a club that wasn't doing anything, and he resented it
but before long he wished he hadn't: but this sentence is getting too long and I will start another. Thunder-Bird put on his
Sunday-best war outfit to let me see him, and he was splendid
to look at, with his face painted red and bright and intense like
a fire-coal and a valance of eagle feathers from the top of his
head all down his back, and he had his tomahawk, too, and
his pipe, which has a stem which is longer than my arm, and I
never had such a good time in an Indian camp in my life, and
I learned a lot of words of the language, and next day BB took
me to the camp out on the Plains, four miles, and I had another
good time and got acquainted with some more Indians and
dogs; and the big chief, by the name of White Cloud, gave
me a pretty little bow and arrows and I gave him my red sash-
ribbon, and in four days I could shoot very well with it and beat
any white boy of my size at the post; and I have been to those
camps plenty of times since; and I have learned to ride, too,
BB taught me, and every day he practises me and praises me,
and every time I do better than ever he lets me have a scamper
on Soldier Boy, and that's the last agony of pleasure! for he is
the charmingest horse, and so beautiful and shiny and black,

and hasn't another color on him anywhere, except a white star in his forehead, not just an imitation star, but a real one, with four points, shaped exactly like a star that's hand-made, and if you should cover him all up but his star you would know him anywhere, even in Jerusalem or Australia, by that. And I got acquainted with a good many of the Seventh Cavalry, and the dragoons, and officers, and families, and horses, in the first few days, and some more in the next few and the next few and the next few, and now I know more soldiers and horses than you can think, no matter how hard you try. I am keeping up my studies every now and then, but there isn't much time for it. I love you so! and I send you a hug and a kiss.

CATHY.

P.S.—I belong to the Seventh Cavalry and Ninth Dragoons, I am an officer, too, and do not have to work on account of not getting any wages.

v *General Alison to Mercedes*

She has been with us a good nice long time, now. You are troubled about your sprite because this is such a wild frontier, hundreds of miles from civilization, and peopled only by wandering tribes of savages? You fear for her safety? Give yourself no uneasiness about her. Dear me, she's in a nursery! and she's got more than eighteen hundred nurses. It would distress the garrison to suspect that you think they can't take care of her. They think they can. They would tell you so themselves. You see, the Seventh Cavalry has never had a child of its very own before, and neither has the Ninth Dragoons; and so they are like all new mothers, they think there is no other child like theirs, no other child so wonderful, none that is so worthy to be faithfully and tenderly looked after and protected. These bronzed veterans of mine are very good mothers, I think, and wiser than some other mothers; for they let her take lots of risks, and it is a good education for her; and the more risks she takes and comes successfully out of, the prouder they are of her. They adopted her, with grave and formal military ceremonies of their own invention—solemnities is the truer word; solemnities that were so profoundly solemn and earnest, that the spectacle would have been comical if it hadn't been so touching. It was a good show, and as stately and complex as guard-mount and the trooping of the colors; and it had its own special music, composed for the occasion by the band-master of the Seventh; and the child was as serious as the most serious war-worn soldier of them all; and finally when they throned her upon the shoulder of the oldest veteran, and pronounced her "well and truly adopted," and the bands struck up and all saluted and she saluted in return, it was better and more moving than any kindred thing I have seen on the stage, because stage things are make-believe, but this was real and the players' hearts were in it.

It happened several weeks ago, and was followed by some additional solemnities. The men created a couple of new ranks, thitherto unknown to the army regulations, and conferred them upon Cathy, with ceremonies suitable to a duke. So now she is Corporal-General of the Seventh Cavalry, and Flag-Lieutenant of the Ninth Dragoons, with the privilege (decreed by the men) of writing U.S.A. after her name! Also, they presented her a pair of shoulder-straps — both dark blue, the one with F. L. on it, the other with C. G. Also, a sword. She wears them. Finally, they granted her the *salute*. I am witness that that ceremony is faithfully observed by both parties — and most gravely and decorously, too. I have never seen a soldier smile yet, while delivering it, nor Cathy in returning it.

Ostensibly I was not present at these proceedings, and am ignorant of them; but I was where I could see. I was afraid of one thing — the jealousy of the other children of the post; but there is nothing of that, I am glad to say. On the contrary, they are proud of their comrade and her honors. It is a surprising thing, but it is true. The children are devoted to Cathy, for she has turned their dull frontier life into a sort of continuous festival; also they know her for a staunch and steady friend, a friend who can always be depended upon, and does not change with the weather.

She has become a rather extraordinary rider, under the tutorship of a more than extraordinary teacher — BB, which is her pet name for Buffalo Bill. She pronounces it *beeby*. He has not only taught her seventeen ways of breaking her neck, but twenty-two ways of avoiding it. He has infused into her the best and surest protection of a horseman—*confidence*. He did it gradually, systematically, little by little, a step at a time, and each step made sure before the next was essayed. And so he inched her along up through terrors that had been discounted by training before she reached them, and therefore were not recognizable as terrors when she got to them. Well, she is a daring little rider, now, and is perfect in what she knows of horsemanship. By-and-by she will know the art like a West Point cadet, and will exercise it as fearlessly. She doesn't know anything about side-saddles. Does that distress you? And she is a fine performer, without any saddle at all. Does that discomfort you? Do not let it; she is not in any danger, I give you my word.

You said that if my heart was old and tired she would refresh it, and you said truly. I do not know how I got along without her, before. I was a forlorn old tree, but now that this blossoming vine has wound itself about me and become the life of my life, it is very different. As a furnisher of business for me and for Mammy Dorcas she is exhaustlessly competent, but I like my share of it and of course Dorcas likes hers, for Dorcas "raised" George, and Cathy is George over again in so many ways that she brings back Dorcas's youth and the joys of that long-vanished time. My father tried to set Dorcas free twenty years ago, when we still lived in Virginia, but without success; she considered herself a member of the family, and wouldn't go. And so, a member of the family she remained, and has held that position unchallenged ever since, and holds it now; for when my mother sent her here from San Bernardino when we learned that Cathy was coming, she only changed from one division of the family to the other. She has the warm heart of her race, and its lavish affections, and when Cathy arrived the pair were mother and child in five minutes, and that is what they are to date and will continue. Dorcas really thinks she raised George, and that is one of her prides, but perhaps it was a mutual raising, for their ages were the same—thirteen years short of mine. But they were playmates, at any rate; as regards that, there is no room for dispute.

Cathy thinks Dorcas is the best Catholic in America except herself. She could not pay any one a higher compliment than that, and Dorcas could not receive one that would please her better. Dorcas is satisfied that there has never been a more wonderful child than Cathy. She has conceived the curious idea that Cathy is *twins*, and that one of them is a boy-twin and failed to get segregated—got submerged, is the idea. To argue with her that this is nonsense is a waste of breath—her mind is made up, and arguments do not affect it. She says:

"Look at her; she loves dolls, and girl-plays, and everything a girl loves, and she's gentle and sweet, and ain't cruel to dumb brutes—now that's the girl-twin, but she loves boy-plays, and drums and fifes and soldiering, and rough-riding, and ain't afraid of anybody or anything—and that's the boy-twin; 'deed you needn't tell *me* she's only *one* child; no, sir, she's twins, and one of them got shet up out of sight. Out of sight, but that don't make any difference, that boy is in there, and you can see him look out of her eyes when her temper is up."

Then Dorcas went on, in her simple and earnest way, to furnish illustrations.

"Look at that raven, Marse Tom. Would anybody befriend a raven but that child? Of course they wouldn't; it ain't natural. Well, the Injun boy had the raven tied up, and was all the time plaguing it and starving it, and she pitied the po' thing, and tried to buy it from the boy, and the tears was in her eyes. That was the girl-twin, you see. She offered him her thimble, and he flung it down; she offered him all the doughnuts she had, which was two, and he flung them down; she offered him half a paper of pins, worth forty ravens, and he made a mouth at her and jabbed one of them in the raven's back. That was the limit, you know. It called for the other twin. Her eyes blazed up, and she jumped for him like a wild-cat, and when she was done with him she was rags and he wasn't anything but an allegory. That was most undoubtedly the other twin, you see, coming to the front. No, sir; don't tell *me* he ain't in there. I've seen him with my own eyes—and plenty of times, at that."

"Allegory? What is an allegory?"

"I don't know, Marse Tom, it's one of her words; she loves

the big ones, you know, and I pick them up from her; they sound good and I can't help it."

"What happened after she had converted the boy into an allegory?"

"Why, she untied the raven and confiscated him by force and fetched him home, and left the doughnuts and things on the ground. Petted him, of course, like she does with every creature. In two days she had him so stuck after her that she—well, *you* know how he follows her everywhere, and sets on her shoulder often when she rides her breakneck rampages—all of which is the girl-twin to the front, you see—and he does what he pleases, and is up to all kinds of devilment, and is a perfect nuisance in the kitchen. Well, they all stand it, but they wouldn't if it was another person's bird."

Here she began to chuckle comfortably, and presently she said:

"Well, you know, she's a nuisance herself, Miss Cathy is, she *is* so busy, and into everything, like that bird. It's all just as innocent, you know, and she don't mean any harm, and is so good and dear; and it ain't her fault, it's her nature; her interest is always a-working and always red-hot, and she *can't* keep quiet. Well, yesterday it was 'Please, Miss Cathy, don't do that'; and, 'Please, Miss Cathy, let that alone'; and, 'Please, Miss Cathy, don't make so much noise'; and so on and so on, till I reckon I had found fault fourteen times in fifteen minutes; then she looked up at me with her big brown eyes that can plead so, and said in that odd little foreign way that goes to your heart,

"'Please, mammy, make me a compliment.'"

"And of course you did it, you old fool?"

"Marse Tom, I just grabbed her up to my breast and says, 'Oh, you po' dear little motherless thing, you ain't got a fault in the world, and you can do anything you want to, and tear the house down, and yo' old black mammy won't say a word!'"

"Why, of course, of course—I knew you'd spoil the child."

She brushed away her tears, and said with dignity:

"Spoil the child? spoil *that* child, Marse Tom? There can't *any-body* spoil her. She's the king bee of this post, and everybody pets her and is her slave, and yet, as you know, your own self, she ain't the least little bit spoiled." Then she eased her mind with this retort: "Marse Tom, she makes you do anything she wants to, and you can't deny it; so if she could be spoilt, she'd been spoilt long ago, because you are the very *worst*! Look at that pile of cats in your chair, and you sitting on a candle-box, just as patient; it's because they're her cats."

If Dorcas were a soldier, I could punish her for such large frankness as that. I changed the subject, and made her resume her illustrations. She had scored against me fairly, and I wasn't going to cheapen her victory by disputing it. She proceeded to offer this incident in evidence on her twin theory:

"Two weeks ago when she got her finger mashed open, she turned pretty pale with the pain, but she never said a word. I took her in my lap, and the surgeon sponged off the blood and took a needle and thread and began to sew it up; it had to have a lot of stitches, and each one made her scrunch a little, but she never let go a sound. At last the surgeon was so full of admiration that he said, 'Well, you *are* a brave little thing!' and she said, just as ca'm and simple as if she was talking about the weather, 'There isn't anybody braver but the Cid!' You see? it was the boy-twin that the surgeon was a-dealing with."

"Who is the Cid?"

"I don't know, sir—at least only what she says. She's always talking about him, and says he was the bravest hero Spain ever had, or any other country. They have it up and down, the children do, she standing up for the Cid, and they working George Washington for all he is worth."

"Do they quarrel?"

"No; it's only disputing, and bragging, the way children do. They want her to be an American, but she can't be anything but a Spaniard, she says. You see, her mother was always longing for home, po' thing! and thinking about it, and so the child is just as much a Spaniard as if she'd always lived there. She thinks she remembers how Spain looked, but I reckon she don't, because she was only a baby when they moved to France. She is very proud to be a Spaniard."

Does that please you, Mercedes? Very well, be content; your

145

niece is loyal to her allegiance: her mother laid deep the foundations of her love for Spain, and she will go back to you as good a Spaniard as you are yourself. She has made me promise to take her to you for a long visit when the War Office retires me.

I attend to her studies myself; has she told you that? Yes, I am her school-master, and she makes pretty good progress, I think, everything considered. Everything considered—being translated—means holidays. But the fact is, she was not born for study, and it comes hard. Hard for me, too; it hurts me like a physical pain to see that free spirit of the air and the sunshine laboring and grieving over a book; and sometimes when I find her gazing far away towards the plain and the blue mountains with the longing in her eyes, I have to throw open the prison doors; I can't help it. A quaint little scholar she is, and makes plenty of blunders. Once I put the question:

"What does the Czar govern?"

She rested her elbow on her knee and her chin on her hand and took that problem under deep consideration. Presently she looked up and answered, with a rising inflection implying a shade of uncertainty,

"The dative case?"

Here are a couple of her expositions which were delivered with tranquil confidence:

"*Chaplain*, diminutive of chap. *Lass* is masculine, *lassie* is feminine."

She is not a genius, you see, but just a normal child; they all make mistakes of that sort. There is a glad light in her eye which is pretty to see when she finds herself able to answer a question promptly and accurately, without any hesitation; as, for instance, this morning:

"Cathy dear, what is a cube?"

"Why, a native of Cuba."

She still drops a foreign word into her talk now and then, and there is still a subtle foreign flavor or fragrance about even her exactest English—and long may this abide! for it has for me a charm that is very pleasant. Sometimes her English is daintily prim and bookish and captivating. She has a child's

sweet tooth, but for her health's sake I try to keep its in-
spirations under check. She is obedient—as is proper for a
titled and recognized military personage, which she is—but
the chain presses sometimes. For instance, we were out for
a walk, and passed by some bushes that were freighted with
wild gooseberries. Her face brightened and she put her hands
together and delivered herself of this speech, most feelingly:

"Oh, if I was permitted a vice it would be the *gourmandise!*"

Could I resist that? No. I gave her a gooseberry.

You ask about her languages. They take care of themselves;
they will not get rusty here; our regiments are not made up
of natives alone—far from it. And she is picking up Indian
tongues diligently.

VI *Soldier Boy and the Mexican Plug*

"When did you come?"

"Arrived at sundown."

"Where from?"

"Salt Lake."

"Are you in the service?"

"No. Trade."

"Pirate trade, I reckon."

"What do you know about it?"

"I saw you when you came. I recognized your master. He is
a bad sort. Trap-robber, horse-thief, squaw-man, renegado—
Hank Butters—I know him very well. Stole you, didn't he?"

"Well, it amounted to that."

"I thought so. Where is his pard?"

"He stopped at White Cloud's camp."

"He is another of the same stripe, is Blake Haskins." (*Aside.*)
They are laying for Buffalo Bill again, I guess. (*Aloud.*) "What
is your name?"

"Which one?"

"Have you got more than one?"

"I get a new one every time I'm stolen. I used to have an honest name, but that was early; I've forgotten it. Since then I've
had thirteen *aliases.*"

"Aliases? What is alias?"

"A false name."

"Alias. It's a fine large word, and is in my line; it has quite a learned and cerebrospinal incandescent sound. Are you educated?"

"Well, no, I can't claim it. I can take down bars, I can distinguish oats from shoe-pegs, I can blaspheme a saddle-boil with the college-bred, and I know a few other things — not many; I have had no chance, I have always had to work; besides, I am of low birth and no family. You speak my dialect like a native, but you are not a Mexican Plug, you are a gentleman, I can see that; and educated, of course."

"Yes, I am of old family, and not illiterate. I am a fossil."

"A which?"

"Fossil. The first horses were fossils. They date back two million years."

"Gr-eat sand and sage-brush! do you mean it?"

"Yes, it is true. The bones of my ancestors are held in reverence and worship, even by men. They do not leave them exposed to the weather when they find them, but carry them three thousand miles and enshrine them in their temples of learning, and worship them."

"It is wonderful! I knew you must be a person of distinction, by your fine presence and courtly address, and by the fact that you are not subjected to the indignity of hobbles, like myself and the rest. Would you tell me your name?"

"You have probably heard of it — Soldier Boy."

"What! — the renowned, the illustrious?"

"Even so."

"It takes my breath! Little did I dream that ever I should stand face to face with the possessor of that great name. Buffalo Bill's horse! Known from the Canadian border to the deserts of Arizona, and from the eastern marches of the Great Plains to the foot-hills of the Sierra! Truly this is a memorable day. You still serve the celebrated Chief of Scouts?"

"I am still his property, but he has lent me, for a time, to the most noble, the most gracious, the most excellent, her Excellency Catherine, Corporal-General Seventh Cavalry and Flag-Lieutenant Ninth Dragoons, U.S.A., — on whom be peace!"

"Amen. Did you say *her* Excellency?"

"The same. A Spanish lady, sweet blossom of a ducal house. And truly a wonder; knowing everything, capable of everything; speaking all the languages, master of all sciences, a mind without horizons, a heart of gold, the glory of her race! On whom be peace!"

"Amen. It is marvellous!"

"Verily. I knew many things, she has taught me others. I am educated. I will tell you about her."

"I listen—I am enchanted."

"I will tell a plain tale, calmly, without excitement, without eloquence. When she had been here four or five weeks she was already erudite in military things, and they made her an officer—a double officer. She rode the drill every day, like any soldier; and she could take the bugle and direct the evolutions herself. Then, on a day, there was a grand race, for prizes— none to enter but the children. Seventeen children entered, and she was the youngest. Three girls, fourteen boys—good riders all. It was a steeplechase, with four hurdles, all pretty high. The first prize was a most cunning half-grown silver bugle, and mighty pretty, with red silk cord and tassels. Buffalo Bill was very anxious; for he had taught her to ride, and he did most dearly want her to win that race, for the glory of it. So he wanted her to ride me, but she wouldn't; and she reproached him, and said it was unfair and unright, and taking advantage; for what horse in this post or any other could stand a chance against me? and she was very severe with him, and said, 'You ought to be ashamed—you are proposing to me conduct unbecoming an officer and a gentleman.' So he just tossed her up in the air about thirty feet and caught her as she came down, and said he was ashamed; and put up his handkerchief and pretended to cry, which nearly broke her heart, and she petted him, and begged him to forgive her, and said she would do anything in the world he could ask but that; but he said he ought to go hang himself, and he *must*, if he could get a rope; it was nothing but right he should, for he never, never could forgive himself; and then *she* began to cry, and they both sobbed, the way you could hear him a mile, and she clinging around

149

his neck and pleading, till at last he was comforted a little, and gave his solemn promise he wouldn't hang himself till after the race; and wouldn't do it at all if she won it, which made her happy, and she said she would win it or die in the saddle; so then everything was pleasant again and both of them content. He can't help playing jokes on her, he is so fond of her and she is so innocent and unsuspecting; and when she finds it out she cuffs him and is in a fury, but presently forgives him because it's *him*; and maybe the very next day she's caught with another joke; you see she can't learn any better, because she hasn't any deceit in her, and that kind aren't ever expecting it in another person.

"It was a grand race. The whole post was there, and there was such another whooping and shouting when the seventeen kids came flying down the turf and sailing over the hurdles — oh, beautiful to see! Half-way down, it was kind of neck and neck, and anybody's race and nobody's. Then, what should happen but a cow steps out and puts her head down to munch grass, with her broadside to the battalion, and they a-coming like the wind; they split apart to flank her, but *she?* — why, she drove the spurs home and soared over that cow like a bird! and on she went, and cleared the last hurdle solitary and alone, the army letting loose the grand yell, and she skipped from the horse the same as if he had been standing still, and made her bow, and everybody crowded around to congratulate, and they gave her the bugle, and she put it to her lips and blew 'boots and saddles' to see how it would go, and BB was as proud as you can't think! And he said, 'Take Soldier Boy, and don't pass him back till I ask for him!' and I can tell you he wouldn't have said that to any other person on this planet. That was two months and more ago, and nobody has been on my back since but the Corporal-General Seventh Cavalry and Flag-Lieutenant of the Ninth Dragoons, U.S.A., — on whom be peace!"

"Amen. I listen — tell me more."

"She set to work and organized the Sixteen, and called it the First Battalion Rocky Mountain Rangers, U.S.A., and she wanted to be bugler, but they elected her Lieutenant-General *and* Bugler. So she ranks her uncle the commandant, who is only a Brigadier. And doesn't she train those little people! Ask the Indians, ask the traders, ask the soldiers; they'll tell you. She has been at it from the first day. Every morning they go clattering down into the plain, and there she sits on my back with her bugle at her mouth and sounds the orders and puts them through the evolutions for an hour or more; and it is too beautiful for anything to see those ponies dissolve from one formation into another, and waltz about, and break, and scatter, and form again, always moving, always graceful, now trotting, now galloping, and so on, sometimes near by, sometimes in the distance, all just like a state ball, you know, and sometimes she can't hold herself any longer, but sounds the 'charge,' and turns me loose! and you can take my word for it, if the battalion hasn't too much of a start we catch up and go over the breastworks with the front line.

"Yes, they are soldiers, those little people; and healthy, too, not ailing any more, the way they used to be sometimes. It's because of her drill. She's got a fort, now—Fort Fanny Marsh. Major-General Tommy Drake planned it out, and the Seventh and Dragoons built it. Tommy is the Colonel's son, and is fifteen and the oldest in the Battalion; Fanny Marsh is Brigadier-General, and is next oldest—over thirteen. She is daughter of Captain Marsh, Company B, Seventh Cavalry. Lieutenant-General Alison is the youngest by considerable; I think she is about nine and a half or three-quarters. Her military rig, as Lieutenant-General, isn't for business, it's for dress parade, because the ladies made it. They say they got it out of the Middle Ages—out of a book—and it is all red and blue and white silks and satins and velvets; tights, trunks, sword, doublet with slashed sleeves, short cape, cap with just one feather in it; I've heard them name these things; they got them out of the book; she's dressed like a page, of old times, they say. It's the daintiest outfit that ever was—you will say so, when you see it. She's lovely in it—oh, just a dream! In some ways she is just her age, but in others she's as old as her uncle, I think. She is very learned. She teaches her uncle his book. I have seen her sitting by with the book and reciting to him what is in it, so that he can learn to do it himself.

"Every Saturday she hires little Injuns to garrison her fort; then she lays siege to it, and makes military approaches by make-believe trenches in make-believe night, and finally at make-believe dawn she draws her sword and sounds the assault and takes it by storm. It is for practice. And she has invented a bugle-call all by herself, out of her own head, and it's a stirring one, and the prettiest in the service. It's to call *me*— it's never used for anything else. She taught it to me, and told me what it says: '*It is I, Soldier—come!*' and when those thrilling notes come floating down the distance I hear them without fail, even if I am two miles away; and then—oh, then you should see my heels get down to business!

"And she has taught me how to say good-morning and good-night to her, which is by lifting my right hoof for her to shake; and also how to say good-bye; I do that with my left foot— but only for practice, because there hasn't been any but make-believe good-byeing yet, and I hope there won't ever be. It would make me cry if I ever had to put up my left foot in earnest. She has taught me how to salute, and I can do it as well as a soldier. I bow my head low, and lay my right hoof against my cheek. She taught me that because I got into disgrace once, through ignorance. I am privileged, because I am known to be honorable and trustworthy, and because I have a distinguished record in the service; so they don't hobble me nor tie me to stakes or shut me tight in stables, but let me wander around to suit myself. Well, trooping the colors is a very solemn ceremony, and everybody must stand uncovered when the flag goes by, the commandant and all; and once I was there, and ignorantly walked across right in front of the band, which was an awful disgrace. Ah, the Lieutenant-General was so ashamed, and so distressed that I should have done such a thing before all the world, that she couldn't keep the tears back; and then she taught me the salute, so that if I ever did any other unmilitary act through ignorance I could do my salute and she believed everybody would think it was apology enough and would not press the matter. It is very nice and distinguished; no other horse can do it; often the men salute me, and I return it. I am privileged to be present when the Rocky Mountain Rangers troop the colors and I stand solemn, like the children, and I salute when the flag goes by. Of course when she goes to her fort her sentries sing out 'Turn out the guard!' and then . . . do you catch that refreshing early-morning whiff from the mountain-pines and the wild flowers? The night is far spent; we'll hear the bugles before long. Dorcas, the black woman, is very good and nice; she takes care of the Lieutenant-General, and is Brigadier-General Alison's mother, which makes her mother-in-law to the Lieutenant-General. That is what Shekels says. At least it is what I think he says, though I never can understand him quite clearly. He—"

"Who is Shekels?"

"The Seventh Cavalry dog. I mean, if he is a dog. His father was a coyote and his mother was a wildcat. It doesn't really make a dog out of him, does it?"

"Not a real dog, I should think. Only a kind of a general dog, at most, I reckon. Though this is a matter of ichthyology, I suppose; and if it is, it is out of my depth, and so my opinion is not valuable, and I don't claim much consideration for it."

"It isn't ichthyology; it is dogmatics, which is still more difficult and tangled up. Dogmatics always are."

"Dogmatics is quite beyond me, quite; so I am not competing. But on general principles it is my opinion that a colt out of a coyote and a wild-cat is no square dog, but doubtful. That is my hand, and I stand pat."

"Well, it is as far as I can go myself, and be fair and conscientious. I have always regarded him as a doubtful dog, and so has Potter. Potter is the great Dane. Potter says he is no dog, and not even poultry—though I do not go quite so far as that."

"And I wouldn't, myself. Poultry is one of those things which no person can get to the bottom of, there is so much of it and such variety. It is just wings, and wings, and wings, till you are weary: turkeys, and geese, and bats, and butterflies, and angels, and grasshoppers, and flying-fish, and—well, there is really no end to the tribe; it gives me the heaves just to think of it. But this one hasn't any wings, has he?"

"No."

"Well, then, in my belief he is more likely to be dog than poultry. I have not heard of poulty that hadn't wings. Wings is the *sign* of poultry; it is what you tell poultry by. Look at the mosquito."

"What do you reckon he is, then? He must be something."

"Why, he could be a reptile; anything that hasn't wings is a reptile."

"Who told you that?"

"Nobody told me, but I overheard it."

"Where did you overhear it?"

"Years ago. I was with the Philadelphia Institute expedition in the Bad Lands under Professor Cope, hunting mastodon bones, and I overheard him say, his own self, that any plantigrade circumflex vertebrate bacterium that hadn't wings and was uncertain was a reptile. Well, then, has this dog any wings? No. Is he a plantigrade circumflex vertebrate bacterium? Maybe so, maybe not; but without ever having seen him, and judging only by his illegal and spectacular parentage, I will bet the odds of a bale of hay to a bran mash that he looks it. Finally, is he uncertain? That is the point—is he uncertain? I will leave it to you if you have ever heard of a more uncertainer dog than what this one is?"

"No, I never have."

"Well, then, he's a reptile. That's settled."

"Why, look here, whatsyourname—"

"Last alias, Mongrel."

"A good one, too. I was going to say, you are better educated than you have been pretending to be. I like cultured society, and I shall cultivate your acquaintance. Now as to Shekels, whenever you want to know about any private thing that is going on at this post or in White Cloud's camp or Thunder-Bird's, he can tell you; and if you make friends with him he'll be glad to, for he is a born gossip, and picks up all the tittle-tattle. Being the whole Seventh Cavalry's reptile, he doesn't belong to anybody in particular, and hasn't any military duties; so he comes and goes as he pleases, and is popular with all the house cats and other authentic sources of private information. He understands all the languages, and talks them all, too. With an accent like gritting your teeth, it is true, and with a grammar that is no improvement on blasphemy—still, with practice you get at the meat of what he says, and it serves. . . . Hark! That's the reveille. . . .

THE REVEILLE*

"Faint and far, but isn't it clear, isn't it sweet? There's no music like the bugle to stir the blood, in the still solemnity of the morning twilight, with the dim plain stretching away to nothing and the spectral mountains slumbering against the sky. You'll hear another note in a minute—faint and far and clear, like the other one, and sweeter still, you'll notice. Wait . . . listen. There it goes! It says, 'It is I, Soldier—come!' . . . Now then, watch me leave a blue streak behind!"

SOLDIER BOY'S BUGLE CALL

*At West Point the bugle is supposed to be saying:
"I can't get 'em up, / I can't get 'em up, / I can't get 'em up in the morning!"

"Did you do as I told you? Did you look up the Mexican Plug?"

"Yes, I made his acquaintance before night and got his friend-ship."

"I liked him. Did you?"

"Not at first. He took me for a reptile, and it troubled me, because I didn't know whether it was a compliment or not. I couldn't ask him, because it would look ignorant. So I didn't say anything, and soon I liked him very well indeed. Was it a compliment, do you think?"

"Yes, that is what it was. They are very rare, the reptiles; very few left, now-a-days."

"Is that so? What is a reptile?"

"It is a plantigrade circumflex vertebrate bacterium that hasn't any wings and is uncertain."

"Well, it—it sounds fine, it surely does."

"And it *is* fine. You may be thankful you are one."

"I am. It seems wonderfully grand and elegant for a person that is so humble as I am; but I am thankful, I am indeed, and will try to live up to it. It is hard to remember. Will you say it again, please, and say it slow?"

"Plantigrade circumflex vertebrate bacterium that hasn't any wings and is uncertain."

"It *is* beautiful, anybody must grant it; beautiful, and of a noble sound. I hope it will not make me proud and stuck-up— I should not like to be that. It is much more distinguished and honorable to be a reptile than a dog, don't you think, Soldier?"

"Why, there's no comparison. It is awfully aristocratic. Often a duke is called a reptile; it is set down so, in history."

"Isn't that grand! Potter wouldn't ever associate with me, but I reckon he'll be glad to when he finds out what I am."

"You can depend upon it."

"I will thank Mongrel for this. He is a very good sort, for a Mexican Plug. Don't you think he is?"

"It is my opinion of him; and as for his birth, he cannot help that. We cannot all be reptiles, we cannot all be fossils; we have to take what comes and be thankful it is no worse. It is the true philosophy."

"For those others?"

"Stick to the subject, please. Did it turn out that my suspicions were right?"

"Yes, perfectly right. Mongrel has heard them planning. They are after BB's life, for running them out of Medicine Bow and taking their stolen horses away from them."

"Well, they'll get him yet, for sure."

"Not if he keeps a sharp lookout."

"He keep a sharp lookout! He never does; he despises them, and all their kind. His life is always being threatened, and so it has come to be monotonous."

"Does he know they are here?"

"Oh yes, he knows it. He is always the earliest to know who comes and who goes. But he cares nothing for them and their threats; he only laughs when people warn him. They'll shoot him from behind a tree the first he knows. Did Mongrel tell you their plans?"

"Yes. They have found out that he starts for Fort Clayton day after to-morrow, with one of his scouts; so they will leave to-morrow, letting on to go south, but they will fetch around north all in good time."

"Shekels, I don't like the look of it."

VIII *The Scout-Start. BB and Lieutenant-General Alison*

BB (*saluting*). "Good! handsomely done! The Seventh couldn't beat it! You do certainly handle your Rangers like an expert, General. And where are you bound?"

"Four miles on the trail to Fort Clayton."

"Glad am I, dear! What's the idea of it?"

"Guard of honor for you and Thorndike."

"Bless—your—heart! I'd rather have it from you than from the Commander-in-Chief of the armies of the United States, you incomparable little soldier!—and I don't need to take any oath to that, for you to believe it."

"I *thought* you'd like it, BB."

"*Like* it? Well, I should say so! Now then—all ready—sound the advance, and away we go!"

"Well, this is the way it happened. We did the escort duty; then we came back and struck for the plain and put the Rangers through a rousing drill—oh, for hours! Then we sent them home under Brigadier-General Fanny Marsh; then the Lieunant-General and I went off on a gallop over the plains for about three hours, and were lazying along home in the middle of the afternoon, when we met Jimmy Slade, the drummer-boy, and he saluted and asked the Lieutenant-General if she had heard the news, and she said no, and he said:

"'Buffalo Bill has been ambushed and badly shot this side of Clayton, and Thorndike the scout, too; Bill couldn't travel, but Thorndike could, and he brought the news, and Sergeant Wilkes and six men of Company B are gone, two hours ago, hotfoot, to get Bill. And they say—'

"'*Go!*' she shouts to me—and I went."

"Fast?"

"Don't ask foolish questions. It was an awful pace. For four hours nothing happened, and not a word said, except that now and then she said, 'Keep it up, Boy, keep it up, sweetheart; we'll save him!' I kept it up. Well, when the dark shut down, in the rugged hills, that poor little chap had been tearing around in the saddle all day, and I noticed by the slack knee-pressure that she was tired and tottery, and I got dreadfully afraid; but every time I tried to slow down and let her go to sleep, so I could stop, she hurried me up again; and so, sure enough, at last over she went!

"Ah, that was a fix to be in! for she lay there and didn't stir, and what was I to do? I couldn't leave her to fetch help, on account of the wolves. There was nothing to do but stand by. It was dreadful. I was afraid she was killed, poor little thing! But she wasn't. She came to, by-and-by, and said, 'Kiss me, Soldier,' and those were blessed words. I kissed her—often; I am used to that, and we like it. But she didn't get up, and I was worried. She fondled my nose with her hand, and talked to me, and called me endearing names—which is her way—but she caressed with the same hand all the time. The other arm was broken, you see, but I didn't know it, and she didn't mention it. She didn't want to distress me, you know.

"Soon the big gray wolves came, and hung around, and you could hear them snarl, and snap at each other, but you couldn't see anything of them except their eyes, which shone in the dark like sparks and stars. The Lieutenant-General said, 'If I had the Rocky Mountain Rangers here, we would make those creatures climb a tree.' Then she made believe that the Rangers were in hearing, and put up her bugle and blew the 'assembly'; and then, 'boots and saddles'; then the 'trot'; 'gallop'; '*charge!*' Then she blew the 'retreat,' and said, 'That's for you, you rebels; the Rangers don't ever retreat!'

"The music frightened them away, but they were hungry, and kept coming back. And of course they got bolder and bolder, which is their way. It went on for an hour, then the tired child went to sleep, and it was pitiful to hear her moan and nestle, and I couldn't do anything for her. All the time I was laying for the wolves. They are in my line; I have had experience. At last the boldest one ventured within my lines, and I landed him among his friends with some of his skull still on him, and they did the rest. In the next hour I got a couple more, and they went the way of the first one, down the throats of the detachment. That satisfied the survivors, and they went away and left us in peace.

"We hadn't any more adventures, though I kept awake all night and was ready. From midnight on the child got very restless, and out of her head, and moaned, and said, 'Water, water—thirsty'; and now and then, 'Kiss me, Soldier'; and sometimes she was in her fort and giving orders to her garrison; and once she was in Spain, and thought her mother was with her. People say a horse can't cry; but they don't know, because we cry inside.

"It was an hour after sunup that I heard the boys coming, and recognized the hoof-beats of Pomp and Cæsar and Jerry, old mates of mine; and a welcomer sound there couldn't ever be.

"Buffalo Bill was in a horse-litter, with his leg broken by a bullet, and Mongrel and Blake Haskins's horse were doing the work. Buffalo Bill and Thorndike had killed both of those toughs.

"When they got to us, and Buffalo Bill saw the child lying

there so white, he said, 'My God!' and the sound of his voice brought her to herself, and she gave a little cry of pleasure and struggled to get up, but couldn't, and the soldiers gathered her up like the tenderest women, and their eyes were wet and they were not ashamed, when they saw her arm dangling; and so weɪᴄ Buffalo Bill's, and when they laid her in his arms he said, 'My darling, how does this come?' and she said, 'We came to save you, but I was tired, and couldn't keep awake, and fell off and hurt myself, and couldn't get on again.' 'You came to save me, you dear little rat? It was too lovely of you!' 'Yes, and Soldier stood by me, which you know he would, and protected me from the wolves; and if he got a chance he kicked the life out of some of them—for you know he would, BB.' The sergeant said, 'He laid out three of them, sir, and here's the bones to show for it.' 'He's a grand horse,' said BB; 'he's the grandest horse that ever was! and has saved your life, Lieutenant-General Alison, and shall protect it the rest of his life—he's yours for a kiss!' He got it, along with a passion of delight, and he said, 'You are feeling better now, little Spaniard—do you think you could blow the advance?' She put up the bugle to do it, but he said wait a minute first. Then he and the sergeant set her arm and put it in splints, she wincing but not whimpering; then we took up the march for home, and that's the end of the tale; and I'm her horse. Isn't she a brick, Shekels?

"Brick? She's more than a brick, more than a thousand bricks —she's a reptile!"

"It's a compliment out of your heart, Shekels. God bless you for it!"

x *General Alison and Dorcas*

"Too much company for her, Marse Tom. Betwixt you, and Shekels, and the Colonel's wife, and the Cid—"

"The Cid? Oh, I remember—the raven."

"—and Mrs. Captain Marsh and Famine and Pestilence the baby *coyotes*, and Sour-Mash and her pups, and Sardanapalus and her kittens—hang these names she gives the creatures, they warp my jaw—and Potter: you—all sitting around in the house, and Soldier Boy at the window the entire time, it's a wonder to me she comes along as well as she does. She—"

"You want her all to yourself, you stingy old thing!"

"Marse Tom, you know better. It's too much company. And then the idea of her receiving reports all the time from her officers, and acting upon them, and giving orders, the same as if she was well! It ain't good for her, and the surgeon don't like it, and tried to persuade her not to and couldn't; and when he *ordered* her, she was that outraged and indignant, and was very severe on him, and accused him of insubordination, and said it didn't become him to give orders to an officer of her rank. Well, he saw he had excited her more and done more harm than all the rest put together, so he was vexed at himself and wished he had kept still. Doctors *don't* know much, and that's a fact. She's too much interested in things—she ought to rest more. She's all the time sending messages to BB, and to soldiers and Injuns and whatnot, and to the animals."

"To the animals?"

"Yes, sir."

"Who carries them?"

"Sometimes Potter, but mostly it's Shekels."

"Now come! who can find fault with such pretty make-believe as that?"

"But it ain't make-believe, Marse Tom. She does send them."

"Yes, I don't doubt that part of it."

"Do you doubt they get them, sir?"

"Certainly. Don't you?"

"No, sir. Animals talk to one another. I know it perfectly well, Marse Tom, and I ain't saying it by guess."

"What a curious superstition!"

"It ain't a superstition, Marse Tom. Look at that Shekels— look at him, *now*. Is he listening, or ain't he? *Now* you see! he's turned his head away. It's because he was caught—caught in the act. I'll ask you—could a Christian look any more ashamed than what he looks now?—*lay down!* You see? he was going to sneak out. Don't tell *me*, Marse Tom! If animals don't talk, I miss *my* guess. And Shekels is the worst. He goes and tells the animals everything that happens in the officers' quarters; and if he's short of facts, he invents them. He hasn't any more principle than a blue jay; and as for morals, he's empty. Look at him now; look at him grovel. He knows what I am saying, and he knows it's the truth. You see, yourself, that he can feel shame; it's the only virtue he's got. It's wonderful how they find out everything that's going on—the animals. They—"

"Do you really believe they do, Dorcas?"

"I don't only just believe it, Marse Tom, I know it. Day before yesterday they knew something was going to happen. They were that excited, and whispering around together; why, anybody could see that they— But my! I must get back to her, and I haven't got to my errand yet."

"What is it, Dorcas?"

"Well, it's two or three things. One is, the doctor don't salute when he comes . . . Now, Marse Tom, it ain't anything to laugh at, and so—"

"Well, then, forgive me; I didn't mean to laugh—I got caught unprepared."

"You see, she don't want to hurt the doctor's feelings, so she don't say anything to him about it; but she is always polite, herself, and it hurts that kind for people to be rude to them."

"I'll have that doctor hanged."

"Marse Tom, she don't *want* him hanged. She—"

"Well, then, I'll have him boiled in oil."

"But she don't *want* him boiled. I—"

"Oh, very well, very well, I only want to please her; I'll have him skinned."

"Why, *she* don't want him skinned; it would break her heart. Now—"

"Woman, this is perfectly unreasonable. What in the nation *does* she want?"

"Marse Tom, if you would only be a little patient, and not fly off the handle at the least little thing. Why, she only wants you to speak to him."

"Speak to him! Well, upon my word! All this unseemly rage and row about such a—a— Dorcas, I never saw you carry on like this before. You have alarmed the sentry; he thinks I am being assassinated; he thinks there's a mutiny, a revolt, an insurrection; he—"

"Marse Tom, you are just putting on; you know it perfectly

well; I don't know what makes you act like that—but you always did, even when you was little, and you can't get over it, I reckon. Are you over it now, Marse Tom?"

"Oh, well, yes; but it would try anybody to be doing the best he could, offering every kindness he could think of, only to have it rejected with contumely and . . . Oh, well, let it go; it's no matter—I'll talk to the doctor. Is that satisfactory, or are you going to break out again?"

"Yes, sir, it is; and it's only right to talk to him, too, because it's just as she says; she's trying to keep up discipline in the Rangers, and this insubordination of his is a bad example for them—now ain't it so, Marse Tom?"

"Well, there *is* reason in it, I can't deny it; so I will speak to him, though at bottom I think hanging would be more lasting. What is the rest of your errand, Dorcas?"

"Of course her room is Ranger headquarters now, Marse Tom, while she's sick. Well, soldiers of the cavalry and the dragoons that are off duty come and get her sentries to let them relieve them and serve in their place. It's only out of affection, sir, and because they know military honors please her, and please the children too, for her sake; and they don't bring their muskets; and so—"

"I've noticed them there, but didn't twig the idea. They are standing guard, are they?"

"Yes, sir, and she is afraid you will reprove them and hurt their feelings, if you see them there; so she begs, if—if you don't mind coming in the back way—"

"Bear me up, Dorcas; don't let me faint."

"There—sit up and behave, Marse Tom. You are not going to faint; you are only pretending—you used to act just so when you was little; it does seem a long time for you to get grown up."

"Dorcas, the way the child is progressing, I shall be out of my job before long—she'll have the whole post in her hands. I must make a stand, I must not go down without a struggle. These encroachments. . . . Dorcas, what do you think she will think of next?"

"Marse Tom, she don't mean any harm."

"Are you sure of it?"

"Yes, Marse Tom."

"You feel sure she has no ulterior designs?"

"I don't know what that is, Marse Tom, but I know she hasn't."

"Very well, then, for the present I am satisfied. What else have you come about?"

"I reckon I better tell you the whole thing first, Marse Tom, then tell you what she wants. There's been an emeute, as she calls it. It was before she got back with BB. The officer of the day reported it to her this morning. It happened at her fort. There was a fuss betwixt Major-General Tommy Drake and Lieutenant-Colonel Agnes Frisbie, and he snatched her doll away, which is made of white kid stuffed with sawdust, and tore every rag of its clothes off, right before them all, and is under arrest, and the charge is conduct un—"

"Yes, I know—conduct unbecoming an officer and a gentleman—a plain case, too, it seems to me. This is a serious matter. Well, what is her pleasure?"

"Well, Marse Tom, she has summoned a court-martial, but the doctor don't think she is well enough to preside over it, and she says there ain't anybody competent but her, because there's a major-general concerned; and so she—she—well, she says, would you preside over it for her? . . . Marse Tom, *sit* up! You ain't any more going to faint than Shekels is."

"Look here, Dorcas, go along back, and be tactful. Be persuasive; don't fret her; tell her it's all right, the matter is in my hands, but it isn't good form to hurry so grave a matter as this. Explain to her that we have to go by precedents, and that I believe this one to be new. In fact, you can say I know that nothing just like it has happened in our army, therefore I must be guided by European precedents, and must go cautiously and examine them carefully. Tell her not to be impatient, it will take me several days, but it will all come out right, and I will come over and report progress as I go along. Do you get the idea, Dorcas?"

"I don't know as I do, sir."

"Well, it's this. You see, it won't ever do for me, a brigadier in the regular army, to preside over that infant court-martial— there isn't any precedent for it, don't you see. Very well. I will go on examining authorities and reporting progress until she is well enough to get me out of this scrape by presiding herself. Do you get it now?"

"Oh, yes, sir, I get it, and it's good, I'll go and fix it with her. *Lay down!* and stay where you are."

"Why, what harm is he doing?"

"Oh, it ain't any harm, but it just vexes me to see him act so."

"What was he doing?"

"Can't you see, and him in such a sweat? He was starting out to spread it all over the post. *Now* I reckon you won't deny, any more, that they go and tell everything they hear, now that you've seen it with yo' own eyes."

"Well, I don't like to acknowledge it, Dorcas, but I don't see how I can consistently stick to my doubts in the face of such overwhelming proof as this dog is furnishing."

"There, now, you've got in yo' right mind at last! I wonder you can be so stubborn, Marse Tom. But you always was, even when you was little. I'm going now."

"Look here; tell her that in view of the delay, it is my judgment that she ought to enlarge the accused on his parole."

"Yes, sir, I'll tell her. Marse Tom?"

"Well?"

"She can't get to Soldier Boy, and he stands there all the time, down in the mouth and lonesome; and she says will you shake hands with him and comfort him? Everybody does."

"It's a curious kind of lonesomeness; but, all right, I will."

XI *Several Months Later, Antonio and Thorndike*

"Thorndike, isn't that Plug you're riding an asset of the scrap you and Buffalo Bill had with the late Blake Haskins and his pal a few months back?"

"Yes, this is Mongrel—and not a half-bad horse, either."

"I've noticed he keeps up his lick first-rate. Say—isn't it a gaudy morning?"

"Right you are!"

"Thorndike, it's Andalusian! and when that's said, all's said."

"Andalusian *and* Oregonian, Antonio! Put it that way, and you have my vote. Being a native up there, I know. You being Andalusian-born—"

"Can speak with authority for that patch of paradise? Well, I can. Like the Don! like Sancho! This is the correct Andalusian dawn now—crisp, fresh, dewy, fragrant, pungent—"

"'What though the spicy breezes
Blow soft o'er Ceylon's isle—'

—*git* up, you old cow! stumbling like that when we've just been praising you! out on a scout and can't live up to the honor any better than that? Antonio, how long have you been out here in the Plains and the Rockies?"

"More than thirteen years."

"It's a long time. Don't you ever get homesick?"

"Not till now."

"Why *now?*—after such a long cure."

"These preparations of the retiring commandant's have started it up."

"Of course. It's natural."

"It keeps me thinking about Spain. I know the region where the Seventh's child's aunt lives; I know all the lovely country for miles around; I'll bet I've seen her aunt's villa many a time; I'll bet I've been in it in those pleasant old times when I was a Spanish gentleman."

"They say the child is wild to see Spain."

"It's so; I know it from what I hear."

"Haven't you talked with her about it?"

"No. I've avoided it. I should soon be as wild as she is. That would not be comfortable."

"I wish I was going, Antonio. There's two things I'd give a lot to see. One's a railroad."

"She'll see one when she strikes Missouri."

"The other's a bull-fight."

"I've seen lots of them; I wish I could see another."

"I don't know anything about it, except in a mixed-up, foggy way, Antonio, but I know enough to know it's grand sport."

"The grandest in the world! There's no other sport that begins with it. I'll tell you what I've seen, then you can judge. It was my first, and it's as vivid to me now as it was when I saw it. It was a Sunday afternoon, and beautiful weather, and my uncle, the priest, took me as a reward for being a good boy and because of my own accord and without anybody asking me I had bankrupted my savings-box and given the money to a mission that was civilizing the Chinese and sweetening their lives and softening their hearts with the gentle teachings of our religion, and I wish you could have seen what we saw that day, Thorndike.

"The amphitheatre was packed, from the bull-ring to the highest row—twelve thousand people in one circling mass, one slanting, solid mass—royalties, nobles, clergy, ladies, gentlemen, state officials, generals, admirals, soldiers, sailors, lawyers, thieves, merchants, brokers, cooks, housemaids, scullery-maids, doubtful women, dudes, gamblers, beggars, loafers, tramps, American ladies, gentlemen, preachers, English ladies, gentlemen, preachers, German ditto, French ditto, and so on and so on, all the world represented: Spaniards to admire and praise, foreigners to enjoy and go home and find fault—there they were, one solid, sloping, circling sweep of rippling and flashing color under the downpour of the summer sun—just a garden, a gaudy, gorgeous flower-garden! Children munching oranges, six thousand fans fluttering and glimmering, everybody happy, everybody chatting gayly with their intimates, lovely girl-faces smiling recognition and salutation to other lovely girl-faces, gray old ladies and gentlemen dealing in the like exchanges with each other—ah, such a picture of cheery contentment and glad anticipation! not a mean spirit, nor a sordid soul, nor a sad heart there—ah, Thorndike, I wish I could see it again.

"Suddenly, the martial note of a bugle cleaves the hum and murmur—clear the ring!

"They clear it. The great gate is flung open, and the procession marches in, splendidly costumed and glittering: the marshals of the day, then the picadores on horseback, then the matadores on foot, each surrounded by his quadrille of *chulos*. They march to the box of the city fathers, and formally salute. The key is thrown, the bull-gate is unlocked. Another bugle blast—the gate flies open, the bull plunges in, furious, trembling, blinking in the blinding light, and stands there, a magnificent creature, centre of those multitudinous and admiring eyes, brave, ready for battle, his attitude a challenge. He sees his enemy: horsemen sitting motionless, with long spears in rest, upon blindfolded broken-down nags, lean and starved, fit only for sport and sacrifice, then the carrion-heap.

"The bull makes a rush, with murder in his eye, but a picador meets him with a spear-thrust in the shoulder. He flinches with the pain, and the picador skips out of danger. A burst of applause for the picador, hisses for the bull. Some shout 'Cow!' at the bull, and call him offensive names. But he is not listening to them, he is there for business; he is not minding the cloak-bearers that come fluttering around to confuse him; he chases this way, he chases that way, and hither and yon, scattering the nimble banderillos in every direction like a spray, and receiving their maddening darts in his neck as they dodge and fly—oh, but it's a lively spectacle, and brings down the house! Ah, you should hear the thundering roar that goes up when the game is at its wildest and brilliant things are done!

"Oh, that first bull, that day, was great! From the moment the spirit of war rose to flood-tide in him and he got down to his work, he began to do wonders. He tore his way through his persecutors, flinging one of them clear over the parapet; he bowled a horse and his rider down, and plunged straight for the next, got home with his horns, wounding both horse and man; on again, here and there and this way and that; and one after another he tore the bowels out of two horses so that they gushed to the ground, and ripped a third one so badly that although they rushed him to cover and shoved his bowels back and stuffed the rents with tow and rode him against the bull again, he couldn't make the trip; he tried to gallop, under the spur, but soon reeled and tottered and fell, all in a heap. For a while, that bull-ring was the most thrilling and glorious and inspiring sight that ever was seen. The bull absolutely cleared it, and stood there alone! monarch of the place. The people went mad for pride in him, and joy and delight, and you couldn't hear yourself think, for the roar and boom and crash of applause."

"Antonio, it carries me clear out of myself just to hear you tell it; it must have been perfectly splendid. If I live, I'll see a bull-fight yet before I die. Did they kill him?"

"Oh yes; that is what the bull is for. They tired him out, and got him at last. He kept rushing the matador, who always slipped smartly and gracefully aside in time, waiting for a sure chance; and at last it came; the bull made a deadly plunge for him—was avoided neatly, and as he sped by, the long sword glided silently into him, between left shoulder and spine—in and in, to the hilt. He crumpled down, dying."

"Ah, Antonio, it *is* the noblest sport that ever was. I would give a year of my life to see it. Is the bull always killed?"

"Yes. Sometimes a bull is timid, finding himself in so strange a place, and he stands trembling, or tries to retreat. Then everybody despises him for his cowardice and wants him punished and made ridiculous; so they hough him from behind, and it is the funniest thing in the world to see him hobbling around on his severed legs; the whole vast house goes into hurricanes of laughter over it; I have laughed till the tears ran down my cheeks to see it. When he has furnished all the sport he can, he is not any longer useful, and is killed."

"Well, it is perfectly grand, Antonio, perfectly beautiful. Burning a nigger don't begin."

XII Mongrel and the Other Horse

"Sage-Brush, you have been listening?"

"Yes."

"Isn't it strange?"

"Well, no, Mongrel, I don't know that it is."

"Why don't you?"

"I've seen a good many human beings in my time. They are created as they are; they cannot help it. They are only brutal because that is their make; brutes would be brutal if it was *their* make."

"To me, Sage-Brush, man is most strange and unaccountable. Why should he treat dumb animals that way when they are not doing any harm?"

"Man is not always like that, Mongrel; he is kind enough when he is not excited by religion."

"Is the bull-fight a religious service?"

"I think so. I have heard so. It is held on Sunday."

(*A reflective pause, lasting some moments.*) Then:

"When we die, Sage-Brush, do we go to heaven and dwell with man?"

"My father thought not. He believed we do not have to go there unless we deserve it."

Part 11: In Spain

XIII *General Alison to His Mother*

It was a prodigious trip, but delightful, of course, through the Rockies and the Black Hills and the mighty sweep of the Great Plains to civilization and the Missouri border—where the railroading began and the delightfulness ended. But no one is the worse for the journey; certainly not Cathy, nor Dorcas, nor Soldier Boy; and as for me, I am not complaining.

Spain is all that Cathy had pictured it—and more, she says. She is in a fury of delight, the maddest little animal that ever was, and all for joy. She thinks she remembers Spain, but that is not very likely, I suppose. The two—Mercedes and Cathy—devour each other. It is a rapture of love, and beautiful to see. It is Spanish; that describes it. Will this be a short visit?

No. It will be permanent. Cathy has elected to abide with Spain and her aunt. Dorcas says she (Dorcas) foresaw that this would happen; and also says that she wanted it to happen, and says the child's own country is the right place for her, and that she ought not to have been sent to me, I ought to have gone to her. I thought it insane to take Soldier Boy to Spain, but it was well that I yielded to Cathy's pleadings; if he had been left behind, half of her heart would have remained with him, and she would not have been contented. As it is, everything has fallen out for the best, and we are all satisfied and comfortable. It may be that Dorcas and I will see America again some day; but also it is a case of maybe not.

We left the post in the early morning. It was an affecting time. The women cried over Cathy, so did even those stern warriors the Rocky Mountain Rangers; Shekels was there, and the Cid, and Sardanapalus, and Potter, and Mongrel, and Sour-

Mash, Famine, and Pestilence, and Cathy kissed them all and wept; details of the several arms of the garrison were present to represent the rest, and say good-bye and God bless you for all the soldiery; and there was a special squad from the Seventh, with the oldest veteran at its head, to speed the Seventh's Child with grand honors and impressive ceremonies; and the veteran had a touching speech by heart, and put up his hand in salute and tried to say it, but his lips trembled and his voice broke, but Cathy bent down from the saddle and kissed him on the mouth and turned his defeat to victory, and a cheer went up.

The next act closed the ceremonies, and was a moving surprise. It may be that you have discovered, before this, that the rigors of military law and custom melt insensibly away and disappear when a soldier or a regiment or the garrison wants to do something that will please Cathy. The bands conceived the idea of stirring her soldierly heart with a farewell which would remain in her memory always, beautiful and unfading, and bring back the past and its love for her whenever she should think of it; so they got their project placed before General Burnaby, my successor, who is Cathy's newest slave, and in spite of poverty of precedents they got his permission. The bands knew the child's favorite military airs. By this hint you know what is coming, but Cathy didn't. She was asked to sound the "reveille," which she did.

REVEILLE

With the last note the bands burst out with a crash: and woke the mountains with the "Star-Spangled Banner" in a way to make a body's heart swell and thump and his hair rise! It was enough to break a person all up, to see Cathy's radiant face shining out through her gladness and tears. By request she blew the "assembly," now. . . .

THE ASSEMBLY

. . . Then the bands thundered in, with "Rally round the flag, boys, rally once again!" Next, she blew another call ("to the Standard") . . .

TO THE STANDARD

. . . and the bands responded with "When we were marching through Georgia." Straightway she sounded "boots and saddles," that thrilling and most expediting call. . . .

BOOTS AND SADDLES

. . . and the bands could hardly hold in for the final note; then they turned their whole strength loose on "Tramp, tramp, tramp, the boys are marching," and everybody's excitement rose to blood-heat.

Now an impressive pause—then the bugle sang "TAPS"—translatable, this time, into "Good-bye, and God keep us all!" for taps is the soldier's nightly release from duty, and farewell: plaintive, sweet, pathetic, for the morning is never sure, for him; always it is possible that he is hearing it for the last time. . . .

TAPS

. . . Then the bands turned their instruments towards Cathy and burst in with that rollicking frenzy of a tune, "Oh, we'll all get blind drunk when Johnny comes marching home—yes, we'll all get blind drunk when Johnny comes marching home!" and followed it instantly with "Dixie," that antidote for melancholy, merriest and gladdest of all military music on any side of the ocean—and that was the end. And so—farewell!

I wish you could have been there to see it all, hear it all, and feel it: and get yourself blown away with the hurricane huzza that swept the place as a finish.

When we rode away, our main body had already been on the road an hour or two—I speak of our camp equipage; but we didn't move off alone: when Cathy blew the "advance" the Rangers cantered out in column of fours, and gave us escort, and were joined by White Cloud and Thunder-Bird in all their gaudy bravery, and by Buffalo Bill and four subordinate scouts. Three miles away, in the Plains, the Lieutenant-General halted, sat her horse like a military statue, the bugle at her lips, and put the Rangers through the evolutions for half an hour; and finally, when she blew the "charge," she led it herself. "Not for the last time," she said, and got a cheer, and we said good-bye all around, and faced eastward and rode away.

Postscript. A Day Later. Soldier Boy was stolen last night. Cathy is almost beside herself, and we cannot comfort her. Mercedes and I are not much alarmed about the horse, although this part of Spain is in something of a turmoil, politically, at present, and there is a good deal of lawlessness. In ordinary times the thief and the horse would soon be captured. We shall have them before long, I think.

XIV *Soldier Boy—To Himself*

It is five months. Or is it six? My troubles have clouded my memory. I think I have been all over this land, from end to end, and now I am back again since day before yesterday, to that city which we passed through, that last day of our long journey, and which is near her country home. I am a tottering ruin and my eyes are dim, but I recognized it. If she could see me she would know me and sound my call. I wish I could hear it once more; it would revive me, it would bring back her face and the mountains and the free life, and I would come—if I were dying I would come! She would not know *me*, looking as I do, but she would know me by my star. But she will never see me, for they do not let me out of this shabby stable—a foul and miserable place, with most two wrecks like myself for company.

How many times have I changed hands? I think it is twelve times—I cannot remember; and each time it was down a step lower, and each time I got a harder master. They have been cruel, every one; they have worked me night and day in degraded employments, and beaten me; they have fed me ill, and some days not at all. And so I am but bones, now, with a rough and frowsy skin humped and cornered upon my shrunken body—that skin which was once so glossy, that skin which she loved to stroke with her hand. I was the pride of the mountains and the Great Plains; now I am a scarecrow and despised.

These piteous wrecks that are my comrades here say we have reached the bottom of the scale, the final humiliation; they say that when a horse is no longer worth the weeds and discarded rubbish they feed to him, they sell him to the bull-ring for a glass of brandy, to make sport for the people and perish for their pleasure.

To die—that does not disturb me; we of the service never care for death. But if I could see her once more! if I could hear her bugle sing again and say, "It is I, Soldier—come!"

XV *General Alison to Mrs. Drake, the Colonel's Wife*
To return, now, to where I was, and tell you the rest. We shall never know how she came to be there; there is no way to account for it. She was always watching for black and shiny and spirited horses—watching, hoping, despairing, hoping again; always giving chase and sounding her call, upon the meagrest chance of a response, and breaking her heart over the disappointment; always inquiring, always interested in sales-stables and horse accumulations in general. How she got there must remain a mystery.

At the point which I had reached in a preceding paragraph of this account, the situation was as follows: two horses lay dying; the bull had scattered his persecutors for the moment, and stood raging, panting, pawing the dust in clouds over his back, when the man that had been wounded returned to the ring on a remount, a poor blind-folded wreck that yet had something ironically military about his bearing—and the next moment the bull had ripped him open and his bowels were dragging upon the ground and the bull was charging his swarm of pests again. Then came pealing through the air a bugle-call that froze my blood—"*It is I, Soldier—come!*" I turned; Cathy was flying down through the massed people; she cleared the parapet at a bound, and sped towards that riderless horse, who staggered forward towards the remembered sound; but his strength failed, and he fell at her feet, she lavishing kisses upon him and sobbing, the house rising with one impulse, and white with horror! Before help could reach her the bull was back again—

She was never conscious again in life. We bore her home, all mangled and drenched in blood, and knelt by her and listened to her broken and wandering words, and prayed for her passing spirit, and there was no comfort—nor ever will be, I think. But she was happy, for she was far away under another sky, and comrading again with her Rangers, and her animal friends, and the soldiers. Their names fell softly and caressingly from her lips, one by one, with pauses between. She was not in pain, but lay with closed eyes, vacantly murmuring, as one who dreams. Sometimes she smiled, saying nothing; sometimes she smiled when she uttered a name—such as Shekels, or BB, or Potter. Sometimes she was at her fort, issuing commands; sometimes she was careering over the plain at the head of her men; sometimes she was training her horse; once she said, reprovingly, "You are giving me the wrong foot; give me the left—don't you know it is good-bye?"

After this, she lay silent some time; the end was near. By-and-by she murmured, "Tired . . . sleepy . . . take Cathy, mamma." Then, "Kiss me, Soldier." For a little time she lay so still that we were doubtful if she breathed. Then she put out her hand and began to feel gropingly about; then said, "I cannot find it; blow 'taps.'" * It was the end.

TAPS

*"Lights out."

Eve's Diary

Eve's Diary (1906) is just one of a number of works in which Twain explores dimensions of Eve's character, her relation to God and Adam, her life in the Garden before the Fall, and her life afterward. Twain's other principal Eve texts are *Eve Speaks* (1923) and *Eve's Autobiography* (1962). In all of the Eve stories Eve is Adam's mate and the "founding mother" of the human race. Twain emphasizes Eve's goodness and innocence in all his versions of Eve and mildly accuses God of unfairly tempting her with the forbidden fruit in the absence of moral and ethical education. Eve possesses an intelligent and inquiring mind and quickly proves her superiority over Adam in the realm of language and speech. Joyce Warren observes that Eve speaks in her own voice and is "one of the few women in Twain's work who tells her own story" (LeMaster and Wilson, 262).

Eve's Diary was written in July 1905, a year after Olivia Clemens's death, and it is widely considered to embody Twain's feelings for his wife. Adam's words about Eve, found at the end of her diary, may well express Twain's painful loss and touching farewell to his wife. Susan Harris judges Eve to be Twain's idealization, not just of his wife but of womankind, pointing out that her life revolves around Adam and that she takes on the challenge of humanizing him and making him happy (123–24). *Eve's Diary* was first published in the Christmas 1905 issue of *Harper's*, then subsequently in book form that was suggestively illustrated and formatted to present the illusion of a privileged glimpse into Eve's life through her own diary entries.

Twain's larger Eve saga portrays her whole life, including

educating and socializing Adam as well as her life after their exit from the Garden and as the bearer of nine children, including Cain and Abel, while *Eve's Diary* focuses almost exclusively on her girlhood. Twain's portrait represents a departure from the female qualities he typically foregrounds in his girl and young women stories, instead extolling the more conventional feminine virtues honored by his Victorian culture. Nonetheless, this charmingly girlish Eve is invested with a restless native intelligence; she is quick to question and to give names to all she encounters. Adam soon discovers that Eve is the keeper of language and that he must master her vocabulary in order to communicate with her. Twain perpetuates many late-Victorian female stereotypes while subtly establishing Eve's challenging curiosity and independence of mind and action.

Twain chose Lester Ralph to illustrate the slim volume, and Ralph's fine art drawings provide interpretive possibilities beyond the scope of the first-person text. With Twain's approval Ralph presented the nude figures of Adam and Eve, but at sufficient distance or with strategic draping in foliage so as to avoid graphic anatomical detail. As Ray Sapirstein observes, Ralph depicts their nudity stylistically, as if part of a "nostalgic paen to Nature in its pristine state, the luxuriant and carefully wrought pastoral landscapes and flora of Eden" (Twain, *Diaries of Adam and Eve*, 22). Twain appears to have laid a trap for the self-righteous censors of the world who would be forced to admit that to denounce nudity would be to contradict the Bible. As he knew from past experience, when *Eve's Diary* was banned by the library in Wooster, Massachusetts, it boosted sales elsewhere.

Translated from the Original

Saturday.—I am almost a whole day old, now.—I arrived yesterday. That is as it seems to me. And it must be so, for if there was a day-before-yesterday I was not there when it happened, or I should remember it. It could be, of course, that it did happen, and that I was not noticing. Very well; I will be very watchful, now, and if any day-before-yesterdays happen I will make a note of it. It will be best to start right and not let the record get confused, for some instinct tells me that these details are going to be important to the historian some day. For I feel like an experiment, I feel exactly like an experiment, it would be impossible for a person to feel more like an experiment than I do, and so I am coming to feel convinced that that is what I *am*—an experiment; just an experiment, and nothing more.

Then if I am an experiment, am I the whole of it? No, I think not; I think the rest of it is part of it. I am the main part of it, but I think the rest of it has its share in the matter. Is my position assured, or do I have to watch it and take care of it? The latter, perhaps. Some instinct tells me that eternal vigilance is the price of supremacy. [That is a good phrase, I think, for one so young.]

Everything looks better to-day than it did yesterday. In the rush of finishing up yesterday, the mountains were left in a ragged condition, and some of the plains were so cluttered with rubbish and remnants that the aspects were quite distressing. Noble and beautiful works of art should not be subjected to haste; and this majestic new world is indeed a most noble and beautiful work. And certainly marvellously near to being perfect, notwithstanding the shortness of the time.

There are too many stars in some places and not enough in others, but that can be remedied presently, no doubt. The moon got loose last night, and slid down and fell out of the scheme—a very great loss; it breaks my heart to think of it. There isn't another thing among the ornaments and decorations that is comparable to it for beauty and finish. It should have been fastened better. If we can only get it back again—

But of course there is no telling where it went to. And besides, whoever gets it will hide it; I know it because I would do it myself. I believe I can be honest in all other matters, but I already begin to realize that the core and centre of my nature is love of the beautiful, a passion for the beautiful, and that it would not be safe to trust me with a moon that belonged to another person and that person didn't know I had it. I could give up a moon that I found in the daytime, because I should be afraid some one was looking; but if I found it in the dark, I am sure I should find some kind of an excuse for not saying anything about it. For I do love moons, they are so pretty and so romantic. I wish we had five or six; I would never go to bed; I should never get tired lying on the moss-bank and looking up at them.

Stars are good, too. I wish I could get some to put in my hair. But I suppose I never can. You would be surprised to find how far off they are, for they do not look it. When they first showed, last night, I tried to knock some down with a pole, but it didn't reach, which astonished me; then I tried clods till I was all tired out, but I never got one. It was because I am left-handed and cannot throw good. Even when I aimed at the one I wasn't after I couldn't hit the other one, though I did make some close shots, for I saw the black blot of the clod sail right into the midst of the golden clusters forty or fifty times, just barely missing them, and if I could have held out a little longer maybe I could have got one.

So I cried a little, which was natural, I suppose, for one of my age, and after I was rested I got a basket and started for a place on the extreme rim of the circle, where the stars were close to the ground and I could get them with my hands, which would be better, anyway, because I could gather them tenderly then, and not break them. But it was farther than I thought, and at last I had to give it up; I was so tired I couldn't drag my feet another step; and besides, they were sore and hurt me very much.

I couldn't get back home; it was too far and turning cold; but I found some tigers and nestled in amongst them and was most adorably comfortable, and their breath was sweet and pleasant, because they live on strawberries. I had never seen a tiger before, but I knew them in a minute by the stripes. If I could have one of those skins, it would make a lovely gown.

To-day I am getting better ideas about distances. I was so eager to get hold of every pretty thing that I giddily grabbed for it, sometimes when it was too far off, and sometimes when it was but six inches away but seemed a foot—alas, with thorns between! I learned a lesson; also I made an axiom, all out of my own head—my very first one: *The scratched Experiment shuns the thorn.* I think it is a very good one for one so young.

I followed the other Experiment around, yesterday afternoon, at a distance, to see what it might be for, if I could. But I was not able to make out. I think it is a man. I had never seen a man, but it looked like one, and I feel sure that that is what it is. I realize that I feel more curiosity about it than about any of the other reptiles. If it is a reptile, and I suppose it is; for it has frowsy hair and blue eyes, and looks like a reptile. It has no hips; it tapers like a carrot; when it stands, it spreads itself apart like a derrick; so I think it is a reptile, though it may be architecture.

I was afraid of it at first, and started to run every time it turned around, for I thought it was going to chase me; but by and by I found it was only trying to get away, so after that I was not timid any more, but tracked it along, several hours, about twenty yards behind, which made it nervous and unhappy. At last it was a good deal worried, and climbed a tree. I waited a good while, then gave it up and went home.

To-day the same thing over. I've got it up the tree again.

Sunday.—It is up there yet. Resting, apparently. But that is a subterfuge: Sunday isn't the day of rest; Saturday is appointed for that. It looks to me like a creature that is more interested in resting than in anything else. It would tire me to rest so much. It tires me just to sit around and watch the tree. I do wonder what it is for; I never see it do anything.

They returned the moon last night, and I was *so* happy! I think it is very honest of them. It slid down and fell off again, but I was not distressed; there is no need to worry when one has that kind of neighbors; they will fetch it back. I wish I could do something to show my appreciation. I would like to send them some stars, for we have more than we can use. I mean I, not we, for I can see that the reptile cares nothing for such things.

It has low tastes, and is not kind. When I went there yesterday evening in the gloaming it had crept down and was trying to catch the little speckled fishes that play in the pool, and I had to clod it to make it go up the tree again and let them alone. I wonder if *that* is what it is for? Hasn't it any heart? Hasn't it any compassion for those little creatures? Can it be that it was designed and manufactured for such ungentle work? It has the look of it. One of the clods took it back of the ear, and it used language. It gave me a thrill, for it was the first time I had ever heard speech, except my own. I did not understand the words, but they seemed expressive.

When I found it could talk I felt a new interest in it, for I love to talk; I talk all day, and in my sleep, too, and I am very interesting, but if I had another to talk to I could be twice as interesting, and would never stop, if desired.

If this reptile is a man, it isn't an *it*, is it? That wouldn't be grammatical, would it? I think it would be *he*. I think so. In that case one would parse it thus: nominative, *he*; dative, *him*; possessive, *his'n*. Well, I will consider it a man and call it he until it turns out to be something else. This will be handier than having so many uncertainties.

Next week Sunday. — All the week I tagged around after him and tried to get acquainted. I had to do the talking, because he was shy, but I didn't mind it. He seemed pleased to have me around, and I used the sociable "we" a good deal, because it seemed to flatter him to be included.

Wednesday.—We are getting along very well indeed, now, and getting better and better acquainted. He does not try to avoid me any more, which is a good sign, and shows that he likes to have me with him. That pleases me, and I study to be useful to him in every way I can, so as to increase his regard. During the last day or two I have taken all the work of naming things off his hands, and this has been a great relief to him, for he has no gift in that line, and is evidently very grateful. He can't think of a rational name to save him, but I do not let him see that I am aware of his defect. Whenever a new creature comes along I name it before he has time to expose himself by an awkward silence. In this way I have saved him many embarrassments. I have no defect like his. The minute I set eyes on an animal I know what it is. I don't have to reflect a moment; the right name comes out instantly, just as if it were an inspiration, as no doubt it is, for I am sure it wasn't in me half a minute before. I seem to know just by the shape of the creature and the way it acts what animal it is.

When the dodo came along he thought it was a wildcat—I saw it in his eye. But I saved him. And I was careful not to do it in a way that could hurt his pride. I just spoke up in a quite natural way of pleased surprise, and not as if I was dreaming of conveying information, and said, "Well, I do declare if there isn't the dodo!" I explained—without seeming to be explaining—how I knew it for a dodo, and although I thought maybe he was a little piqued that I knew the creature when he didn't, it was quite evident that he admired me. That was very agreeable, and I thought of it more than once with gratification before I slept. How little a thing can make us happy when we feel that we have earned it.

Thursday.—My first sorrow. Yesterday he avoided me and seemed to wish I would not talk to him. I could not believe it, and thought there was some mistake, for I loved to be with him, and loved to hear him talk, and so how could it be that he could feel unkind toward me when I had not done anything? But at last it seemed true, so I went away and sat lonely in the place where I first saw him the morning that we were made and I did not know what he was and was indifferent about him; but now it was a mournful place, and every little thing spoke of him, and my heart was very sore. I did not know why very clearly, for it was a new feeling; I had not experienced it before, and it was all a mystery, and I could not make it out.

But when night came I could not bear the lonesomeness, and went to the new shelter which he has built, to ask him what I had done that was wrong and how I could mend it and get back his kindness again; but he put me out in the rain, and it was my first sorrow.

Sunday.—It is pleasant again, now, and I am happy; but those were heavy days; I do not think of them when I can help it.

I tried to get him some of those apples, but I cannot learn to throw straight. I failed, but I think the good intention pleased him. They are forbidden, and he says I shall come to harm; but so I come to harm through pleasing him why shall I care for that harm?

Monday.—This morning I told him my name, hoping it would interest him. But he did not care for it. It is strange. If he should tell me his name, I would care. I think it would be pleasanter in my ears than any other sound.

He talks very little. Perhaps it is because he is not bright, and is sensitive about it and wishes to conceal it. It is such a pity that he should feel so, for brightness is nothing; it is in the heart that the values lie. I wish I could make him understand that a loving good heart is riches, and riches enough, and that without it intellect is poverty.

Although he talks so little he has quite a considerable vocabulary. This morning he used a surprisingly good word. He evidently recognized, himself, that it was a good one, for he worked it in twice afterward, casually. It was not good casual art, still it showed that he possesses a certain quality of perception. Without a doubt that seed can be made to grow, if cultivated.

Where did he get that word? I do not think I have ever used it.

No, he took no interest in my name. I tried to hide my disappointment, but I suppose I did not succeed. I went away and sat on the moss-bank with my feet in the water. It is where I go when I hunger for companionship, some one to look at, some one to talk to. It is not enough—that lovely white body painted there in the pool—but it is something, and something is better than utter loneliness. It talks when I talk; it is sad when I am sad; it comforts me with its sympathy; it says, "Do not be downhearted, you poor friendless girl; I will be your friend." It is a good friend to me, and my only one; it is my sister.

That first time that she forsook me! ah, I shall never forget that—never, never. My heart was lead in my body! I said, "She was all I had, and now she is gone!" In my despair I said, "Break, my heart; I cannot bear my life any more!" and hid my face in my hands, and there was no solace for me. And when I took them away, after a little, there she was again, white and shining and beautiful, and I sprang into her arms!

That was perfect happiness; I had known happiness before, but it was not like this, which was ecstasy. I never doubted her afterwards. Sometimes she stayed away—maybe an hour, maybe almost the whole day, but I waited and did not doubt; I said, "She is busy, or she is gone a journey, but she will come." And it was so: she always did. At night she would not come if it was dark, for she was a timid little thing; but if there was a moon she would come. I am not afraid of the dark, but she is younger than I am; she was born after I was. Many and many are the visits I have paid her; she is my comfort and my refuge when my life is hard—and it is mainly that.

Tuesday.—All the morning I was at work improving the estate; and I purposely kept away from him in the hope that he would get lonely and come. But he did not.

At noon I stopped for the day and took my recreation by flitting all about with the bees and the butterflies and revelling in the flowers, those beautiful creatures that catch the smile of

God out of the sky and preserve it! I gathered them, and made them into wreaths and garlands and clothed myself in them whilst I ate my luncheon—apples, of course; then I sat in the shade and wished and waited. But he did not come.

But no matter. Nothing would have come of it, for he does not care for flowers. He calls them rubbish, and cannot tell one from another, and thinks it is superior to feel like that. He does not care for me, he does not care for flowers, he does not care for the painted sky at eventide—is there anything he does care for, except building shacks to coop himself up in from the good clean rain, and thumping the melons, and sampling the grapes, and fingering the fruit on the trees, to see how those properties are coming along?

I laid a dry stick on the ground and tried to bore a hole in it with another one, in order to carry out a scheme that I had, and soon I got an awful fright. A thin, transparent bluish film rose out of the hole, and I dropped everything and ran! I thought it was a spirit, and I *was* so frightened! But I looked back, and it was not coming; so I leaned against a rock and rested and panted, and let my limbs go on trembling until they got steady again; then I crept warily back, alert, watching, and ready to fly if there was occasion; and when I was come near, I parted the branches of a rose-bush and peeped through—wishing the man was about, I was looking so cunning and pretty—but the sprite was gone. I went there, and there was a pinch of delicate pink dust in the hole. I put my finger in, to feel it, and said *ouch!* and took it out again. It was a cruel pain. I put my finger in my mouth; and by standing first on one foot and then the other, and grunting, I presently eased my misery; then I was full of interest, and began to examine.

I was curious to know what the pink dust was. Suddenly the name of it occurred to me, though I had never heard of it before. It was *fire!* I was as certain of it as a person could be of anything in the world. So without hesitation I named it that—fire.

I had created something that didn't exist before; I had added a new thing to the world's uncountable properties; I realized this, and was proud of my achievement, and was going to run and find him and tell him about it, thinking to raise myself in his esteem, — but I reflected, and did not do it. No — he would not care for it. He would ask what it was good for, and what could I answer? for if it was not *good* for something, but only beautiful, merely beautiful —

So I sighed, and did not go. For it wasn't good for anything; it could not build a shack, it could not improve melons, it could not hurry a fruit crop; it was useless, it was a foolishness and a vanity; he would despise it and say cutting words. But to me it was not despicable; I said, "Oh, you fire, I love you, you dainty pink creature, for you are *beautiful* — and that is enough!" and was going to gather it to my breast. But refrained. Then I made another maxim out of my own head, though it was so nearly like the first one that I was afraid it was only a plagiarism: "*The burnt Experiment shuns the fire.*"

I wrought again; and when I had made a good deal of fire-dust I emptied it into a handful of dry brown grass, intending to carry it home and keep it always and play with it; but the wind struck it and it sprayed up and spat out at me fiercely, and I dropped it and ran. When I looked back the blue spirit was towering up and stretching and rolling away like a cloud, and instantly I thought of the name of it — *smoke!* — though, upon my word, I had never heard of smoke before.

Soon, brilliant yellow and red flares shot up through the smoke, and I named them in an instant — *flames!* — and I was right, too, though these were the very first flames that had ever been in the world. They climbed the trees, they flashed splendidly in and out of the vast and increasing volume of tumbling smoke, and I had to clap my hands and laugh and dance in my rapture, it was so new and strange and so wonderful and so beautiful!

He came running, and stopped and gazed, and said not a word for many minutes. Then he asked what it was. Ah, it was too bad that he should ask such a direct question. I had to answer it, of course, and I did. I said it was fire. If it annoyed him that I should know and he must ask, that was not my fault; I had no desire to annoy him. After a pause he asked,

"How did it come?"

Another direct question, and it also had to have a direct answer.

"I made it."

The fire was travelling farther and farther off. He went to the edge of the burnt place and stood looking down, and said,

"What are these?"

"Fire-coals."

He picked up one to examine it, but changed his mind and put it down again. Then he went away. *Nothing* interests him.

But I was interested. There were ashes, gray and soft and delicate and pretty—I knew what they were at once. And the embers; I knew the embers, too. I found my apples, and raked them out, and was glad; for I am very young and my appetite is active. But I was disappointed; they were all burst open and spoiled. Spoiled apparently; but it was not so; they were better than raw ones. Fire is beautiful; some day it will be useful, I think.

Friday.—I saw him again, for a moment, last Monday at nightfall, but only for a moment. I was hoping he would praise me for trying to improve the estate, for I had meant well and had worked hard. But he was not pleased, and turned away and left me. He was also displeased on another account: I tried once more to persuade him to stop going over the Falls. That was because the fire had revealed to me a new passion—quite new, and distinctly different from love, grief, and those others which I had already discovered—*fear.* And it is horrible!—I wish I had never discovered it; it gives me dark moments, it spoils my happiness, it makes me shiver and tremble and shudder. But I could not persuade him, for he has not discovered fear yet, and so he could not understand me.

Tuesday—Wednesday—Thursday—and to-day: all without seeing him. It is a long time to be alone; still, it is better to be alone than unwelcome.

I *had* to have company—I was made for it, I think,—so I made friends with the animals. They are just charming, and they have the kindest disposition and the politest ways; they never look sour, they never let you feel that you are intruding, they smile at you and wag their tail, if they've got one, and they are always ready for a romp or an excursion or anything you want to propose. I think they are perfect gentlemen. All these days we have had such good times, and it hasn't been lonesome for me, ever. Lonesome! No, I should say not. Why, there's always a swarm of them around—sometimes as much as four or five acres—you can't count them; and when you stand on a rock in the midst and look out over the furry expanse it is so mottled and splashed and gay with color and frisking sheen and sun-flash, and so rippled with stripes, that you might think it was a lake, only you know it isn't; and there's storms of sociable birds, and hurricanes of whirring wings; and when the sun strikes all that feathery commotion, you have a blazing up of all the colors you can think of, enough to put your eyes out.

We have made long excursions, and I have seen a great deal of the world; almost all of it, I think; and so I am the first traveller, and the only one. When we are on the march, it is an imposing sight—there's nothing like it anywhere. For comfort I ride a tiger or a leopard, because it is soft and has a round back that fits me, and because they are such pretty animals; but for long distance or for scenery I ride the elephant. He hoists me up with his trunk, but I can get off myself; when we are ready to camp, he sits and I slide down the back way.

The birds and animals are all friendly to each other, and there are no disputes about anything. They all talk, and they all talk to me, but it must be a foreign language, for I cannot make out a word they say; yet they often understand me when I talk back, particularly the dog and the elephant. It makes me ashamed. It shows that they are brighter than I am, and are therefore my superiors. It annoys me, for I want to be the principal Experiment myself—and I intend to be, too.

I have learned a number of things, and am educated, now, but I wasn't at first. I was ignorant at first. At first it used to vex me because, with all my watching, I was never smart enough to be around when the water was running up-hill; but now I do not mind it. I have experimented and experimented until now

I know it never does run up-hill, except in the dark. I know it does in the dark, because the pool never goes dry; which it would, of course, if the water didn't come back in the night. It is best to prove things by actual experiment; then you *know*; whereas if you depend on guessing and supposing and con- jecturing, you will never get educated.

Some things you *can't* find out; but you will never know you can't by guessing and supposing: no, you have to be patient and go on experimenting until you find out that you can't find out. And it is delightful to have it that way, it makes the world so interesting. If there wasn't anything to find out, it would be dull. Even trying to find out and not finding out is just as interesting as trying to find out and finding out, and I don't know but more so. The secret of the water was a treasure until I *got* it; then the excitement all went away, and I recognized a sense of loss.

By experiment I know that wood swims, and dry leaves, and feathers, and plenty of other things; therefore by all that cumu- lative evidence you know that a rock will swim; but you have to put up with simply knowing it, for there isn't any way to prove it—up to now. But I shall find a way—then *that* excitement will go. Such things make me sad; because by and by when I have found out everything there won't be any more excitements, and I do love excitements so! The other night I couldn't sleep for thinking about it.

At first I couldn't make out what I was made for, but now I think it was to search out the secrets of this wonderful world and be happy and thank the Giver of it all for devising it. I think there are many things to learn yet—I hope so; and by econo- mizing and not hurrying too fast I think they will last weeks and weeks. I hope so. When you cast up a feather it sails away on the air and goes out of sight; then you throw up a clod and it doesn't. It comes down, every time. I have tried it and tried it, and it is always so. I wonder why it is? Of course it *doesn't* come down, but why should it *seem* to? I suppose it is an opti- cal illusion. I mean, one of them is. I don't know which one. It may be the feather, it may be the clod; I can't prove which it is, I can only demonstrate that one or the other is a fake, and let a person take his choice.

By watching, I know that the stars are not going to last. I have seen some of the best ones melt and run down the sky. Since one can melt, they can all melt; since they can all melt, they can all melt the same night. That sorrow will come—I know it. I mean to sit up every night and look at them as long as I can keep awake; and I will impress those sparkling fields on my memory, so that by and by when they are taken away I can by my fancy restore those lovely myriads to the black sky and make them sparkle again, and double them by the blur of my tears.

After the Fall

When I look back, the Garden is a dream to me. It was beautiful, surpassingly beautiful, enchantingly beautiful; and now it is lost, and I shall not see it any more.

The Garden is lost, but I have found *him*, and am content. He loves me as well as he can; I love him with all the strength of my passionate nature, and this, I think, is proper to my youth and sex. If I ask myself why I love him, I find I do not know, and do not really much care to know; so I suppose that this kind of love is not a product of reasoning and statistics, like one's love for other reptiles and animals. I think that this must be so. I love certain birds because of their song; but I do not love Adam on account of his singing—no, it is not that; the more he sings the more I do not get reconciled to it. Yet I ask him to sing, because I wish to learn to like everything he is interested in. I am sure I can learn, because at first I could not stand it, but now I can. It sours the milk, but it doesn't matter; I can get used to that kind of milk.

It is not on account of his brightness that I love him—no, it is not that. He is not to blame for his brightness, such as it is, for he did not make it himself; he is as God made him, and that is sufficient. There was a wise purpose in it, *that* I know. In time it will develop, though I think it will not be sudden; and besides, there is no hurry; he is well enough just as he is.

It is not on account of his gracious and considerate ways

and his delicacy that I love him. No, he has lacks in these regards, but he is well enough just so, and is improving.

It is not on account of his industry that I love him—no, it is not that. I think he has it in him, and I do not know why he conceals it from me. It is my only pain. Otherwise he is frank and open with me, now. I am sure he keeps nothing from me but this. It grieves me that he should have a secret from me, and sometimes it spoils my sleep, thinking of it, but I will put it out of my mind; it shall not trouble my happiness, which is otherwise full to overflowing.

It is not on account of his education that I love him—no, it is not that. He is self-educated, and does really know a multitude of things, but they are not so.

It is not on account of his chivalry that I love him—no, it is not that. He told on me, but I do not blame him; it is a peculiarity of sex, I think, and he did not make his sex. Of course I would not have told on him, I would have perished first; but that is a peculiarity of sex, too, and I do not take credit for it, for I did not make my sex.

Then why is it that I love him? *Merely because he is masculine*, I think.

At bottom he is good, and I love him for that, but I could love him without it. If he should beat me and abuse me, I should go on loving him. I know it. It is a matter of sex, I think.

He is strong and handsome, and I love him for that, and I admire him and am proud of him, but I could love him without those qualities. If he were plain, I should love him; if he were a wreck, I should love him; and I would work for him, and slave over him, and pray for him, and watch by his bedside until I died.

Yes, I think I love him merely because he is *mine*, and is *masculine*. There is no other reason, I suppose. And so I think it is as I first said: that this kind of love is not a product of reasonings and statistics. It just *comes*—none knows whence—and cannot explain itself. And doesn't need to.

It is what I think. But I am only a girl, and the first that has examined this matter, and it may turn out that in my ignorance and inexperience I have not got it right.

Forty Years Later

It is my prayer, it is my longing, that we may pass from this life together—a longing which shall never perish from the earth, but shall have place in the heart of every wife that loves, until the end of time; and it shall be called by my name.

But if one of us must go first, it is my prayer that it shall be I; for he is strong, I am weak, I am not so necessary to him as he is to me—life without him would not be life; how could I endure it? This prayer is also immortal, and will not cease from being offered up while my race continues. I am the first wife; and in the last wife I shall be repeated.

At Eve's Grave

Adam: Wheresoever she was, *there* was Eden.

Saint Joan of Arc

Although it is difficult to separate myth from historical accounts, it is generally accepted that Joan of Arc, an illiterate peasant girl from Domrémy, France, commanded the French armies and, with great courage and tactical skill, forced the defeat and retreat of the English army from most of France, paving the way for the complete liberation of France from English rule two decades after her execution. At the age of seventeen Joan took command of French military forces and, through a series of inspired victories, broke the back of the Hundred Years' War and escorted the King of France to the newly liberated cathedral at Rheims for his coronation. Joan accomplished in thirteen months what France without her had been unable to do in the previous ninety years. Although she was tried by a French ecclesiastical court and sentenced to be burned at the stake, she was "officially rehabilitated" in 1456 as a national hero and eventually canonized Saint Joan of Arc.

Mark Twain was powerfully attracted to Joan of Arc's story, particularly to her personal qualities of character, her unflinching commitment to her convictions, and her martyrdom for a noble cause. As a youth he came across a stray page from a history book detailing Joan's captivity; this stray page marked the beginning of Twain's lifelong fascination with and attraction to the young woman. There are many references to her accomplishments in his speeches, but in the early 1880s he began work on what would become his last novel. Published in 1896, *The Personal Recollections of Joan of Arc* is both his longest novel and the one he regarded as his best.

Unlike the novel, which was written as a memoir "related" by Joan's lifelong friend and secretary, Sieur Louis De Conte, the story included here is told directly by Twain as a first-person, story-length account of her life. The first-person narration gives him the opportunity for a direct summation of her life and character from his perspective. The biographical story was written long after the completed novel and published in *The $30,000 Bequest and Other Stories* in 1906. It is Twain's last and most openly personal statement about the heroic maiden. He speaks of her courage on the battlefield, but also of her "forgiving, generous, unselfish" nature. Though she wore armor and commanded armies, Twain wants us to see her always as a girl, "a lithe young slender figure . . . dear and bonny and loveable." She embodies what he held highest among human qualities: intellect, moral conviction, youthful beauty, and an "unquenchable spirit." Of course, he distributes these qualities liberally upon his other young female protagonists as well.

I

The evidence furnished at the Trials and Rehabilitation sets forth Joan of Arc's strange and beautiful history in clear and minute detail. Among all the multitude of biographies that freight the shelves of the world's libraries, this is the only one *whose validity is confirmed to us by oath*. It gives us a vivid picture of a career and a personality of so extraordinary a character that we are helped to accept them as actualities by the very fact that both are beyond the inventive reach of fiction. The public part of the career occupied only a mere breath of time — it covered but two years; but what a career it was! The personality which made it possible is one to be reverently studied, loved, and marvelled at, but not to be wholly understood and accounted for by even the most searching analysis.

In Joan of Arc at the age of sixteen there was no promise of a romance. She lived in a dull little village on the frontiers of civilization; she had been nowhere and had seen nothing; she knew none but simple shepherd folk; she had never seen

Note. — The Official Record of the Trials and Rehabilitation of Joan of Arc is the most remarkable history that exists in any language; yet there are few people in the world who can say they have read it: in England and America it has hardly been heard of.

Three hundred years ago Shakespeare did not know the true story of Joan of Arc; in his day it was unknown even in France. For four hundred years it existed rather as a vaguely defined romance than as definite and authentic history. The true story remained buried in the official archives of France from the Rehabilitation of 1456 until Quicherat dug it out and gave it to the world two generations ago, in lucid and understandable modern French. It is a deeply fascinating story. But only in the Official Trials and Rehabilitation can it be found in its entirety. — M. T.

a person of note; she hardly knew what a soldier looked like; she had never ridden a horse, nor had a warlike weapon in her hand; she could neither read nor write: she could spin and sew; she knew her catechism and her prayers and the fabulous histories of the saints, and this was all her learning. That was Joan at sixteen. What did she know of law? of evidence? of courts? of the attorney's trade? of legal procedure? Nothing. Less than nothing. Thus exhaustively equipped with ignorance, she went before the court at Toul to contest a false charge of breach of promise of marriage; she conducted her cause herself, without any one's help or advice or any one's friendly sympathy, and won it. She called no witnesses of her own, but vanquished the prosecution by using with deadly effectiveness its own testimony. The astonished judge threw the case out of court, and spoke of her as "this marvellous child."

She went to the veteran Commandant of Vaucouleurs and demanded an escort of soldiers, saying she must march to the help of the King of France, since she was commissioned of God to win back his lost kingdom for him and set the crown upon his head. The Commandant said, "What, you? you are only a child." And he advised that she be taken back to her village and have her ears boxed. But she said she must obey God, and would come again, and again, and yet again, and finally she would get the soldiers. She said truly. In time he yielded, after months of delay and refusal, and gave her the soldiers; and took off his sword and gave her that, and said, "Go—and let come what may." She made her long and perilous journey through the enemy's country, and spoke with the King, and convinced him. Then she was summoned before the University of Poitiers to prove that she *was* commissioned of God and not of Satan, and daily during three weeks she sat before that learned congress unafraid, and capably answered their deep questions out of her ignorant but able head and her simple and honest heart; and again she won her case, and with it the wondering admiration of all that august company.

And now, aged seventeen, she was made Commander-in-Chief, with a prince of the royal house and the veteran generals of France for subordinates; and at the head of the first army she had ever seen, she marched to Orleans, carried the commanding fortresses of the enemy by storm in three desperate assaults, and in ten days raised a siege which had defied the might of France for seven months.

After a tedious and insane delay caused by the King's instability of character and the treacherous counsels of his ministers, she got permission to take the field again. She took Jargeau by storm; then Meung; she forced Beaugency to surrender; then—in the open field—she won the memorable victory of Patay against Talbot, "the English lion," and broke the back of the Hundred Years' War. It was a campaign which cost but seven weeks of time; yet the political results would have been cheap if the time expended had been fifty years. Patay, that unsung and now long-forgotten battle, was the Moscow of the English power in France; from the blow struck that day it was destined never to recover. It was the beginning of the end of an alien dominion which had ridden France intermittently for three hundred years.

Then followed the great campaign of the Loire, the capture of Troyes by assault, and the triumphal march past surrendering towns and fortresses to Rheims, where Joan put the crown upon her King's head in the Cathedral, amid wild public rejoicings, and with her old peasant father there to see these things and believe his eyes if he could. She had restored the crown and the lost sovereignty; the King was grateful for once in his shabby poor life, and asked her to name her reward and have it. She asked for nothing for herself, but begged that the taxes of her native village might be remitted forever. The prayer was granted, and the promise kept for three hundred and sixty years. Then it was broken, and remains broken today. France was very poor then, she is very rich now; but she has been collecting those taxes for more than a hundred years.

Joan asked one other favor: that now that her mission was fulfilled she might be allowed to go back to her village and take up her humble life again with her mother and the friends of her childhood; for she had no pleasure in the cruelties of war, and the sight of blood and suffering wrung her heart. Sometimes in battle she did not draw her sword, lest in the splendid madness of the onset she might forget herself and take an enemy's life with it. In the Rouen Trials, one of her quaintest speeches—coming from the gentle and girlish source it did— was her naïve remark that she had "never killed any one." Her prayer for leave to go back to the rest and peace of her village home was not granted.

Then she wanted to march at once upon Paris, take it, and drive the English out of France. She was hampered in all the ways that treachery and the King's vacillation could devise, but she forced her way to Paris at last, and fell badly wounded in a successful assault upon one of the gates. Of course her men lost heart at once—she was the only heart they had. They fell back. She begged to be allowed to remain at the front, saying victory was sure. "I will take Paris now or die!" she said. But she was removed from the field by force; the King ordered a retreat, and actually disbanded his army. In accordance with a beautiful old military custom Joan devoted her silver armor and hung it up in the Cathedral of St. Denis. Its great days were over.

Then, by command, she followed the King and his frivolous court and endured a gilded captivity for a time, as well as her free spirit could; and whenever inaction became unbearable she gathered some men together and rode away and assaulted a stronghold and captured it.

At last in a sortie against the enemy, from Compiègne, on the 24th of May (when she was turned eighteen), she was herself captured, after a gallant fight. It was her last battle. She was to follow the drums no more.

Thus ended the briefest epoch-making military career known to history. It lasted only a year and a month, but it found France an English province, and furnishes the reason that France is France to-day and not an English province still. Thirteen months! It was, indeed, a short career; but in the centuries that have since elapsed five hundred millions of Frenchmen have lived and died blest by the benefactions it conferred; and so long as France shall endure, the mighty debt must grow. And France is grateful; we often hear her say it. Also thrifty: she collects the Domrémy taxes.

Joan was fated to spend the rest of her life behind bolts and bars. She was a prisoner of war, not a criminal, therefore hers was recognized as an honorable captivity. By the rules of war she must be held to ransom, and a fair price could not be refused if offered. John of Luxembourg paid her the just compliment of requiring a prince's ransom for her. In that day that phrase represented a definite sum—61,125 francs. It was, of course, supposable that either the King or grateful France, or both, would fly with the money and set their fair young benefactor free. But this did not happen. In five and a half months neither King nor country stirred a hand nor offered a penny. Twice Joan tried to escape. Once by a trick she succeeded for a moment, and locked her jailer in behind her, but she was discovered and caught; in the other case she let herself down from a tower sixty feet high, but her rope was too short, and she got a fall that disabled her and she could not get away.

Finally, Cauchon, Bishop of Beauvais, paid the money and bought Joan—ostensibly for the Church, to be tried for wearing male attire and for other impieties, but really for the English, the enemy into whose hands the poor girl was so piteously anxious not to fall. She was now shut up in the dungeons of the Castle of Rouen and kept in an iron cage, with her hands and feet and neck chained to a pillar; and from that time forth during all the months of her imprisonment, till the end, several rough English soldiers stood guard over her night and day—and not outside her room, but in it. It was a dreary and hideous captivity, but it did not conquer her: nothing could break that invincible spirit. From first to last she was a prisoner a year; and she spent the last three months of it on trial for her life before a formidable array of ecclesiastical judges, and disputing the ground with them foot by foot and inch by inch with brilliant generalship and dauntless pluck. The spectacle of that solitary girl, forlorn and friendless, without advocate or adviser, and without the help and guidance of any copy of the charges brought against her or rescript of the complex and voluminous daily proceedings of the court to modify the crushing strain upon her astonishing memory, fighting that long battle serene and undismayed against these colossal odds, stands alone in its pathos and its sublimity; it has nowhere its mate, either in the annals of fact or in the inventions of fiction.

And how fine and great were the things she daily said, how fresh and crisp—and she so worn in body, so starved, and tired, and harried! They run through the whole gamut of feeling and expression—from scorn and defiance, uttered with soldierly fire and frankness, all down the scale to wounded dignity clothed in words of noble pathos; as, when her patience was exhausted by the pestering delvings and gropings and searchings of her persecutors to find out what kind of devil's witchcraft she had employed to rouse the war spirit in her timid soldiers, she burst out with, "What I said was, '*Ride these English down*'—and I did it myself!" and as, when insultingly asked why it was that *her* standard had place at the crowning of the King in the Cathedral of Rheims rather than the standards of the other captains, she uttered that touching speech, "*It had borne the burden, it had earned the honor*"—a phrase which fell from her lips without premeditation, yet whose moving beauty and simple grace it would bankrupt the arts of language to surpass.

Although she was on trial for her life, she was the only witness called on either side; the only witness summoned to testify before a packed jury commissioned with a definite task: to find her guilty, whether she was guilty or not. She must be convicted out of her own mouth, there being no other way to accomplish it. Every advantage that learning has over ignorance, age over youth, experience over inexperience, chicane over artlessness, every trick and trap and gin devisable by malice and the cunning of sharp intellects practised in setting snares for the unwary—all these were employed against her without shame; and when these arts were one by one defeated by the marvellous intuitions of her alert and penetrating mind, Bishop Cauchon stooped to a final baseness which it degrades human speech to describe: a priest who pretended to come from the region of her own home and to be a pitying friend and anxious to help her in her sore need was smuggled into her cell, and he misused his sacred office to steal her confidence; she confided to him the things sealed from revealment by her Voices, and which her prosecutors had tried so long in vain to trick her into betraying. A concealed confederate set it all down and delivered it to Cauchon, who used Joan's secrets, thus obtained, for her ruin.

Throughout the Trials, whatever the foredoomed witness said was twisted from its true meaning when possible, and made to tell against her; and whenever an answer of hers was beyond the reach of twisting it was not allowed to go upon the record. It was upon one of these latter occasions that she uttered that pathetic reproach—to Cauchon: "Ah, you set down everything that is against me, but you will not set down what is for me."

That this untrained young creature's genius for war was wonderful, and her generalship worthy to rank with the ripe products of a tried and trained military experience, we have the sworn testimony of two of her veteran subordinates— one, the Duc d'Alençon, the other the greatest of the French generals of the time, Dunois, Bastard of Orleans; that her genius was as great—possibly even greater—in the subtle warfare of the forum we have for witness the records of the Rouen Trials, that protracted exhibition of intellectual fence maintained with credit against the master-minds of France; that her moral greatness was peer to her intellect we call the Rouen Trials again to witness, with their testimony to a fortitude which patiently and steadfastly endured during twelve weeks the wasting forces of captivity, chains, loneliness, sickness, darkness, hunger, thirst, cold, shame, insult, abuse, broken sleep, treachery, ingratitude, exhausting sieges of cross-examination, the threat of torture, with the rack before her and the executioner standing ready: yet never surrendering, never asking quarter, the frail wreck of her as unconquerable the last day as was her invincible spirit the first.

Great as she was in so many ways, she was perhaps even greatest of all in the lofty things just named—her patient endurance, her steadfastness, her granite fortitude. We may not hope to easily find her mate and twin in these majestic qualities; where we lift our eyes highest we find only a strange and curious contrast—there in the captive eagle beating his broken wings on the Rock of St. Helena.

III

The Trials ended with her condemnation. But as she had conceded nothing, confessed nothing, this was victory for her, defeat for Cauchon. But his evil resources were not yet exhausted. She was persuaded to agree to sign a paper of slight import, then by treachery a paper was substituted which contained a recantation and a detailed confession of everything which had been charged against her during the Trials and denied and repudiated by her persistently during the three months; and this false paper she ignorantly signed. This was a victory for Cauchon. He followed it eagerly and pitilessly up by at once setting a trap for her which she could not escape. When she realized this she gave up the long struggle, denounced the treason which had been practised against her, repudiated the false confession, reasserted the truth of the testimony which she had given in the Trials, and went to her martyrdom with the peace of God in her tired heart, and on her lips endearing words and loving prayers for the cur she had crowned and the nation of ingrates she had saved.

When the fires rose about her and she begged for a cross for her dying lips to kiss, it was not a friend but an enemy, not a Frenchman but an alien, not a comrade in arms but an English soldier, that answered that pathetic prayer. He broke a stick across his knee, bound the pieces together in the form of the symbol she so loved, and gave it her; and his gentle deed is not forgotten, nor will be.

IV

Twenty-five years afterwards the Process of Rehabilitation was instituted, there being a growing doubt as to the validity of a sovereignty that had been rescued and set upon its feet by a person who had been proven by the Church to be a witch and a familiar of evil spirits. Joan's old generals, her secretary, several aged relations and other villagers of Domrémy, surviving judges and secretaries of the Rouen and Poitiers Processes—a cloud of witnesses, some of whom had been her enemies and persecutors,—came and made oath and testified; and what they said was written down. In that sworn testimony the moving and beautiful history of Joan of Arc is laid bare, from her childhood to her martyrdom. From the verdict she rises stainlessly pure, in mind and heart, in speech and deed and spirit, and will so endure to the end of time.

She is the Wonder of the Ages. And when we consider her origin, her early circumstances, her sex, and that she did all the things upon which her renown rests while she was still a young girl, we recognize that while our race continues she will be also the *Riddle* of the Ages. When we set about accounting for a Napoleon or a Shakespeare or a Raphael or a Wagner or an Edison or other extraordinary person, we understand that the measure of his talent will not explain the whole result, nor even the largest part of it; no, it is the atmosphere in which the talent was cradled that explains; it is the training which it received while it grew, the nurture it got from reading, study, example, the encouragement it gathered from self-recognition and recognition from the outside at each stage of its development: when we know all these details, then we know why the man was ready when his opportunity came. We should expect Edison's surroundings and atmosphere to have the largest share in discovering him to himself and to the world; and we should expect him to live and die undiscovered in a land where an inventor could find no comradeship, no sympathy, no ambition-rousing atmosphere of recognition and applause—Dahomey, for instance. Dahomey could not find an Edison out; in Dahomey an Edison could not find himself out. Broadly speaking, genius is not born with sight, but blind; and it is not itself that opens its eyes, but the subtle influences of a myriad of stimulating exterior circumstances.

We all know this to be not a guess, but a mere commonplace fact, a truism. Lorraine was Joan of Arc's Dahomey. And there the Riddle confronts us. We can understand how she could be born with military genius, with leonine courage, with incomparable fortitude, with a mind which was in several particulars a prodigy—a mind which included among its specialties the lawyer's gift of detecting traps laid by the adversary in cunning and treacherous arrangements of seemingly innocent words, the orator's gift of eloquence, the advocate's gift of presenting a case in clear and compact form, the judge's gift of sorting and weighing evidence, and finally, something recognizable as more than a mere trace of the statesman's gift of understanding a political situation and how to make profitable use of such opportunities as it offers; we can comprehend how she could be born with these great qualities, but we cannot comprehend how they became immediately usable and effective without the developing forces of a sympathetic atmosphere and the training which comes of teaching, study, practice—years of practice,—and the crowning and perfecting help of a thousand mistakes. We can understand how the possibilities of the future perfect peach are all lying hid in the humble bitter-almond, but we cannot conceive of the peach springing directly from the almond without the intervening long seasons of patient cultivation and development. Out of a cattle-pasturing peasant village lost in the remoteness of an unvisited wilderness and atrophied with ages of stupefaction and ignorance we cannot see a Joan of Arc issue equipped to the last detail for her amazing career and hope to be able to explain the riddle of it, labor at it as we may.

It is beyond us. All the rules fail in this girl's case. In the world's history she stands alone—quite alone. Others have been great in their first public exhibitions of generalship, valor, legal talent, diplomacy, fortitude; but always their previous years and associations had been in a larger or smaller degree a preparation for these things. There have been no exceptions to the rule. But Joan was competent in a law case at sixteen without ever having seen a law-book or a courthouse before; she had no training in soldiership and no associations with it, yet she was a competent general in her first campaign; she was brave in her first battle, yet her courage had had no education—not even the education which a boy's courage gets from never-ceasing reminders that it is not permissible in a boy to be a coward, but only in a girl; friendless, alone, ignorant, in the blossom of her youth, she sat week after week, a prisoner in chains, before her assemblage of judges, enemies hunting her to her death, the ablest minds in France, and answered them out of an untaught wisdom which overmatched their learning, baffled their tricks and treacheries with a native sagacity which compelled their wonder, and scored every day a victory against these incredible odds and camped unchallenged on the field. In the history of the human intellect, untrained, inexperienced, and using only its birthright equipment of untried capacities, there is nothing which approaches this. Joan of Arc stands alone, and must continue to stand alone, by reason of the unfellowed fact that in the things wherein she was great she was so without shade or suggestion of help from preparatory teaching, practice, environment, or experience. There is no one to compare her with, none to measure her by; for all others among the illustrious *grew* towards their high place in an atmosphere and surroundings which discovered their gift to them and nourished it and promoted it, intentionally or unconsciously. There have been other young generals, but they were not girls; young generals, but they had been soldiers before they were generals: she *began* as a general; she commanded the first army she ever saw; she led it from victory to victory, and never lost a battle with it; there have been young commanders-in-chief, but none so young as she: she is the only soldier in history who has held the supreme command of a nation's armies at the age of seventeen.

Her history has still another feature which sets her apart and leaves her without fellow or competitor: there have been many uninspired prophets, but she was the only one who ever ventured the daring detail of naming, along with a foretold event, the event's precise nature, the special time-limit within which it would occur, and the place—and *scored fulfilment*. At Vaucouleurs she said she must go to the King and be made his general, and break the English power, and crown her sovereign—"at Rheims." It all happened. It was all to happen "next year"— and it did. She foretold her first wound and its character and date a month in advance, and the prophecy was recorded in a public record-book three weeks in advance. She repeated it the morning of the date named, and it was fulfilled before night. At Tours she foretold the limit of her military career—saying it would end in one year from the time of its utterance—and she was right. She foretold her martyrdom—using *that word*, and naming a time three months away—and again she was right. At a time when France seemed hopelessly and permanently in the hands of the English she twice asserted in her prison before her judges that within seven years the English would meet with a mightier disaster than had been the fall of Orleans: it happened within five—the fall of Paris. Other prophecies of hers came true, both as to the event named and the time-limit prescribed.

She was deeply religious, and believed that she had daily speech with angels; that she saw them face to face, and that they counselled her, comforted and heartened her, and brought commands to her direct from God. She had a childlike faith in the heavenly origin of her apparitions and her Voices, and not any threat of any form of death was able to frighten it out of her loyal heart. She was a beautiful and simple and lovable character. In the records of the Trials this comes out in clear and shining detail. She was gentle and winning and affectionate; she loved her home and friends and her village life; she was miserable in the presence of pain and suffering; she was full of compassion: on the field of her most splendid victory she forgot her triumphs to hold in her lap the head of a dying enemy and comfort his passing spirit with pitying words; in an age when it was common to slaughter prisoners she stood dauntless between hers and harm, and saved them alive; she was forgiving, generous, unselfish, magnanimous; she was pure from all spot or stain of baseness. And always she was a *girl*; and dear and worshipful, as is meet for that estate: when she fell wounded, the first time, she was frightened, and cried when she saw her blood gushing from her breast; but she was Joan of Arc! and when presently she found that her generals were sounding the retreat, she staggered to her feet and led the assault again and took that place by storm.

There is no blemish in that rounded and beautiful character. How strange it is!—that almost invariably the artist remem-

bers only one detail—one minor and meaningless detail of
the personality of Joan of Arc: to wit, that she was a peasant girl—and forgets all the rest; and so he paints her as a
strapping middle-aged fishwoman, with costume to match,
and in her face the spirituality of a ham. He is slave to his one
idea, and forgets to observe that the supremely great souls are
never lodged in gross bodies. No brawn, no muscle, could endure the work that their bodies must do; they do their miracles
by the spirit, which has fifty times the strength and staying
power of brawn and muscle. The Napoleons are little, not big;
and they work twenty hours in the twenty-four, and come up
fresh, while the big soldiers with the little hearts faint around
them with fatigue. We know what Joan of Arc was like, without asking—merely by what she did. The artist should paint
her *spirit*—then he could not fail to paint her body aright. She
would rise before us, then, a vision to win us, not repel: a
lithe young slender figure, instinct with "the unbought grace
of youth," dear and bonny and lovable, the face beautiful, and
transfigured with the light of that lustrous intellect and the
fires of that unquenchable spirit.

Taking into account, as I have suggested before, all the circumstances—her origin, youth, sex, illiteracy, early environment, and the obstructing conditions under which she ex-
ploited her high gifts and made her conquests in the field and
before the courts that tried her for her life,—she is easily and
by far the most extraordinary person the human race has ever
produced.

Little Bessie

Twain began work on "Little Bessie" in February 1908 during a yachting trip off the Bermuda coast with his good friend and financial advisor, H. H. Rogers. The cover sheet of the typescript contains the following note, written in Twain's hand: "It is dull, & I need wholesome excitement & distraction, so I will go lightly excursioning along the primrose path of theology" (*Fables*, 8). The text takes the form of a condensed novel and continues Twain's practice of satirizing unquestioned heritage —in this instance the major theological events of the Christian faith. There is no indication he intended to publish "Little Bessie," and it is more likely he created her precocious irreverence solely for his personal pleasure and that of like-minded friends. During this same period Twain was trading letters and pranks with his Angel-Fish, and like Little Bessie they gave him new insight into the nimble and questioning minds of adolescent girls.

For additional stories about precocious children see "The Story of Mamie Grant, the Child Missionary" (1868), and "Little Nelly Tells a Story out of Her Own Head" (1907).

CHAPTER I: *Little Bessie Would Assist Providence*

Little Bessie was nearly three years old. She was a good child, and not shallow, not frivolous, but meditative and thoughtful, and much given to thinking out the reasons of things and trying to make them harmonise with results. One day she said—

"Mamma, why is there so much pain and sorrow and suffering? What is it all for?"

It was an easy question, and mamma had no difficulty in answering it:

"It is for our good, my child. In His wisdom and mercy the Lord sends us these afflictions to discipline us and make us better."

"Is it *He* that sends them?"

"Yes."

"Does He send *all* of them, mamma?"

"Yes, dear, all of them. None of them comes by accident; He alone sends them, and always out of love for us, and to make us better."

"Isn't it strange!"

"Strange? Why, no, I have never thought of it in that way. I have not heard any one call it strange before. It has always seemed natural and right to me, and wise and most kindly and merciful."

"Who first thought of it like that, mamma? Was it you?"

"Oh, no, child, I was taught it."

"Who taught you so, mamma?"

"Why, really, I don't know—I can't remember. My mother, I suppose; or the preacher. But it's a thing that everybody knows."

"Well, anyway, it does seem strange. Did He give Billy Norris the typhus?"

"Yes."

"What for?"

"Why, to discipline him and make him good."

"But he died, mamma, and so it *couldn't* make him good."

"Well, then, I suppose it was for some other reason. We know it was a *good* reason, whatever it was."

"What do you think it was, mamma?"

"Oh, you ask so many questions! I think it was to discipline his parents."

"Well, then, it wasn't fair, mamma. Why should *his* life be taken away for their sake, when he wasn't doing anything?"

"Oh, I don't know! I only know it was for a good and wise and merciful reason."

"What reason, mamma?"

"I think—I think—well, it was a judgment; it was to punish them for some sin they had committed."

"But *he* was the one that was punished, mamma. Was that right?"

"Certainly, certainly. He does nothing that isn't right and wise and merciful. You can't understand these things now, dear, but when you are grown up you will understand them, and then you will see that they are just and wise."

After a pause:

"Did He make the roof fall in on the stranger that was trying to save the crippled old woman from the fire, mamma?"

"Yes, my child. *Wait!* Don't ask me why, because I don't know. I only know it was to discipline some one, or be a judgment upon somebody, or to show His power."

"That drunken man that stuck a pitchfork into Mrs. Welch's baby when—"

"Never mind about it, you needn't go into particulars; it was to discipline the child—*that* much is certain, anyway."

"Mamma, Mr. Burgess said in his sermon that billions of little creatures are sent into us to give us cholera, and typhoid, and lockjaw, and more than a thousand other sicknesses and—mamma, does He send them?"

"Oh, certainly, child, certainly. Of course."

"What for?"

"Oh, to discipline us! haven't I told you so, over and over again?"

"It's awful cruel, mamma! And silly! and if I—"

"Hush, oh hush! do you want to bring the lightning?"

"You know the lightning did come last week, mamma, and struck the new church, and burnt it down. Was it to discipline the church?"

(Wearily). "Oh, I suppose so."

"But it killed a hog that wasn't doing anything. Was it to discipline the hog, mamma?"

"Dear child, don't you want to run out and play a while? If you would like to—"

"Mamma, only think! Mr. Hollister says there isn't a bird or fish or reptile or any other animal that hasn't got an enemy that Providence has sent to bite it and chase it and pester it, and kill it, and suck its blood and discipline it and make it good and religious. Is that true, mother—because if it is true, why did Mr. Hollister laugh at it?"

"That Hollister is a scandalous person, and I don't want you to listen to anything he says."

"Why, mamma, he is very interesting, and I think he tries to be good. He says the wasps catch spiders and cram them down into their nests in the ground—*alive*, mamma!—and there they live and suffer days and days and days, and the hungry little wasps chewing their legs and gnawing into their bellies all the time, to make them good and religious and praise God for His infinite mercies. I think Mr. Hollister is just lovely, and ever so kind; for when I asked him if *he* would treat a spider like that, he said he hoped to be damned if he would; and then he—"

"My child! oh, do for goodness' sake—"

"And mamma, he says the spider is appointed to catch the fly, and drive her fangs into his bowels, and suck and suck and suck his blood, to discipline him and make him a Christian; and whenever the fly buzzes his wings with the pain and misery of it, you can see by the spider's grateful eye that she is thanking the Giver of All Good for—well, she's saying grace, as *he* says; and also, he—"

"Oh, aren't you *ever* going to get tired chattering! If you want to go out and play—"

"Mamma, he says himself that all troubles and pains and miseries and rotten diseases and horrors and villainies are sent to us in mercy and kindness to discipline us; and he says it is the duty of every father and mother to *help* Providence, every way they can; and says they can't do it by just scolding and whipping, for that won't answer, it is weak and no good—Providence's way is best, and it is every parent's duty and every *person's* duty to help discipline everybody, and cripple them and kill them, and starve them, and freeze them, and rot them with diseases, and lead them into murder and theft and dishonor and disgrace; and he says Providence's invention for disciplining us and the animals is the very brightest idea that ever was, and not even an idiot could get up anything shinier. Mamma, brother Eddie needs disciplining, right away; and I know where you can get the smallpox for him, and the itch, and the diphtheria, and bone-rot, and heart disease, and consumption, and—*Dear* mamma, have you fainted! I will run and bring help! Now this comes of staying in town this hot weather."

CHAPTER 2: *Creation of Man*

Mamma. You disobedient child, have you been associating with that irreligious Hollister again?

Bessie. Well, mamma, he is interesting, anyway, although wicked, and I can't help loving interesting people. Here is the conversation we had:

Hollister. Bessie, suppose you should take some meat and bones and fur, and make a cat out of it, and should tell the cat, Now you are not to be unkind to any creature, on pain of punishment and death. And suppose the cat should disobey, and catch a mouse and torture it and kill it. What would you do to the cat?

Bessie. Nothing.

H. Why?

B. Because I know what the cat would say. She would say, It's my nature, I couldn't help it; I didn't make my nature, *you* made it. And so you are responsible for what I've done—I'm not. I couldn't answer that, Mr. Hollister.

H. It's just the case of Frankenstein and his Monster over again.

B. What is that?

H. Frankenstein took some flesh and bones and blood and made a man out of them; the man ran away and fell to raping and robbing and murdering everywhere, and Frankenstein was horrified and in despair, and said, I made him, without asking his consent, and it makes me responsible for every crime he commits. I am the criminal, he is innocent.

B. Of course he was right.

H. I judge so. It's just the case of God and man and you and the cat over again.

B. How is that?

H. God made man, without man's consent, and made his nature, too; made it vicious instead of angelic, and then said, Be angelic, or I will punish you and destroy you. But no matter, God is responsible for everything man does, all the same; He can't get around that fact. There is only one Criminal, and It is not man.

Mamma. This is atrocious! it is wicked, blasphemous, irreverent, horrible!

Bessie. Yes'm, but it's true. And I'm not going to make a cat. I would be above making a cat if I couldn't make a good one.

CHAPTER 3

Mamma, if a person by the name of Jones kills a person by the name of Smith just for amusement, it's murder, isn't it, and Jones is a murderer?

Yes, my child.

And Jones is punishable for it?

Yes, my child.

Why, mamma?

Why? Because God has forbidden homicide in the Ten Commandments, and therefore whoever kills a person commits a crime and must suffer for it.

But mamma, suppose Jones has by birth such a violent temper that he can't control himself?

He *must* control himself. God requires it.

But he doesn't make his own temper, mamma, he is born with it, like the rabbit and the tiger; and so, why should he be held responsible?

Because God *says* he is responsible and *must* control his temper.

But he *can't,* mamma; and so, don't you think it is God that does the killing and is responsible, because it was *He* that gave him the temper which he couldn't control?

Peace, my child! He *must* control it, for God requires it, and that ends the matter. It settles it, and there is no room for argument.

(*After a thoughtful pause.*) It doesn't seem to me to settle it. Mamma, murder is murder, isn't it? and whoever commits it is a murderer? That is the plain simple fact, isn't it?

(*Suspiciously.*) What are you arriving at now, my child?

Mamma, when God designed Jones He could have given him a rabbit's temper if He had wanted to, couldn't He?

Yes.

Then Jones would not kill anybody and have to be hanged?

True.

But He chose to give Jones a temper that would *make* him kill Smith. Why, then, isn't *He* responsible?

Because He also gave Jones a Bible. The Bible gives Jones ample warning not to commit murder; and so if Jones commits it he alone is responsible.

(*Another pause.*) Mamma, did God make the house-fly?

Certainly, my darling.

What for?

For some great and good purpose, and to display His power.

What is the great and good purpose, mamma?

We do not know, my child. We only know that He makes *all* things for a great and good purpose. But this is too large a subject for a dear little Bessie like you, only a trifle over three years old.

Possibly, mamma, yet it profoundly interests me. I have been reading about the fly, in the newest science-book. In that book he is called "the most dangerous animal and the most murderous that exists upon the earth, killing hundreds of thousands of men, women and children every year, by distributing deadly diseases among them." Think of it, mamma, the *most* fatal of all the animals! by all odds the most murderous of all the living things created by God. Listen to this, from the book:

> Now, the house fly has a very keen scent for filth of any kind. Whenever there is any within a hundred yards or so, the fly goes for it to smear its mouth and all the sticky hairs of its six legs with dirt and disease germs. A second or two suffices to gather up many thousands of these disease germs, and then off goes the fly to the nearest kitchen or dining room. There the fly crawls over the meat, butter, bread, cake, anything it can find in fact, and often gets into the milk pitcher, depositing large numbers of disease germs at every step. The house fly is as disgusting as it is dangerous.

Isn't it horrible, mamma! One fly produces fifty-two billions of descendants in 60 days in June and July, and they go and crawl over sick people and wade through pus, and sputa, and foul matter exuding from sores, and gaum themselves with every kind of disease-germ, then they go to everybody's dinner-table and wipe themselves off on the butter and the other food, and many and many a painful illness and ultimate death results from this loathsome industry. Mamma, they murder seven thousand persons in New York City alone, every year—people against whom they have no quarrel. To kill without cause is murder—nobody denies that. Mamma?

Well?

Have the flies a Bible?

Of course not.

You have said it is the Bible that makes man responsible. If God didn't give him a Bible to circumvent the nature that

223

He deliberately gave him, God would be responsible. He gave the fly his murderous nature, and sent him forth unobstructed by a Bible or any other restraint to commit murder by wholesale. And so, therefore, God is Himself responsible. God is a murderer. Mr. Hollister says so. Mr. Hollister says God can't make one moral law for man and another for Himself. He says it would be laughable.

Do shut up! I wish that that tiresome Hollister was in H—amburg! He is an ignorant, unreasoning, illogical ass, and I have told you over and over again to keep out of his poisonous company.

CHAPTER 4

"Mamma, what is a virgin?"

"A maid."

"Well, what is a maid?"

"A girl or woman that isn't married."

"Uncle Jonas says that sometimes a virgin that has been having a child—"

"Nonsense! A virgin can't have a child."

"Why can't she, mamma?"

"Well, there are reasons why she can't."

"What reasons, mamma?"

"Physiological. She would have to cease to be a virgin before she could have the child."

"How do you mean, mamma?"

"Well, let me see. It's something like this: a Jew couldn't be a Jew after he had become a Christian; he couldn't be Christian and Jew at the same time. Very well, a person couldn't be mother and virgin at the same time."

"Why, mamma, Sally Brooks has had a child, and she's a virgin."

"Indeed? Who says so?"

"She says so herself."

"Oh, no doubt! Are there any other witnesses?"

"Yes—there's a dream. She says the governor's private secretary appeared to her in a dream and told her she was going to have a child, and it came out just so."

"I shouldn't wonder! Did he say the governor was the corespondent?"

CHAPTER 5

B. Mamma, didn't you tell me an ex-governor, like Mr. Burlap, is a person that's been governor but isn't a governor any more?

M. Yes, dear.

B. And Mr. Williams said "ex" always stands for a Has Been, didn't he?

M. Yes, child. It is a vulgar way of putting it, but it expresses the fact.

B, (eagerly). So then Mr. Hollister was right, after all. He says the Virgin Mary isn't a virgin any more, she's a Has Been. He says—

M. It is false! Oh, it was just like that godless miscreant to try to undermine an innocent child's holy belief with his foolish lies; and if I could have my way, I—

B. But mamma,—honest and true—*is* she still a virgin—a *real* virgin, you know?

M. Certainly she is; and has never been anything but a virgin—oh, the adorable One, the pure, the spotless, the undefiled!

B. Why, mamma, Mr. Hollister says she *can't* be. That's what he says. He says she had five children after she had the One that was begotten by absent treatment and didn't break anything and he thinks such a lot of child-bearing, spread over years and years and years, would ultimately wear a virgin's virginity so thin that even Wall street would consider the stock too lavishly watered and you couldn't place it there at any discount you could name, because the Board would say it was wildcat, and wouldn't list it. That's what *he* says. And besides—

M. Go to the nursery, instantly! Go!

CHAPTER 6

Mamma, is Christ God?

Yes, my child.

Mamma, how can He be Himself and Somebody Else at the same time?

He isn't, my darling. It is like the Siamese twins—two persons, one born ahead of the other, but equal in authority, equal in power.

I understand it, now, mamma, and it is quite simple. One twin has sexual intercourse with his mother, and begets himself and his brother; and next he has sexual intercourse with his grandmother and begets his mother. I should think it would be difficult, mamma, though interesting. Oh, ever so difficult. I should think that the Corespondent—

All things are possible with God, my child.

Yes, I suppose so. But not with any other Siamese twin, I suppose. You don't think any ordinary Siamese twin could beget himself and his brother on his mother, do you, mamma, and then go on back while his hand is in and beget *her*, too, on his grandmother?

Certainly not, my child. None but God can do these wonderful and holy miracles.

And enjoy them. For of course He enjoys them, or He wouldn't go foraging around among the family like that, *would* He, mamma?—injuring their reputations in the village and causing talk. Mr. Hollister says it was wonderful and awe-inspiring in those days, but wouldn't work now. He says that if the Virgin lived in Chicago now, and got in the family way and explained to the newspaper fellows that God was the Corespondent, she couldn't get two in ten of them to believe it. He says they are a hell of a lot!

My child!

Well, that is what he says, anyway.

Oh, I do *wish* you would keep away from that wicked, wicked man!

He doesn't *mean* to be wicked, mamma, and he doesn't blame God. No, he doesn't blame Him; he says they all do it— gods do. It's their habit, they've always been that way.

What way, dear?

Going around unvirgining the virgins. He says our God did not invent the idea—it was old and mouldy before He happened on it. Says He hasn't invented anything, but got His Bible and His Flood and His morals and all His ideas from earlier gods, and they got them from still earlier gods. He says there never was a god yet that wasn't born of a Virgin. Mr. Hollister says no virgin is safe where a god is. He says he wishes he was a god; he says he would make virgins so scarce that—

Peace, peace! Don't run on so, my child. If you—

—and he advised me to lock my door nights, because—

Hush, *hush*, will you!

—because although I am only three and a half years old and quite safe from *men*—

Mary Ann, come and get this child! There, now, go along with you, and don't come near me again until you can interest yourself in some subject of a lower grade and less awful than theology.

Bessie, (disappearing.) Mr. Hollister says there *ain't* any.

Mark Twain, Rebellious Girls, and Daring Young Women

Fondly recalling his daughters' teenage years, Samuel Clemens between 1895 and 1910 made friendships with adolescent girls, his "Angel-Fish," and created a host of young female protagonists in his fiction. Some connections between the Angel-Fish, Twain's stories of girls and young women, and Clemens's daughters are direct and well-documented. For example, in his autobiographical dictations Clemens declared that several Angel-Fish reminded him of his daughter Susy, particularly Carlotta Welles and the young writer and Angel-Fish Dorothy Quick. He also commented that he had fashioned Cathy Alison, the protagonist of *A Horse's Tale*, as a posthumous tribute to Susy. He began writing *The Personal Recollections of Joan of Arc* at Susy's bidding, read passages of the manuscript-in-progress for her editorial suggestions, and viewed the finished novel as a tribute to her brief but exceptional life. Clemens's richest memories of his daughters' childhood focus on Susy, with her "intense" personality and her precocious talents, rather than on Clara or Jean. This is understandable, given Susy's early promise as a writer and her tragic death. Susy's younger sister, Clara, may also have influenced the shape and direction of the girl and young woman stories. More strong-willed than Susy, she became interested in men at the age of sixteen, then aspired to independence and a career—desires which vexed her father for the next twenty years. Assertive and rebellious female characters like Joan of Arc and Cathy Alison appear to have been inspired not only by Susy but also incorporated aspects of Clara's personality and relationship with her father.

Clemens had not been prepared for the maturation of his daughters, as they became interested in young men and in education and training outside their happy but protective family environs. He was perhaps least ready to be no longer at the center of their worlds. He resisted Susy's and then Clara's desires to leave home for further education and, in keeping with his stalwart perpetuation of the Victorian code, forbade them to go out unchaperoned or appear conspicuously in public. Exceeding even the rigid expectations of his society regarding the proper protection of young women, Clemens insisted that Clara travel with and be accompanied at all times by a suitable chaperone until she married. Clara eventually married at the age of thirty-five.

The battle for freedom and independence was waged more vigorously by Clara than by Susy, reflecting Clara's stronger health and more rebellious nature. In 1890, at the age of sixteen, Clara received reluctant family permission to enroll in the Willard School in Berlin for music training. (The family was living in Italy at the time.) Clara wrote home excitedly about the many social events she was attending and casually mentioned that she had been the sole female at a banquet held by forty young German officers. Although the event was entirely innocent, she assured her parents, Clemens's lengthy reply was witheringly vindictive, registering his concern about his own reputation as much as hers. It began: "If you would not have yourself and us talked about, there is but one course for you—to make yourself acquainted at the earliest moment, with the nicest shades of what is allowable by German custom and keep strictly within the boundaries of it for the future. We want you to be a lady—a lady beyond reproach" (Harnsberger, 140–41). Both parents expressed their fears that she had injured her reputation.

On another occasion Clemens locked Clara in her hotel room as punishment for exchanging glances with a young man. Even as late as 1904, when Clara was thirty years old, this protectiveness continued. Once while Clemens and Clara were having tea in a Florence tearoom, he noticed a table of Italian officers looking at his daughter with amorous interest, obviously attracted to Clara's dark beauty. Enraged, Clemens hastily returned to their rented villa and cut the artificial fruit away from the rim of Clara's hat, declaring it coquettishly provocative.

Threats of further punishment did not constrain "Blackie" — as her family called Clara — for long. As the fair-haired Susy was effectively confined to home due to her delicate health, the more robust and sultry Blackie clashed openly with her father and painfully elbowed her way to semi-independence. This independence came gradually and only after bitter battles between their headstrong personalities. Although none of Twain's female protagonists in these stories live in family circumstances resembling those of the Clemens girls, they express an independence of thought and action that Clemens was unwilling to give his own daughters.

In 1905 Samuel Clemens began seeking the friendships of young schoolgirls, in effect collecting girls the way other famous collectors accumulated rare stamps or precious art objects. He did not show any secrecy or embarrassment in writing about his living collection of thirteen adolescent girls as if they were pets or gems. The schoolgirls had to be admirable specimens of childhood, girls for whom life was "a perfect joy," girls who had not suffered extensively from physical injury, grief, or bitterness. His enterprise was not entirely an effort to shore up companionship against his loneliness, but rather to gather about himself schoolgirls who reminded him of his daughters when they were children. Clemens insisted that the members of his Aquarium Club possess the very qualities that reminded him of Susy but were now missing in his life. By the spring of 1908 Clemens was calling these girls his Angel-Fish.

The Aquarium Club became "life's chief delight" for Clemens during his last years. Between 1905 and his death in 1910, approximately three hundred letters were written to and from the Angel-Fish, and Clemens wrote several essays about them. Although his last years were often plagued by loneliness, illness, and depression, Clemens's Angel-Fish letters are consistently optimistic, loving, and playful. They reveal the depths of

his emptiness from the deaths of Susy and Olivia, his wife, and
the magnitude of his need for attention and affection. Given
his losses and change in outlook on life and the human condition, it is remarkable that Clemens possessed the resilience
to rekindle his sense of humor, to write hundreds of playful,
loving letters, and to "suffer" numerous visits from his schoolgirl friends.

Clemens met Gertrude Natkin, his first Angel-Fish, in December 1905 after a concert at Carnegie Hall. Noting her name
and address, he started up a correspondence and friendship
that lasted through the first half of 1906. A second and then
a third schoolgirl friend were added a year later, in June 1907
during Clemens's voyage to England to receive an honorary
degree from Oxford University. Frances Nunnally, soon nicknamed "Francesca," became one of his most faithful Angel-
Fish. The next schoolgirl drawn into Clemens's magnetic orb,
Carlotta "Charlie" Welles, further evoked memories of Susy.
Margaret Blackmer, Irene Gerkin, and Helen Allen joined the
Aquarium Club in late 1907 and 1908. In Bermuda, Irene
played billiards with Clemens and his friends so often that,
long after her return home they still referred to a certain position of the balls as "an Irene." Margaret, Helen, and Clemens
took frequent trips by donkey cart to a picturesque spot on the
coast called "Spanish Point." At an aquarium located nearby
Clemens viewed the brilliantly colored angelfish native to the
Bermuda waters and realized they would make a perfect em-
blem for his club of schoolgirls.

On his return trip from England in 1907, Clemens met ten-
year-old Dorothy Quick, who had been watching him for some
time parade about the decks of the S. S. *Minnetonka* in a scarlet-
colored Oxford robe. Eventually Clemens said to Dorothy,
"Aren't you going to speak to me, little girl?" They became fast
friends, deciding to wear only white clothing during the remainder of the voyage to honor their friendship. On their ar-
rival in New York a session was arranged for the news photog-
raphers, and the results were widely published, with captions
like this one: "Mark Twain Home—Captive of Little Girl."

Dorothy Quick replied lovingly to every letter sent by Clemens, and sealed their friendship with a visit to Clemens's rented home at Tuxedo Park in August 1907, and another in September. During these visits, which must have evoked the childhood of his own girls, Clemens and Dorothy played card games and charades, accompanied by members of his amiable staff led by Isabel Lyon and Robert Ashcroft. Since Dorothy wanted to be a writer, they formed an "author's league of two" in which Clemens gave advice and took dictation as Dorothy concocted stories. Clemens was so amused by Dorothy's stories with their "punctuationless prose" and "adorably lawless spelling" that he would suppress his laughter until his stomach ached. When Dorothy's first visit came to an end he recorded that he was recovering from a "tremendous week" that left him feeling as if he "had been through a storm in heaven."

One can imagine how letters from and visits with Dorothy must have felt like flashbacks to Susy's childhood. Like Dorothy, Susy was a "slender little maid with plaited tails of copper-tinged brown hair down her back and was perhaps the busiest bee in the household hive" (Autobiographical dictations, 201). Even Dorothy's writing reminded him of Susy's: "The spelling is frequently desperate but it was Susy's and it shall stand. . . . To me it is gold. To correct it would alloy it, not refine it. It would spoil it. It is Susy's spelling and she was doing the best she could—and nothing could better it for me" (Autobiographical dictations, 202). Clemens's acceptance of—even affection for—undisciplined writing is a far cry from his anger and punitive measures of a few years later, when his daughters began to attract the attention of men.

The Angel-Fish were not a ragtag bunch of the first dozen girls who doted on a famous old man. They came from affluent families, traveled extensively, attended private schools, and were well protected from life's rough edges. Clemens met and entertained them in the "right" places—at concert halls and theaters, on ocean liners, in Bermuda hotels, and at his own imposing estate. It is not surprising that Clemens selected for his club only girls who had grown up in family circumstances similar to those of his daughters. He was quick to point out that although he could carefully choose his Angel-Fish, real parents and grandparents had to accept what fate provided, good, bad, or indifferent.

Since Clemens was burdened with none of the responsibilities and worries he once had for his own daughters, he could say of all his Angel-Fish: "Dorothy is perfect, just as she is; Dorothy the child cannot be improved; let Dorothy the woman wait until the proper time comes." "Letting the woman wait" became a persistent subtheme in his remarks to and about the Angel-Fish. To him they likely represented a timeless adolescence he had not been able to experience with Susy, Clara, and Jean or, for that matter, in his own childhood. He believed that if he could keep these "angels" perpetually young and if they would visit and write him frequently, their innocent fire and unruly spontaneity would continue to warm his heart and imagination.

Clemens advised the Aquarium girls that adulthood was a dreadful place, a place best avoided. "Cling to your blessed youth—the valuable time of life—don't part with it till you must," he warned. This offhand comment profoundly reflects Clemens's vision of the desirable innocence of girlhood. Such protective happiness also stands in stark contrast to the lives of the adolescent female protagonists in his fiction.

Gertrude Natkin was fifteen when Clemens met her and turned sixteen in April 1906. When Clemens heard the shattering news he wrote: "So you are 16 to-day, you dear little rascal! Oh come, this won't do—you mustn't move along so fast, at any rate you will soon be a young lady and next you'll be getting married. . . . *Sixteen!* Ah, what has become of my little girl? I am almost afraid to send a blot, but I will venture it. It comes within an ace of being improper! Now back you go to 14— then there's no impropriety" (*Aquarium*, 24–25).

Clemens struck a chord here that he repeated with other Angel-Fish: they should not turn sixteen, for then it might be improper for him to kiss them, appear in public with them, or even send them a "blot" by letter.

Gertrude began to fear, from Clemens's failure to write, that somehow sixteen was a mysterious divide in the mind of her famous pen pal. She pleaded, "Dear Grandpa, please don't love me any less because I am sixteen . . . I shall always be your little Marjorie [his nickname for her] as long as you wish it." Her response expresses an understanding of his fetish: even though she could not stop time or her sexual maturation, Gertrude was willing to play the fourteen-year-old part in his schoolgirl play in order to maintain their friendship.

The female protagonists in this collection of Twain's stories are young (ranging between three and seventeen years of age) and assume personality traits and behaviors that Twain and his society typically reserved for young males. During his last fifteen years as a writer his male characters, regardless of age or intentions, are correspondingly characterized by ineptitude and cowardliness. In five tales—"A Mediæval Romance," "Saint Joan of Arc," "Hellfire Hotchkiss," "How Nancy Jackson Married Kate Wilson," and *A Horse's Tale*—Twain's young women adopt men's clothing and roles in order to more fully realize certain dimensions of their personalities or to accomplish challenging tasks. In every story Twain's female protagonists challenge and offend patriarchal authority through transgressive actions such as cross-dressing and cross-acting. Some of Twain's heroic maidens pay the highest price for their gender transgressions, with their lives.

One of Twain's most interesting excursions into the arena of the inept male and assertive female appears in "A Story without an End." In the opening paragraphs Twain appears to be relating a conventional courtship tale about any young couple in the 1890s. But he quickly whips the lap robe of convention from this storiette by revealing that the personalities of the protagonists are reversed from traditional gender expectations. Despite his advantage of age (thirty-one), John Brown is hardly a dominant personality, but instead is "gentle, bashful, timid." Young Mary Taylor is "gentle and sweet" but also clear-headed, adept at problem solving, and decisive in implementation.

In "Story without an End" Twain dramatizes the predicament of the indecisive male and the capable maiden by using an anecdote clever enough to amuse female readers but meant to be acutely embarrassing to their male counterparts. This "traditional" courtship romance runs amuck when shy and timid John Brown arrives by carriage at the appointed place to meet his fianceé, Mary Taylor, but in a state of "dis-dress" as well as distress. As a result of a series of comic misadventures, John arrives clothed from the waist down in nothing but a lap robe. As Mary announces that she needs the carriage to transport two elderly women who are cold and hungry, John clutches the lap robe, speechless with embarrassment, hoping he will not be exposed. As the curtain falls on this unresolved gender-bender, Mary asks for the lap robe and "put out her hand to take it." Twain declares he leaves to the reader "the privilege to determine for himself how the thing comes out," thus preserving the humor of the tale while avoiding authorial involvement in the humiliation of a male character. Readers aware of the sexual double-entendres that punctuate Twain's notebooks would have to suspect duplicity in the phrases "how the thing comes out" and "put out her hand to take it."

In this microcosmic gender tale John Brown (with possible ironic allusion to his abolitionist, revolutionary namesake) has relinquished his trousers without a fight and awaits full exposure of his masculine inadequacy by a young woman with whom he is no match.

Another of Twain's comedies of switched genders, "Hellfire Hotchkiss," explores the dilemma of Rachel (nicknamed "Hellfire"), a classic tomboy, and her weak male counterpart, Oscar "Thug" Carpenter. While Hellfire exhibits "manly" toughness and heroics, as well as a "good business head and practical sense," it is generally conceded in her hometown of Dawson's Landing that Oscar "ought to put on petticoats." In the climactic scene of the story a fearless Hellfire rescues a frightened and weeping Oscar from drowning in the Mississippi River. When she hears of his peril she gallops astride her "great black horse" to the river's edge, swims in the frigid, winter river to the ice floe on which Oscar is marooned, straps a life preserver to the stricken Thug, and then swims with him to shore. Her heroism points to his cowardice; her tomboy nature counterpoints his effeminacy.

But Hellfire's independent wings appear to be clipped by the end of this unfinished story. In her sixteenth year Rachel comes upon an ugly street scene in which two village tough guys, the Stover brothers, are bullying a stranger. As she watches they put a gun to his head. When the revolver misfires, Rachel pulls out her wooden bat and knocks the brothers senseless. Several days later her "Aunt Betsy" informs her that the brothers are circulating rumors in an effort to smear her reputation as a young woman. Her aunt suggests that Rachel has enjoyed sixteen years as a boy and now it's time to begin to conform to the expectations of her gender.

Alone with her thoughts in the final scene, Rachel admits that at sixteen she is too old to merely play with boys as "good company." She will attempt to change her way of life, and act and dress as a young woman. Yet there is a fatalism to her thoughts; deep inside she knows that "Thug Carpenter is out of his sphere, I am out of mine. Neither of us can arrive at any success in life, we shall be hampered and fettered and kept back by our misplaced sexes, and in the end defeated by them." Both Hellfire and Twain seem to be admitting that in their society, with its rigid gender divisions, a failure to conform will bring defeat.

In a burst of insight, however, Hellfire makes her private peace with her misplaced gender. She will dress and act as a girl except when duty demands otherwise. As she explains it, "Before this I would have horsewhipped the Stovers just as a pleasure; but now it will be for a higher motive . . . and in every way a worthier one." Hellfire appears more determined than ever to dress and act like a man in the pursuit of fairness and justice when duty demands it. Otherwise, she will try her best to wear skirts and act as a woman.

Twain gives his evolving vision of the heroic female its fullest treatment in *Personal Recollections of Joan of Arc* (the story "Saint

Joan of Arc," included in this edition, is a short version of the novel, so the context is essentially the same). Twain's inflated estimate of Joan ("I liked *Joan of Arc* best of all my books; and it is the best; I know it perfectly well") is best explained by the author's deep, perhaps obsessive love for his eldest daughter (Autobiographical dictations, 1034). Susy's early death in 1896 no doubt elevated his emotional attachment to Joan, whom he considered "the mystery of the ages." After Susy's death he declared, "Susy died at the right time, the fortunate time of life, the happy age—twenty-four years" (Gillman, 106).

Significantly, Twain's version of Joan of Arc is told as if by her former servant and devoted follower. The elderly narrator, presumably Twain's amanuensis, observes that although she dressed and behaved as a man at age sixteen and had rejected her parents' arrangement for her marriage, Joan was also a "shapely and graceful" maiden. Twain's characterization of Joan blends qualities traditionally associated in Victorian culture with the feminine (shapely, graceful, innocent, pure, uncorrupted, compassionate), with those connected with the masculine (courageous, inspiring, intelligent, daring, skill at horsemanship and swordsmanship). In a nation of weak-willed and cowardly men, including the king, Joan pleads, "if there are a dozen of you who are not cowards, it is enough—follow me!" (*Joan of Arc*, 78).

As Twain blurs the traditional gender divisions of his society, the weakening of the male role invites, perhaps necessitates, the emergence of heroic and masculine young women. Yet, as suggested by Twain's transvestite tales, there is always a price to be paid for such violations of gender boundaries—social misplacement, possible loss of sexual identity, and the likelihood of punishment, including violent death.

Echoing Clemens's stern advice to Clara during the years before her marriage, Joan's father warns her that by refusing to marry and by dressing and behaving like a young man she will "unsex herself," and therefore ruin her reputation and attractiveness (102). Joan adopts the clothing of men of war in order to be accepted by them, thus gaining empowerment to act in their world. Joan's costume is no hesitant excursion into the realm of the male: it includes breeches, shirt, doublet, hose, a short mantle falling to above the knee, short cropped hair, tight-fitting boots, long spurs, sword, breastplate, and dagger—the entire outfit of a fifteenth-century man of war. After she is elevated to the realm of military leadership, Joan keeps a stable of fine horses, collects swords, and maintains in her retinue a squire, a knight, and four servants. Twain's Joan of Arc never hides her sexual identity, though she deliberately confuses or violates the boundary lines between constructed gender identities. At her trial, for example, she challenges any woman in Rouen to compete with her in sewing and spinning—just as she had challenged countless men at their own games.

In contrast to the multiple capabilities bestowed upon Joan, Clemens stated publicly (in testimony before a House Copyright Committee in December 1906) that "I have carefully raised them [his daughters] as young ladies, who don't know anything and can't do anything." Even though he may have been speaking hyperbolically before a house of "good old boys" who would be receptive to Gilded Age stereotyping of young ladies, this vision of female gentility contrasts starkly with the lives of his "new girl" characters and the life of Clara Clemens, who by 1906 was pursuing a singing career and living away from home though still financially dependent upon her father. Susy Clemens inspired her father's labor of fictional love, she read and marveled over the manuscript as it emerged, and she resembled the Maid from Orleans in intellect. But Joan's character may also register Twain's concerns about Clara, who provoked his disapproval and punishment on various occasions for transgressing his own boundaries of acceptable female behavior.

"How Nancy Jackson Married Kate Wilson," a story that hints at the possibility of a lesbian marriage, remained unpublished until it appeared in the *Missouri Review* in 1987. One reason it would have remained unpublished in Clemens's lifetime, and a possible autobiographical connection, is his oldest daughter's passionate friendship with Louise Brownell. The two met during Susy's first year away from home, at Bryn Mawr College in 1891. According to Andrew Hoffman's biography of Twain, Susy and Louise wanted to share a house during their second college year, but the Clemenses withdrew their daughter from college and decided to settle in Florence for the year in hopes that Susy would cure herself of her "illness" and misdirected friendship. While living in their secluded Florence villa Susy felt like a prisoner under closely watched house arrest, a punishment, perhaps, for her romantic transgression. During the Florence year she warned her sister, Clara, to guard her freedom, since their parents wished to rein her in as well.

In the Nancy Jackson–Kate Wilson story, Twain's punishment may have worked by reversal, forcing two young heterosexual women into a same-sex marriage, with the suggestion that they deserved their strange domestic alliance or far worse for their breaches of decorum. Intent on saving her neck from the gallows' noose, Nancy's imposture completely fools the family and village who give her refuge. She even tricks, we are led to believe, Kate Wilson, who appears to fall in love with her in her disguise as Robert Finlay. Kate's romantic attachment to Nancy's transvestite role argues for the power of inspired acting, but also speaks to the relative and protean nature of gender identity. In the light of Susy's relationship with Louise Brownell, one can imagine a lesbian subtext beneath what is for Twain a fairly commonplace plot of switched identities.

Because of her sexual promiscuity Kate has become pregnant and subsequently jilted by "a sincere young man with the best of intentions." Forced by the pregnancy to change her strategy, Kate shifts from flirtation to entrapment and soon catches the poor changeling, Robert Finlay (Nancy Jackson). The text takes pleasure in a discourse of double entendres between two young women who may or may not know they are both women—one of whom is trying to preserve her imposture and gain a secure haven, while the other is trying to preserve her reputation and secure a father for her expected child. Kate mistakes Nancy's "friendship" and "affection" for signs of a passionate commitment to marriage. Unable, or perhaps unwilling, to extricate herself from the sticky meshes of this trap, Nancy submits to the "shotgun" marriage that follows, probably considering it a far better fate than exposure, trial, and punishment.

Nancy's physical and Kate's sexual assertiveness counterbalance each other, resulting in a possible double warning to transgressive women that they will become unmarriageable, at least heterosexually, because of their violations of acceptable behavior. Twain further compounds the punishment by requiring that Nancy keep her trousers up along with her disguise. Thus, Nancy and Kate are at least officially denied either the friendly partnership of sisters in adversity or, God and Twain forbid, the lesbian marriage the title certainly suggests to contemporary readers. However, Twain's last lines preserve the possibility that even the author is struggling to imagine a lesbian partnership. When one of Kate's old friends asks why she and her "husband" seem so distant, Kate lays a hand on her friend's knee and replies "How would it do to say it is none of your business?" Twain's inconclusive and ambiguous tale can be read two ways: a warning and punishment to physically or sexually transgressive women and, simultaneously, the covert suggestion that two women (with a child to raise) might forge a secret and possibly satisfying marriage. Despite the social taboos of his era, Twain may have been attempting to imagine the possibility of such a partnership for young women like Susy Clemens and Louise Brownell.

Like "Nancy Jackson," *Wapping Alice* also violates conventions by deliberately confusing gender categories. Intermittently between 1877 and 1907 Twain continued to gender bend "Alice," rendering a true incident that involved a faulty burglar alarm, a young serving girl in Twain's employ, and a mechanic into first a story centering on the unreliable alarm ("The McWilliamses and the Burglar Alarm"), then converting it into a male transvestite farce. For the latter he changed the names of the participants to fictional ones and distanced himself and his household from the story by setting it in the Deep South, casting the narrator as a plantation owner named Jackson who tells the story during an ocean cruise.

Through double-entendres, graphic or suggestive symbolism, and sexual references Twain establishes a subtext that explores the hidden and forbidden world of homosexual attraction, friendship, and sexual relations, including "sodomy." As Hamlin Hill pointed out in his afterword to the only published version of the story, Twain's choice of the London borough of Wapping as both the home and nickname for Alice allows for suggestive play with the verb "to wap" or "wrap around," and the noun "wap"—a tossing or thumping movement. Twain would have known Wapping as the Docklands, a district that sorely challenged Victorian morality and a likely place of origin for a young transvestite wishing to seek his fortune in the New World. Equally poignant is Twain's change of name for his "straight" male character, from an American Willie Taylor to a Swede named Bjorgensen Bjuggerson. While the name Wapping Alice might suggest a sexually aggressive young woman looking for a man, the young Swede's name signals an inordinate interest in organs and buggery, not philandering. By barely disguised suggestion Twain is making light of a sexual practice that in 1870 he asserted was "never named among women and children, and is . . . only mentioned in rare books of the law, and then as 'the crime without a name'—a term with a shudder in it" (*Wapping Alice*, 78).

Twain's sound-alike narrator, Jackson, discloses at the beginning of his amazing narration that Alice's disguise and acting was so successful, "no suspicion of the fraud he was playing ever crossed our minds." Twain's narrator dismisses the switched identity, observing that "why he unsexed himself was his own affair," a comment that suggests private reasons not yet explored and a motivation that was either sexual attraction or entrapment. The Alice who so successfully deceived the Jackson household would have charmed Clemens as well, one suspects; "her" outfit is a "white summer gown with a pink ribbon at the throat, and another one around her waist and [she] looked very neat, and comely and attractive and modest." Twain is probably identifying the pink ribbons with those worn by gay residents to identify themselves in the San Francisco of his bohemian days. By contrast to Alice in drag with pink ribbons, her covert lover is described as a "good hearted and manly young fellow," and a "joiner" (carpenter) by trade.

The farcical elements of the tale turn extensively on the architectural and mechanical features of Jackson's house. Alice lives in the kitchen wing that is joined to the main house only at the dining room and the cellar levels. On the night that Alice arranges to open the lower rear door for the young Swede, Bjuggerson, to enter, "she" does not realize that the house is protected by a burglar (or is it buggerler?) alarm, which silently records the entry. After three nights of the Swede's late-night rear entries, Alice overhears a family conversation about the seemingly malfunctioning alarm. "She" informs her friend, who is, after all, a joiner by day if not nocturnally as well, and thus ever-handy with tools. Bjuggerson files the pegs off Alice's lock (chastity belt?), allowing himself freedom to enter and stay at will, as he does for the next six months.

The text is rife with references to the open laundry room door, the unprotected household, and the unlawful cellar entries, as well as with play on wapping and joining, burglary and buggery. The sexual shorthand for this story might read: as Alice waps, Bjorn Bjuggers—the title all but eliminates any uncertainty. Despite the light and humorous tone Twain sets with his homosexual innuendoes, he is presumably admitting that gay sexuality exists, perhaps even within the shadows or lower reaches of the American family household, though in a shadowed and clandestine relationship to the upper chambers of acceptable sexual practice.

In 1895 at the conclusion of the third trial of Oscar Wilde, a British court found him guilty of "gross Indecency" with another male. The trials and their outcome attracted such extraordinary attention on both sides of the Atlantic that Twain could not have been unaware of the proceedings and some of the details. By the time the dust of scandal and notoriety had settled and the press had digested what was known and conjectured, the public had become educated about a dimension of male behavior that had up to that time been kept from widespread public knowledge. Even in its coverage of the Wilde trials the press avoided reporting on the details of homosexual behavior under the presumption that it was, as Twain himself had earlier commented, "too horrible to be named" or described (Sinfield, 140).

It is a widely held view among historians of sexuality that Wilde's public personality, described as "effeminate" and "aesthete," was largely responsible for the effeminate homosexual stereotype through which heterosexuals have since viewed gay culture. As Alan Sinfield expresses it, "until the Wilde trials, effeminacy and homosexuality did not correlate in the way they have done subsequently" (4). Sinfield holds to Foucault's constructionist theory "that sexualities are not essential, but constructed within an array of prevailing social possibilities," a theory opposed to Twain's essentialist inheritance, the essence of which was beginning to find expression in his writing. Unjustly or not, Wilde became identified with an effeminate homosexual stereotype and was recognized as the main cause of its formation.

A year after the Wilde trials Twain began work on "Hellfire Hotchkiss." As already mentioned, this comedy of confused genders explores the dilemma of an aggressive and masculine young woman and her best friend, the effeminate Oscar Carpenter. Pitiful Oscar, ironically nicknamed "Thug," possesses qualities that Twain and perhaps American society in the post–Wilde-trial years derisively identified with the feminine, including indecisiveness and changeability.

Several years later, when Twain converted the essence of the Oscar Carpenter personality into Wapping Alice, he further suggested that an effeminate male might find cover under the protective "skirts" of transvestism. By creating a same-sex couple composed of a feminine male (the Oscar component) and a very masculine male (the working-class tradesman), Twain perpetuated both his and his society's bifurcated vision of gender, but also allowed for gender differences within a same-sex relationship and perhaps by implication within a gay (and lesbian) subculture.

The story's poignant moment of revelation charmingly parallels the original moment of discovery in the Clemens household. Once confronted, Alice swears (as did Lizzy) that "she" intended only to offer the otherwise homeless Swede a place to sleep during the previous six months, but that the cur took advantage of him. "Oh, dear-dear, it is too true, sir [a pregnant pause ensues] — and now he won't marry me." A skillful trickster, Alice turns near disaster to final advantage, hoping to force his reluctant lover to the altar.

Alice's false claim of pregnancy is, of course, the furthest advance a male transvestite can make into a conventional heterosexual plot of this sort, without actually producing the baby. The idea of a gay couple forced by "her" employer to marry because of a false pregnancy and a double legal bind for the Swede (considering the illegal rear entries: burglary and buggery) also serves as an amusing counterpart to the false pregnancy of Lizzy the real serving girl in Clemens's employ, whose disclosure and shotgun marriage is the nucleus of the Wapping Alice story. The story's narrator, Jackson, falls for Alice's final trick: assuming she is a young woman, he produces a clergyman and a policeman, and offers Bjuggerson the choice between jail or marriage to Alice. The young Swede's reluctant decision results in a same-sex marriage, witnessed and sanctioned by the clergy and the law, a rare outcome in America even a century later.

Twain engaged in deception or self-delusion when in 1907 he stated that the transvestite element was a "non-essential detail" designed to "soften the little drama sufficiently to enable me to exploit it in a magazine" without "over shocking" the readers (Autobiographical dictations, 9 April 1907). Since "Alice" was rejected by two publishers during a time when virtually everything Twain wrote found publication, one can surmise that Twain had broached a subject his editors felt would "over shock" their readers.

In these two transvestite tales we are led to believe Nancy Jackson has successfully deceived an entire community, her "wife's" family, and possibly her same-sex partner, Kate, as to her female identity. Equally as intriguing is the idea that Wapping Alice could have passed so successfully and for so long as a female domestic servant, while under the careful scrutiny of a family not unlike the Clemenses. Twain explores the ways in which a feminine man might attract and win his "manly" counterpart, a strategy that preserves Twain's more traditional concept of two distinct gender personalities that can be identified as "feminine" and "masculine." In so doing, however, Twain participates in deconstructing the notion that men are always masculine and women always feminine, and the belief that one can presume to know a person's gender identity or sexual orientation even after daily familiarity.

A Horse's Tale is woven with textual connections to *The Personal Recollections of Joan of Arc*, to the Angel-Fish, and to Clemens's recollections of his daughters. Twain declares his deep personal involvement with *A Horse's Tale* in a 1907 letter to his publisher: "The heroine is my daughter Susy whom we lost. It [the portrait of Susy] was not intentional—It was a good while before we found it out" (*Letters* 2:997). Like Susy and Angel-Fish Dorothy Quick, Cathy Alison flits about at "firefly" pace, putting those near her through a perpetual double-time of "thunderstorms and sunshine." When Clemens pleads with Dorothy to quiet down, he echoes General Alison's pleading: "Oh, you bewitching little scamp, can't you be quiet just a minute or two." When Buffalo Bill calls her "you dear little rat" he uses one of Clemens's favorite expressions for his young friends. Even the names of General Alison's cats (Mongrel, Sour-Mash, Famine, and Pestilence) are drawn from the Clemens family's cat menagerie. Here the similarities seem to end, however. Cathy's physical daring takes her into territory unknown to Clemens's daughters or to the Angel-Fish.

Through the androgynous female figure Twain also links Cathy with Joan of Arc. Cathy's ceremonial costume of velvet tights, sword, and "doublet with slashed sleeves" is reminiscent of Joan's, as is her personality, which similarly merges traditionally held female and male gender traits. Cathy "loves everything a girl loves" but she also adores "boy-plays and drums and fifes and soldiering and rough riding, and ain't afraid of anybody or anything." This observable androgyny is enlarged by General Allison's African-American servant, Dorcas, who theorizes that "Cathy is twins, and that one of them is a boy-twin and failed to get segregated." (Poignant malapropism indeed!) Though the boy-child is invisible, as Dorcas tells it, "that boy is in there, and you can see him look out of her eyes when her temper is up" (*Short Stories*, 566). The entire garrison loves and admires Cathy's curious combination of feminine and masculine personalities.

In a scene of unusually suggestive eroticism for Twain, the girl side of Cathy appears to be engaged in "innocent" sexual foreplay with Buffalo Bill. She sits in Buffalo Bill's lap and looks up lovingly into his brave eyes and rugged face. She plays with his long hair, admires his big hands, the long barrel of his dangerous carbine, and protests her love for him. Somewhat later in the story Cathy has apparently transferred her adolescent love for Buffalo Bill to a more suitable object, Bill's horse, the faithful and obedient gelding, Soldier Boy. As they ride across the plains he transports her (by the rapture of the saddle?) to "the last agony of pleasure." The boy-twin in Cathy's personality rides Soldier Boy at breakneck speed and, as if he were Tom Sawyer, pulverizes any other boy who will challenge him.

Although Cathy Alison's cause appears trivial by comparison to Joan's, Twain's announced purpose for producing the tale was to support the Anti-Vivisection movement. It was commissioned by animal rights activist Minnie Maddern Fiske and appeared as a banner for her cause in the August and September 1906 issues of *Harper's Monthly*. Because of its melodramatic sentimentality, *A Horse's Tale* is probably more interesting to contemporary readers as a story about assertive girls and male authority than about cruelty to animals. Undercutting its declared purpose, the tale presents indiscriminate masculine cruelty to animals and the eventual cruel punishment of a heroic young girl who intervenes unquestioningly where no males dare tread.

The story also dramatizes the vulnerability of daring young women when assaulted by bullish, unrestrained male behavior. Cathy's hideous death in the bullring, while being watched by her uncle and a stadium of shocked onlookers, may be Twain's symbolic representation of rape, as her vulnerable girl's body is pierced by the horns of the enraged bull. (Note the suggestive parallels between Cathy's hideous death and the rape of Peggy, a girl character in Twain's unfinished novel *Huck and Tom among the Indians*.) Twain's chilling conclusion elicits emotional sympathy for Cathy and her cause. As in his other stories of girls and young women, men are incompetent or absent when heroic action is called for. At the same time, the ending asserts the crushing power of unrestrained masculinity and its ability to destroy even girls who, by circumstance or by some aberration of personality, are driven to act like males.

It is tempting to speculate that Twain's portraits of assertive maidens like Mary Taylor, Hellfire Hotchkiss, Joan of Arc, and Cathy Alison reflect his awareness of a national debate over issues of gender and the place of women in his society. During the 1890s and in the decades following, a growing number of young women who were generally college-educated, single, and economically independent began to make their presence felt in American life. Variously referred to as the "new women" or "angry young women," they began to assert their desires for greater independence and autonomy, especially regarding sexual practices and legal and reproductive rights. In part the emergence of the new woman can be directly associated with the rise to prominence of women's colleges in the later nineteenth century—colleges like Bryn Mawr, which Susy Clemens attended against her father's wishes.

If one accepts Twain's comments at surface value, several of the young women in his Aquarium Club and the fictional heroines Joan of Arc and Cathy Alison reminded him of and served as tribute to his daughter Susy. As previously noted, though, the daughter who most assertively defied her father's rules and wishes and thus more closely resembles Joan, Cathy, and the others is Clara Clemens, not Susy. As she grew more independent of her father she became his rival for family honors. As Clemens remarked to the press after one of Clara's early vocal concerts, "Yes, I am passing off the stage, and now my daughter is the famous member of the family" (Harnsberger,

208). More than that, Clara, who disapproved of the Aquarium Club from its inception in 1907, began to assert her authority as head of the family, clamping down on her father's drinking, smoking, late hours, and happy times with schoolgirls. Fearing that any impropriety on his part would tarnish the family reputation, she essentially closed down the Aquarium Club in November 1908 and changed the name of his new home from "Innocence at Home" to "Stormfield." Soon after she "convinced" Clemens to fire his chiefs of staff and close friends Isabel Lyon and Ralph Ashcroft, who had facilitated his "autumn summer" of happiness. The assertive daughter effectively turned the tables and imposed control over her aging and ailing father.

Late in his remarkable life Samuel Clemens surrounded himself with adolescent females, both living and fictional, some of whom reflected happy memories of bygone years. His life and his stories of girls and young women also reflect uncertainty regarding female suffrage and independence, and thus may encapsulate the gender growth pains of a society in transition. Twain's assertive female stories honor his loving memory of the perfect and fair-haired daughter, Susy, but they also warn against the dangers that the rebellious sister could encounter and the havoc she could wreak. These texts recognize the intellects and capabilities of young women, yet warn of the willingness of a patriarchal society to punish transgressive female behavior. They evoke the memory of lost daughters, they deliver a warning about rebellious females, and they establish an inconclusive discourse connecting Twain's personal and fictional experiences—a discourse about gains and losses, about opportunities being realized, and about the damage incurred in the process of redefining female and male roles in the modern era.

Works Cited

Fishkin, Shelly Fisher. "Mark Twain and Women." *Mark Twain's Humor: Critical Essays.* Ed. David E. E. Sloane. New York: Garland, 1993. 52–73.

Gillman, Susan. *Dark Twins: Imposture and Identity in Mark Twain's America.* Chicago: U of Chicago P, 1989.

Harnsberger, Caroline T. *Mark Twain, Family Man.* New York: Citadel, 1960.

Harris, Susan K. *Mark Twain's Escape from Time: A Study of Patterns and Images.* Columbia: U of Missouri P, 1982.

Henderson, Archibold. *Mark Twain.* Philadelphia: Folcroft, 1969.

Hoffman, Andrew Jay. *Inventing Mark Twain: The Lives of Samuel Langhorne Clemens.* New York: Morrow, 1997.

LeMaster, J. R., and James D. Wilson, eds. *The Mark Twain Encyclopedia.* New York: Garland, 1993.

Neider, Charles. *Papa: An Intimate Biography of Mark Twain.* New York: Doubleday, 1985.

Sinfield, Alan. *The Wilde Century: Effeminacy, Oscar Wilde and the Queer Movement.* New York: Columbia UP, 1994.

Skandera-Trombley, Laura. *Mark Twain in the Company of Women.* Philadelphia: U of Pennsylvania P, 1994.

Stahl, J. D. *Mark Twain, Culture, and Gender: Envisioning America through Europe.* Athens: U of Georgia P, 1994.

Stoneley, Peter. *Mark Twain and the Feminine Aesthetic.* New York: Cambridge UP, 1992.

Twain, Mark. Autobiographical dictations. Mark Twain Papers. Bancroft Library, University of California, Berkeley.

———. *The Complete Works of Mark Twain.* 24 vols. New York: Harper, 1923.

———. *The Diaries of Adam and Eve.* New York: Oxford UP, 1996.

———. "How Nancy Jackson Married Kate Wilson." Ed. Robert Sattelmeyer. *The Missouri Review* March 1987.

251

———. *Huck Finn and Tom Sawyer among the Indians and Other Unfinished Stories*. Ed. Dahlia Armon and Walter Blair. Berkeley: U of California P, 1989.

———. *The Love Letters of Mark Twain*. Ed. Dixon Wecter. New York: Harper, 1949.

———. *Mark Twain's Aquarium: The Samuel Clemens–Angelfish Correspondence, 1905–1910*. Ed. John Cooley. Athens: U of Georgia P, 1991.

———. *Mark Twain's Fables*. Ed. John S. Tuckey, Kenneth M. Sanderson, and Bernard L. Stein. Berkeley: U of California P, 1972.

———. *Mark Twain's Letters*. 2 vols. Ed. Albert Bigelow Paine. New York: Harper, 1917.

———. *Mark Twain's Satires and Burlesques*. Ed. Franklin R. Rogers. Berkeley: U of California P, 1967.

———. *The Personal Recollections of Joan of Arc*. New York: Harper, 1896.

———. *The Signet Classic Book of Mark Twain's Short Stories*. Ed. Justin Kaplan. New York: New American Library, 1985.

———. *Wapping Alice*. Introduction and afterword by Hamlin Hill. Berkeley: Friends of the Bancroft Library, University of California, 1981.

Warren, Joyce W. "Mark Twain and the Three R's." In *The American Narcissus: Individualism and Women in Nineteenth-Century American Fiction*. New Brunswick: Rutgers UP, 1984.

Suggestions for Further Reading

Other Works by Mark Twain

"The $30,000 Bequest." In *The Signet Classic Book of Mark Twain's Short Stories.* Ed. Justin Kaplan. New York: New American Library, 1985. A gender-switching story involving a married couple.

"1,002d Arabian Night" (1883). In *Mark Twain's Satires and Burlesques.* Ed. Franklin R. Rogers. Berkeley: U of California P, 1967. The tale of a happily married couple content in their gender-switched roles.

"Huck Finn and Tom Sawyer among the Indians." In *Huck Finn and Tom Sawyer among the Indians and Other Unfinished Stories.* Berkeley: U of California P, 1989. This unfinished manuscript foregrounds Huck and Tom, but implies that young Peggy Mills has been raped, and possibly murdered, by Indians.

[*The Tragedy of*] *Pudd'nhead Wilson.* Mineola, N.Y.: Dover, 1999. Twain's novel about the switching at birth of male infants of different races also involves transvestism and its plot is activated by the female slave Roxy, Twain's most calculating and assertive woman character.

"The Story of Mamie Grant, the Child-Missionary." In *Mark Twain's Satires and Burlesques.* Ed. Franklin R. Rogers. Berkeley: U of California P, 1967. This condensed burlesque features a nine-year-old version of the theologically precocious "Little Bessie."

Studies of Gender and Women's Issues in Mark Twain's Life and Works

Cooley, John, ed. *Mark Twain's Aquarium: The Samuel Clemens–Angelfish Correspondence, 1905–1910.* Athens: U of Georgia P, 1991.

Gillman, Susan. *Dark Twins: Imposture and Identity in Mark Twain's America.* Chicago: U of Chicago P, 1989.

Harnsberger, Caroline T. *Mark Twain, Family Man*. New York: Citadel, 1960.

Mark Twain and Women. Spec. issue of *Mark Twain Journal* 34.2 (fall 1996).

Salsbury, Edith Colgate. *Susy and Mark Twain: Family Dialogues*. New York: Harper, 1965.

Skandera-Trombley, Laura E. *Mark Twain and the Company of Women*. Philadelphia: U of Pennsylvania P, 1994.

Stahl, J. D. *Mark Twain: Culture and Gender: Envisioning America through Europe*. Athens: U of Georgia P, 1994.

Stone, Albert E. *The Innocent Eye: Childhood in Mark Twain*. New Haven: Yale UP, 1992.

Stonely, Peter. *Mark Twain and the Feminine Aesthetic*. New York: Cambridge UP, 1992.

Willis, Resa. *Mark and Livy: The Story of Mark Twain and the Woman Who Almost Tamed Him*. New York: Atheneum, 1992.

Other Studies of Gender and Women's Issues

Showalter, Elaine, ed. *Scribbling Women: Short Stories by Nineteenth-Century American Women*. New Brunswick: Rutgers UP, 1996.

———, ed. *Speaking of Gender*. New York: Routledge, 1989.

Smith-Rosenberg, Carol. *Disorderly Conduct*. New York: Knopf, 1985.

Sources

Stories in this collection were previously published as:

"Lucretia Smith's Soldier." *Californian* 3 December 1864.

"Aurelia's Unfortunate Young Man." As "Whereas" in *Californian* 22 October 1864.

"A Mediæval Romance." As "An Awful Terrible Mediæval Romance" in *Buffalo Express* 1870.

"The Esquimau Maiden's Romance." *Cosmopolitan Magazine* 1893.

"Hellfire Hotchkiss." In *Huck Finn and Tom Sawyer among the Indians and Other Unfinished Stories*. Ed. Dahlia Armon and Walter Blair. Berkeley: U California P, 1989. Published with permission from the University of California Press.

"A Story without an End." In *Following the Equator: A Journey around the World*. Hartford, Conn.: American Publishing Company, 1897.

"Wapping Alice." *Wapping Alice*. Berkeley: The Friends of the Bancroft Library, University of California, 1981. Published with permission from the University of California Press.

"How Nancy Jackson Married Kate Wilson." Ed. Robert Sattelmeyer. *The Missouri Review* March 1987. Published with permission from the University of California Press.

"A Horse's Tale." *A Horse's Tale*. New York: Harper, 1907.

"Eve's Diary." *Eve's Diary*. New York: Harper, 1906.

"Saint Joan of Arc." In *The $30,000 Bequest and Other Stories*. New York: Harper, 1906.

"Little Bessie." In *Mark Twain's Fables of Man*. Ed. John S. Tuckey, Kenneth M. Sanderson, and Bernard L. Stein. Berkeley: U of California P, 1972. Published with permission from the University of California Press.